WHEN THE LIGHT TURNED RED

WHEN THE LIGHT TURNED RED

SIMI JOEL

Paperback: 978-1-0674536-0-2
eBook: 978-1-0674536-1-9

Published by Simi Joel
Edmonton, Alberta, Canada
www.simistories.com
contact@simistories.com

First edition, April 2026

Cover design: Pixels and Vector
Interior design and layout: Adebayo Gbenga

For every longing heart daring to believe it's worthy of love, learning to hush the voices of doubt, and choosing at last to live unafraid.

TABLE OF CONTENTS

PROLOGUE

Sola Adesesan sat at the extreme left of the 250-seater capacity hall, hanging on to every word uttered by the stout man addressing the orderly rows of students in brown and white coloured uniforms. His voice boomed from the stage, dispelling thoughts of the just concluded WASSCE from his mind.

"Today marks the beginning of the rest of your lives. You'll all do well to remember the lessons imparted to you in this prestigious citadel of learning. They will carry you to success in the real world if you ride on their great wings of wisdom. Till we meet again, my dear graduating class of 2010, *adios*. Good luck!"

The headteacher left, and the other teachers followed with the pile of submitted answer scripts and performative shouts of well-wishes and goodbye to the students. As the last teacher disappeared through the exit, the students filled the air with loud chants of exhilaration, flinging their pens and question papers. Some climbed their tables while others drummed loudly. Sola leaned his back against the wall, tapping his pen repeatedly against the desk, as he watched his classmates troop out of the hall, with clear groups and friendship divides coming through. The girls formed clusters outside the hall, chatting animatedly. Most male students headed toward the school field, while a few singles could be seen hanging around or heading home.

Sola could relate to their excitement. The end of his secondary school journey meant freedom from his parents' rules once he was off to university. Although a part of him appreciated the rules and the strong sense of morality and pride his parents had instilled in him over the years, he couldn't stand the constant comparison to his elder brother and golden child of the family, Teju.

His best friend Derin approached and tapped his shoulder.

"Hey!" he said, grabbing the chair on Sola's right and turning it to sit in reverse, facing him. Resting his elbows on the chair's back, he adjusted his thick-lens glasses. "We're finally free!"

Sola smiled, sticking his pen in his trademark afro.

Of his friends, Derin was the street smart one who spearheaded most of their mischief, which they'd lost count of. He and Sola were drawn to each other from their first day at the school. In their science class, Derin shot up his hand to answer every question the teacher asked. But during lunch, when he brought out garri and groundnut to eat, their classmates made fun of him. Sola had jumped to the rescue of the 'scholarship kid,' and they'd been inseparable since.

Before Sola could respond with a comment of his own, the other two that completed their friend group showed up. Suleiman, the fifth son of a sitting senator with his lazy eye, shaven head, tall, lanky frame, and one hand in his pocket; then Chude, the class comedian loved by everyone who walked like he knew it, the son of entrepreneurs and car manufacturers.

Chude pulled up a chair while Suleiman sat on Sola's desk.

"Don't look back," Derin signalled. "We have a diva approaching."

The rest of the guys assumed a semblance of indifference while Sola tried to act cool. Moments later, he felt a tap on his shoulder. He looked to his right and swallowed.

Samira.

Her braided hair framed her oblong face perfectly, and her small gold earrings glistened in the light.

"Hi, Sola," she said, looking straight at him like he was the only one in the room.

"Hey, Sammie," he replied, pushing his seat back and getting up. He stood above her, but she was still tall enough for a girl. "How did you find today's finals?"

"That's why I am here. To thank you for being the best study partner a girl could ask for and holding my hand along the way," she handed him a small bag. To his surprise, she followed that move with a light embrace before walking off to join her friends.

Chude cleared his throat. "All hail the study partner of the year."

Sola's silence wasn't a deterrent for the teasing of his friends, but he didn't mind it. The opposite in fact.

Derin leaned forward with mischief on his face. "You know what this means, right? We have to attend Mek's party tonight."

He knew why Derin was bringing up the party, and he would have liked to see Sammie, but he didn't have permission from his parents to go, which was a big deal. He would be scolded—or worse, if they got caught.

Derin continued. "School is over now, so you can drop the good boy thing for one day. Your parents are out of town, so you can drive one of the cars and be back later tonight. No one will know, so let's rock this party."

Suleiman lazily raised an eyebrow. "What's in the bag the diva brought you?"

The boys looked around to make sure that Sammie and her girls were out of sight. Confident that they were unobserved, they opened the gift bag. It contained a large bottle of very expensive looking perfume.

As his friends softly gasped, Sola made his decision.

He looked at Derin. "We will need a good cover story for the domestic staff," he said.

Laughing, Derin clapped his shoulder again. "Leave it to me."

That night, in Sola's multi-room mansion, escaping the housekeeper, Yewande, didn't end up being so tricky. Getting past Yakubu the gateman on the other hand was only possible when they used Derin's rehearsed threat. It turned out the nightwatchman had a penchant for one of the maids. He let them through in exchange for his secret being kept safe.

Sola drove. He was only fifteen but was tall enough to pass for a nineteen-year-old. His afro dimmed some of his babyish handsomeness. At the party somewhere in the middle of Ibadan, he didn't spot Samira at first. When he did, about thirty minutes later, the hype and encouragement from his friends bolstered his confidence to approach her.

"What's up, Sammie?"

"Hey, Sola. I didn't expect to see you here," she replied, giggling. A small cohort of not-as-pretty girls surrounded her.

"Um, yeah, I came with my friends. So, I just wanted to say thanks for the gift earlier," he stammered.

"Sure, it's nothing."

"Also, can I talk to you ... privately?"

"Well, this is as private as it gets. My friends are fine; you can say anything."

"Okay ... I was wondering if you'd like to hang out sometime, now that school is over."

"Wait, are you asking me out?" she blurted, a hint of pity in her eyes. "Because we were study partners?"

"Uh...Well—"

"I'm sorry," she said gently. "You're a nice guy, but I like you as a friend, so let's keep it that way, okay?"

Sola felt his self-esteem pool and crash into the floor around his feet.

"I understand," he said, then he turned around to see his friends' crestfallen faces looking back at him.

For the next hour, Sola tried to dislodge the feeling in his chest with alcohol, tried to sway away the rejection to the music, and tried to allow the hype his friends continued to pile on him to warm up his insides. But it didn't work.

"I have to go," he slurred. Chude told him to just hang out a bit more, but all Sola wanted was his bed.

"We'll go together," Derin said to the guys. "Don't worry."

In the car, they turned up the music. The last thing Sola remembered was Derin teasing him about being a lightweight.

When he came to, he found himself on a narrow gurney. Somewhere, a shrill female voice screamed, over and over:

"Murderer!"

"You killed my husband!"

"You deserved to die, not him!"

Tears streaked down her face, her head tie swooped sideways on her head. "Look at what you've done to me and my family!" she wailed. "Kill me too because there's nothing left for me in this life! Kill me, ooooh!"

Sola looked at the woman, unable to turn away due to the brace holding his neck, his gaze fixed hopelessly as he was wheeled without choice in the opposite direction.

He was faintly aware of the nurses pushing the stretcher and yelling orders. His head was pounding, and he couldn't feel his feet, but he saw one thing clearly. This woman, with flailing arms, down on her knees, weeping uncontrollably, and a little girl at her side pulling at the wrapper, which had loosened from her waist and now lay at her side.

The memories of what happened began to claw back, slowly wrapping its fingers around his throat, choking him. Flashing images and sounds of unending screams and blinding lights forced him to shut his eyes.

He couldn't accept what he was seeing and feeling.

Did they really kill a man?

He clenched his fists beside him and started to cry, hoping desperately it was all a bad dream and that when he opened his eyes, it would all be over. After what seemed like an eternity, he dared to look again. But when his eyes fluttered open, they locked with the piercing innocence of the little girl from whom he'd just stolen.

The stretcher turned a corner, cutting his gaze, but the sight of that girl stayed with him for years to come.

I

RUPTURE

one

INTERSECTION

MAY 2024

An hour after his plane landed at the Murtala Muhammed Airport, Sola waited impatiently by the conveyor belt for his baggage. As the harmonious voice of the female announcer trailed on through the airport intercom, his eyes searched for his green suitcase. The belt had already gone around twice, and he hoped he wouldn't have to file a baggage claim.

"There!" He grabbed his case at last and headed briskly for the exit.

He was a frequent traveller, and a tall man with shoulder length locs. These two things alone drew the attention of the security staff and hangers-on. Luckily, he kept small foreign currency on him for things like this.

At the car park, he spotted a casually dressed, well-presented driver among the other vendors and headed over to him. "Is your car close by?"

"Yes, sir. Let me help you with your bag."

They walked together to his neat, blue Toyota Camry, and the driver placed his suitcase in the trunk.

"Let me pay for parking first," the driver said. Sola nodded and got into the passenger seat that had already been opened. Alone, he turned his phone on. Almost immediately, he was bombarded with multiple WhatsApp alerts and text messages.

The driver pulled out and began their journey.

As they drove off, Ebenezer Obey's *Ketekete* greeted his ears. Sola nodded approvingly. The song was one of his father's favourites and a staple from his childhood. It told the story of a donkey, a man, and his son, and how it's impossible to please everyone.

Scrolling through his messages, he saw that his Mum, Derin and Stalin had tried to reach him. He paused to decide whose message he wanted to read first. Stalin.

Man! It was great catching up with you at the reunion and seeing you're doing well. I always knew you would do great. Call me if you ever come to Sweden, and we'll have some drinks and talk more. And who knows, maybe business will bring me to Nigeria before then.

Sola smiled and typed in response:

Yeah, man. Glad to see that you've grown some hair, and it was nice to meet your lovely wife. Send my love to her, will you? I'd love to host you if you're ever on my side of the world.

Returning to the notification tab, he laughed at the red-highlighted fifty-six message notification next to his mother's name. He reminded himself to call her when he got home.

Speeding down the stretch of the Third Mainland Bridge in Lagos, amid the familiar honking sounds and music in the background, he reflected on his MBA reunion trip to Poland. It was an unequivocal success. He got to see old classmates who were now working in industries worldwide ranging from consulting, healthcare, non-profit, and sports entertainment. Some, like himself, had started their own companies. He pitched his financial merchant service startup, *Luna Pay*, which was in the middle of a venture capital raise. Their business promise was to deliver secure, seamless transactions in physical stores and online, e-commerce solutions, inventory management, and loyalty programs for small businesses and large enterprises.

He and Derin had worked hard to create differentiation for their product and had successfully onboarded multiple small businesses. After several tests, iterations, hirings, and firings, things finally took shape, and there was a productive structure. Their next goal was to onboard large enterprises. For that, they needed more funding. It was in this regard that the trip went better than he expected, securing more commitments and references to a broader range of contacts.

He still had emails and meetings to follow up with but for now, he was content to celebrate the wins and get some rest.

His phone buzzed with a notification from Derin:
Have you landed?

Yeah, I have. Got some good news from the guys I met. I'll call you when I'm settled, and we can meet up sometime tomorrow.

Derin sent a GIF of a dancing polar bear in response then followed with:

Get some rest. I'll come over to yours tomorrow.

Perfect.

The moment he sent the last response, his phone immediately rang. Sweet Momma appeared on the screen. He hesitated but thought it was best to get the conversation over with; or otherwise, his mother wouldn't let up.

"Hello, Mum"

"Sola, you've landed. You were online on WhatsApp but didn't reply to my messages. You had me worried."

"I landed some minutes ago and I'm on my way home now. I was going to call you when I got there."

"You should have called me when you landed. I'd have sent the driver to come and meet you at the airport. I even sent you a message. If only you'd read it."

"Sorry, Mum, but I'd told you not to worry about it."

"You aren't the one to tell me what to do or what not to do. Do you even have food at home?"

"No, but I'll order some. It's no big deal."

"Okay, make sure you order good food, not burgers and chips that you're always eating. I'm sure you had a lot of junk when you travelled. Then come over tomorrow. Yewande cooked some soups today, so I packed some in the freezer for you. Come and get them."

"Can't the driver bring them?"

"I said you should come and get them. Are you the one who put the driver in the house for me? Ah ahn. Omo yi sha," she chided him. "I didn't even say you should come and see me, yet you're throwing a tantrum over coming to pick up food."

"But coming to pick up food is the same as seeing you, Mum."

"And is it a bad thing to visit your mother?"

"No, that's not what I'm saying." Realising that he wasn't going to win the conversation, he relented. "Okay, I'll come."

"That's better."

"Will your husband be home tomorrow?" he asked. She didn't respond for two heartbeats. When she finally spoke, her tone was sombre.

"Your father has been out of town for a week, so Yewande and I have been home alone. Neither you nor your brother have visited."

He sighed in relief. "Don't worry, Mum, I'll come tomorrow, okay?"

"O ṣe, Oko mi," she crooned like a little girl who just got candy.

About an hour later, they pulled up to his house.

"Home sweet home. Time to get some food and sleep. Tomorrow is another day," he said to himself.

Rebecca Arinze paced Jibowu motor park as her daily affirmations—a mixture of positive quotes and Bible verses—rolled off her tongue.

"I'm excellent, confident, and successful. I'm not a woman who runs from challenges, but I face them and surmount them."

Her tall silhouette was elegant against the chaotic backdrop of the park as she looked around for the driver who had called her thirty minutes ago. An atypical cold wind swirled. She pulled her shawl tighter around her shoulders, although it barely covered her arms and tank top. The wind grew stronger, the dark clouds above promising rain. She had been on her morning run when a dispatch driver called to let her know the consignment her mother sent had arrived. She'd rushed back home to pick up her car keys, throwing a light shawl over herself at the last moment before heading out.

She should have worn something warmer.

"Surely there's an end, and my expectation will not be cut short."

Rebecca always struggled with this Proverbs verse. So far in her twenty-four years of life, experience had taught her to manage her expectations or risk disappointment. Hope often felt like trying to hold smoke in her hands.

All good things must come to an end.

How many things in her life had gone wrong when she expected too much? Graduated almost top of the class, she watched others with worse grades snag admirable positions while she piled up rejection upon rejection when it came to finding a job. So, she turned to business—helping her mum sell fashion wares in Lagos and gradually building an online brand. That went well enough, so she started creating content that resonated with followers, which resulted in small brand partnerships. In between, she got a job and gave her all and everything to manage both well. She built her social media accounts to about 30k followers, and just as she made moves to connect with the entertainment industry, she lost them.

Thankfully, she built her page back up, getting a trickle of influencer deals. It was far from enough, but is it delusional to keep telling herself her expectations won't be cut short?

Whatever ...

The park was already abuzz with the small shops starting to open, passengers hustling to catch the first morning buses, and hawkers walking around with their wares. The air was thick with the aroma of hot akara, eggs, roasted fish, and yam, nipping at Rebecca's senses and gnawing at her empty stomach. White, blue, and red buses lined both sides of the park, while wooden stalls displayed goods and hot meals for travellers and weary drivers in need of a bite before their journeys.

A hawker approached Rebecca with an array of wristwatches.

"Fine girl, I have beautiful wristwatches for you; look and take your pick. Very affordable," he exclaimed. She shook her head, dismissing him quickly. Just then, a car drove past, raising dust. She jumped to the side, looking around, panic rising. *Where was this driver?*

She checked her phone and redialled his number, starting to fret about arriving at work late. Imade, her Cruella incarnate manager, would tear her into pieces if she was even two minutes late.

"Mama the mama!"

She looked to the side to see one of the park conductors, Wasiu, hailing her. He was a familiar face, but the clock was ticking, so she didn't stop walking toward the line of buses that arrived from the Eastern route to Lagos.

"Anything for your boy?" Wasiu was still trailing her.

"Wasiu, it's early, I don't have time to chat, abeg."

"No time is better than the present, Mama. Bless your boy and show me some love."

This dance was a regular occurrence. Finally, Rebecca stopped.

"Okay, but you have to work for it. I'm looking for Oga Emeka, one of the drivers from the east. He's not picking his phone, and I'm in a hurry."

"No wahala, Mama, I sabi am, he go chop."

He ran off in the opposite direction to find the driver while she paced.

She checked her watch again and groaned. All this could have been avoided if her mother had sent the load over the weekend. Now, she barely had two hours to collect the bale of clothes, get back home, freshen up, and make it to work. Despite her repeated pleas for her mother to send goods on a Friday or Saturday, she insisted on sending them on the Sunday night bus, often with little or no notice. And now, the driver was nowhere to be found.

"Thank God," she muttered when she spotted Wasiu from a distance, walking toward her with a small older man beside him.

"Oga Emeka, where have you been? I've been looking for you since."

"No vex o," he apologised when they got close, wiping his hands on his shorts. "My phone is faulty, no vex. Follow me."

They headed over to his bus and Wasiu moved quickly to offload the bale that the man pointed to. The driver also handed her a smaller black nylon wrapped bag.

"Your mother said there's dried fish here. Thank her for me o, she gave me some, too. My wife will be happy with this one." He laughed, flashing his kola-nut-stained teeth.

She thanked him and walked toward her parked car with Wasiu, who had carried the load. Handing Wasiu a tip, he immediately saluted her, waving and hailing her as she pulled out of the park.

On the drive back home, she listened to more affirmation messages hoping for a miracle to help offload the bale when she got there. When she parked in front of her flat, and tried to remove the huge bale, it fell to the ground with a thud, raising dust in the process.

"Rebecca!"

She turned to see her landlord's son, Muyiwa, walking toward her. Seeing him made her feel conflicted. On the one hand, he would definitely help her, on the other hand, she didn't necessarily *want* his help.

"I'm surprised to see you home on a Monday morning at this time. Is everything okay?"

He was nicely kitted for work in a crisp, black suit perfectly tailored to his frame, paired with a light blue shirt and checkered tie. He closed the distance between them in a few long strides, his clean-shaven face stretching into a smile as he got closer.

She straightened up. "Yeah, don't mind me. I had to pick up some items from the park." She bent forward and dragged the bag on the floor.

Muyiwa bent to stop her. He smelled musky, aromatic, and clean.

"Let me help you with that."

"No o, bro Muyiwa. You're already dressed for work. I wouldn't want to ruin your suit because the bag is heavier than it looks."

He ignored her protest and instead removed his suit jacket and draped it on her driver's seat.

"Don't worry about it, I'll be careful. You should have called me in the first place."

"It's too early on a Monday morning to start asking for favours. You're obviously heading to work."

He rolled up his trousers and carried the load to avoid staining his shirt, dusting his hands as he returned. When she handed him a wet wipe; their hands brushed against each other lightly. She shivered a little, but was unsure if it was in response to the touch or if the wind. It isn't clear. She chose the latter.

"Thank you so much. You literally took a load off me," Rebecca chuckled.

"You're welcome." He grabbed his jacket.

"I see your plant is thriving." He pointed at her apartment. "I thought it'd be dead by now. You must be doing something right."

She was pleased with the compliment and herself. Muyiwa had given her the plant a few months ago as a birthday gift along with plant care instructions, which she'd kept devotedly.

"You underestimate me, sir. But you get some credit. Your tips are working," she said.

"Uncle Flabbergasted. Good morning," a child's voice called excitedly in their direction.

They both looked over to see the giggling eight-year-old girl running up to the gate, her struggling mother, Anita, running behind to catch her.

"Good morning, Bro Muyiwa, Rebecca," the child's mother greeted, grabbing the child by her arm and chastising her softly for running.

They both waved and shouted greetings in response.

"Uncle Flabbergasted?" Rebecca asked after the mother and child duo exited. "That's new."

Muyiwa chuckled. "It's our word for the week. I guess she's excited about it."

"Your weekend lessons for the kids are going strong. That's impressive."

"It's nothing. I enjoy the time with them, it helps me unwind from work and other stress."

"It's not nothing, but you're trying to stay humble, right? So, it's alright," she teased. He let out a little laugh and Rebecca found herself thinking: *That's a laugh I wouldn't mind hearing every day.*

She immediately chastised herself in her head.

"Aren't you going to work today?" he asked.

"I am, but I had to pick this up first. I'll go prepare now."

"Okay, don't be late."

"Sure thing." She turned to leave.

"Rebecca?"

"Yes?"

"Are you free this weekend? My invitation to hang out is still open. You promised to think about it, but haven't said anything," his voice was dripping with gentle accusation, but his eyes were playful. "I want to say you can think about it for as long as you need, but I see you almost every day, and we do our sis Rebecca and bro Muyiwa dance, which is downright painful," he clutched his chest in mock hurt.

She chuckled, distracted by the dark freckles around his eyes on his fair skin.

"I'm thinking about it, seriously; unfortunately, this weekend is pretty busy. I'm volunteering at an event, but I'll let you know if anything changes."

"Of course, busy bee. I'll keep hope alive. Next weekend?" His eyes were pleading.

She shrugged. "Yeah, maybe, we'll see."

"All right, take it easy and have a great day."

"You too."

She waved, sighing as he finally left.

They'd built a comfortable friendship, which started with requests about house maintenance. He was the de facto caretaker of the house since his parents were hardly ever around. Quick knocks on his flat to complain about the occasional water outage or waste problem had gradually turned into longer chats over her two-year stay. Then, a few months ago, she suffered a massive embarrassment in front of him and other neighbours. She had almost moved out, but the ridiculous cost of Lagos rent and the infuriating antics of agents convinced her that shame was a cheaper price to pay. She'd tried to avoid her neighbours since then, especially Muyiwa, but he was difficult to evade.

She stepped into her apartment, and except for the bales on the floor, the rest of the house is exactly how she likes it: Tidy, not a throw pillow out of place, her plant thriving by the window, and her vision board in the corner near her bookshelf. There's a picture of a woman in a suit, dollar signs and the word LOVE written in bold red letters, but she'd crossed it out in a thick black line after her public disgrace. The text underneath it reads, *If you can see it, you can have it.* The board and her routine remind her to be optimistic about life and the future.

For Rebecca, that's a tall order.

Getting ready was a breeze. Her routine is consistent, and outfits and shoes are picked out the day before. Today's pick is a purple midi pencil dress that flatters her dark complexion and a pair of black heels. She pulls out two packs of the prepped meals for the week—stir-fried pasta or yam with fish stew? She decides on the pasta, packs her laptop in a large handbag, and mutters a quick prayer and affirmation with forced enthusiasm before stepping out of the house.

two

UPHEAVAL

It ended up not being a great day.

As Rebecca rushed from the car park into the office, she stumbled on the stairs, bumped into a colleague, and landed bum-first on the floor. The Oregon group was nestled among others in an impressive building at the heart of Lagos Island, where they occupied two of the seven floors. The 'accident' happened just as she got to her floor.

After apologizing to the poor victim of her clumsiness, she made another affirmation in her head:

"Be positive. Remember, your thoughts and words define your reality. Death and life are in the power of the tongue, and those who love it shall eat of its fruit thereof."

When she walked into her office, she dropped her bag at her station, and hurried over to Imade's office, feigning an outward composure that she most certainly did not feel on the inside. All the delays meant that there was no time for her morning coffee before she had to face her manager.

"Good morning, boss," she said, forcing the most pleasant and happy sing-song tone she could muster into her voice.

Imade didn't look up from her laptop as she responded.

"Good morning to you, Miss Best Regional Analyst. While I'm all about recognition for great work, being awarded last week doesn't give you the leeway to come in late to work."

"Actually, I wasn't late," Rebbeca whispered. "I arrived a few minutes before 8 AM."

Imade pursed her lips, then looked up at her with an expression that echoed the word she didn't say: *So?*

Rebecca backtracked. She has tried everything she can to please her, but even doing her job well seemed to bring Imade little pleasure. Hard work should equal progress, but she hasn't figured out what will actually move the needle with her superior officer.

"My apologies for the tardiness."

"Better. Now, what do you want?"

"I thought I should inform you that the regulatory meeting is in less than ninety minutes, so it's best to leave now so you won't be late."

"Ugh, I am not looking forward to that meeting, but it is what it is. Call Patrick and have him bring the car out front."

"Okay." She turned to leave.

"Also, grab your things; we are going to the meeting together."

Oh, no! There went the dream of her morning coffee.

"Me?"

"Did I stutter?" Imade stopped typing, closed her laptop, and dropped it into her bag. She barely looked at Rebecca, sending a disapproving nod toward her as she walked briskly past instead, handing her bag over in one swift gesture.

That was Rebecca's cue to hurry to her station and grab her items.

She stumbled behind, trying to balance both bags and catch up to Imade's pace; the stilettos shoes she had on proving to be a wrong choice for the day. But they say beauty is pain, so it was just like Rebecca to never sacrifice her fashion choices for comfort.

"Keep up, Rebecca, we can't be late."

"Yes, Ma, I'm right behind you."

She hobbled, struggling under the weight of her handbag, Imade's bag, laptop, and files for their meeting.

She paused to catch her breath as they finally got to the car.

"Good morning, Mr Patrick," she greeted the driver as she climbed in.

The genial elderly man smiled at her. "Good morning, dear."

"How is the family?"

Before he could respond, Imade, her voice high with irritation, said: "Rebecca, shut the door and hand over my bag."

"Sorry, ma'am." Rebecca settled in fully behind the driver, shut the door, and shoved one of the bags toward Imade.

"This isn't my ba—"

"Sorry," Rebecca stammered, retrieving her bag and handing the correct one over.

Imade's eyes narrowed to slits. "Is that Fendi?"

Rebecca bit her lip to keep from laughing and pulled her best poker face. "This? Uh, yeah, it's just something I picked up recently."

"How can you even afford that?" Imade rolled her eyes.

Not with the salary you pay me, Rebecca thought. But she didn't say that, offering a sage smile in response instead.

Rebecca joined Oregon as a business analyst, but two months into the role, her manager—an amiable, round-bellied man she absolutely adored—was swapped for this Ice Queen. Now, her role mirrored that of an advanced personal assistant while her core business analyst responsibilities had become a side gig. Yet Imade hardly acknowledged her progress, only pushing her harder and harder, to what end, Rebecca had no clue.

"I haven't received your updated training tracker for the quarter," Imade cut into her thoughts.

"Uh, so sorry, you'll get it today."

At first, Rebecca looked forward to learning a lot from her, but lately she has begun actively searching for roles in other departments. The problem with that was all other department heads are scared of Imade, and worried about getting on her bad side. Imade has been in the company for over twelve years, working across states and abroad, with her most recent stint in East Africa. On paper, she's the perfect role model. But in real life, she's the draining kind of fierce. She hasn't been unkind to Rebecca personally, but her intimidating presence makes it hard for people to actually like her.

"Anyway," Imade continued, "did you remember to call ahead to confirm that the meeting will hold as scheduled? I won't be very pleased if it turns out that this meeting has been cancelled again."

"Yes, you are still scheduled for 10:30 AM."

Imade huffed in response and turned to her iPad.

Thankful for the silence, Rebecca pulled up her to-do list on her phone. She had to find time today to call her mother to let her know she'd received the bale, go through her Instagram messages to respond to orders, follow up on the deliveries to go out before noon, and sort through the deliveries she took this morning. Scratch that—the sorting can wait until tomorrow.

Then, on the 9–5 side of things, she needed to go through Imade's schedule to confirm everything was going according to plan, update her on any changes, send out their close-out analytics for the previous week, and connect with the other commercial director on some of his pending requests.

As she was going through the list, Rebecca's phone buzzed with an email notification, and her heart skipped a beat. She quickly read the email, then shut her eyes, pressing them tightly against the tears threatening to spill. Another rejection. It was familiar at this point. For the past quarter, she has spent her weekends sending out countless job applications, each time hopeful. Each time, with eventual dashed hopes.

What was it going to take for her career to truly progress? Her situation was impossible. In her current job, there was an invisible barrier holding her back—one that formed when Imade arrived. The frustration pushed her to seek opportunities elsewhere. But despite her relentless efforts, every lead so far has fallen through. This one had felt different—after three gruelling panel interviews and a one-on-one meeting with the department head, she was confident. That's why this rejection stung. She swallowed down the impulse to fire off a blistering response.

"Whew!"

Imade shot her a scathing look. "What was that?"

"Oh, nothing. Sorry, I was just taking a breath."

"Tone it down, you're messing with my concentration."

Rebecca rolled her eyes and made an exaggerated mumming motion. At this rate, she could hardly wait for her vacation next week to start.

She understood that Imade hated meetings with government officials, but unfortunately, they were key stakeholders, and face-to-face meetings with them helped fast-track approval processes. Among other things that happen behind closed doors.

TelOne has been a major player in the telecom industry from the outset, and they have a new innovative service and product they want to roll out. However, the regulatory approval was taking longer than usual, so her boss was under pressure. Unfortunately, the regulators tended to cancel meetings on a whim, like they did two weeks ago. They spent almost two hours in traffic only to get there and find out it had been rescheduled. Rebecca has had to call every day all week to ensure no repeat of that incident.

"Have you checked in with Director Jimi?

"Yes, he'll be joining us at the venue. His flight arrived this morning from their summit in Port Harcourt."

"Okay, he shouldn't be late. This meeting has been on his schedule for over a week, and we need him there."

The rest of their trip went on in silence except for the persistent honking of cars, which was unavoidable on Lagos roads. Imade took calls and worked on her laptop while Rebecca tried not to breathe too loudly.

An hour later, they pulled up to the Ministry.

They both got out of the car, and as usual, Rebecca carried all the bags and files and followed Imade.

Imade stopped abruptly, turned back, and gave Rebecca a cursory look from top to bottom. "When we walk in there, I want you to exude the highest level of confidence, okay? No bending or stuttering or whatever else you have going on. And when the questions come, always have an answer handy. You know the numbers, so be ready to provide them if I nod or gesture at you. Is that clear?"

"Yes, ma'am."

"Hand me my bag and files and keep your phone close."

"Okay."

Imade nodded approvingly. "Let's go."

Once again, Rebecca rolled her eyes and picked up the things she had dropped on the car seat, shutting the door with the back of her heels.

As they both walked up to the entrance, Rebecca caught their reflection in the tall, polished reflective glass doors. They both looked good, but Imade looked the epitome of a confident top executive. She carried herself like a celebrity all day, every day—with effortless grace. She was one of the few women Rebecca knew who could pull off her height in perfect outfits. The pencil style, blue skirt, beige checkered jacket, nude heeled sandals, and back-length straight-cut auburn human hair wig Imade put together for the meeting delivered effortless sophistication with absolute flair. It was so sleek, Rebecca planned to use it for one of her style inspo videos.

"I don't look too bad myself," Rebecca thought. Her look was tamer but no less chic. She adjusted her ponytail, tugged at her dress, and straightened her posture, immediately feeling better. She headed to the reception desk and smiled at the middle-aged woman in an ankara outfit.

"Good morning, Ma. We have an appointment for 10:30 AM, the Oregon Group."

"Okay, you can go to your right in the second meeting room."

She turned to Imade. "Second meeting room on the right."

Imade nodded and walked ahead, with Rebecca following closely.

They walked into the room and met Director Jimi waiting alone with a lady setting up a coffee stand.

"Rebecca," his throaty voice echoed around the large room.

Rebecca smiled. He had such a welcoming, fatherly aura. "You look well my dear," he said. Glancing at Imade, he nodded noncommittally. "Imade, good morning."

"Morning, Jimi."

Their terse exchange wasn't unusual. There has been a long-standing rivalry between the department heads. But to be fair to Jimi, Imade was a rival to most of the department heads, except their collective boss, who positively beams whenever Imade is around. Another reason they detested her so much. Although rumours have it that with Jimi, it's different; they used to be close until she left for Kenya some years ago on an international assignment.

They waited for another fifteen minutes before the other attendees arrived. The meeting then dragged on for an hour and thirty minutes. Rebecca shot out numbers, while Imade led an incredible pitch and moderated the meeting like a pro.

At the end of the meeting, Imade asked Rebecca to wait for her outside so she and Jimi could speak to the committee head.

Another Monday had snuck up on Sola, and while he was up early to send emails to follow up on the conversations he had at the reunion, he's not too happy about it. No thanks to having only had a few hours of fitful sleep due to a bad dream.

New day, same troubles, he thought.

He headed to the gym to clear his head, and upon his return, met Derin waiting in his parked almost new SUV. With a clean-shaven face and glasses perched on his nose, he looked as serious as always in his button-up-patterned T-shirt.

"You're early," Sola said, knocking gently on the car window to grab Derin's attention. "I didn't think you'd come over until late afternoon."

"I was eager. You have good news?"

"Yeah. Let's go in."

Over steaming cups of coffee, Sola gave him a rundown of the conversations and those who agreed to invest.

"That's amazing. We are getting the funds, but now we need to scale with customers."

"Yeah, have you heard back from any of the clients we pitched to?"

"Just one, but it makes for even better news. Do you remember the managing director of the Tabano chain that we met some months back?"

"Yes?"

"She reached out while you were out of the country. She's in town with her father today and wants a physical meeting."

"*The* Tabano?" Sola gawked at Derin. "Are you serious?"

"Yes, I am. You should have gotten the email, too. You are on cc."

"That's amazing. So much was going on that I glossed over it. We already wrote them off as a dead end; we've been chasing them for almost half of the year, and now they want to meet?" Sola pumped the air in celebration.

"I already made a reservation at the Pisces restaurant. Figured we could have the discussion over lunch," Derin said.

"That makes sense, at least until our new space is fully renovated."

They just leased a new space and moved their operations from Sola's house, as their team was expanding with additional account managers and product designers.

They settled to review the sketch for their discussion and operational details.

"By the way, I have some ideas for a new service or business," Sola hinted. "We could integrate them with Luna Pay or set them up separately."

Derin groaned. "You're doing it again."

"Doing what?"

"Sola, you know what. We are in a good space with the business, and both agreed on the next step, which is expansion, but you're ready to run off with a new idea. You need to see this through."

"Of course. I'm seeing it through, but there's nothing wrong with pursuing new challenges. You haven't even heard the ideas."

"And I don't want to. Let's just focus on this first, okay?"

Sola's phone rang, cutting his response short. It was his mother. He didn't answer but took that as his cue to head out. "I need to go out now, but we'll pick this up later. I'll catch you at the office."

"Okay, where are you headed?

Sola paused before responding, "Uh, my mum has been calling, so I want to pop in and say hello before coming to the office."

"I'll go with you, and then we can head to the office together in my car. There's no point driving apart."

"Uh, nah, don't stress about it. You have things to do, so I'll meet you at the office."

"No, I insist. I haven't seen your mum in such a long time. It'll be nice to surprise her and say hello."

Sola shrugged and gave in.

When they got to his childhood home about an hour later, his mother ran to the entrance to envelop him in a hug.

"Ọkọ mi, welcome…" She trailed off when she spotted Derin, who'd been parking the car while Sola went ahead.

Derin approached and bent his head in greeting. "Good afternoon, Ma, how have you been?"

She looked curiously between Sola and Derin.

"Welcome, ọrẹ Sola. I wasn't expecting you," she said, sending an accusing gaze toward Sola, who pleaded with his eyes. She switched back to being upbeat, "Come in, come in. She ushered them into the house. "Yewande!" she called. "Serve Sola and his friend." She turned to Sola. "Ehm, Sola, before

Yewande brings your food, come quick. I have something to show you." She shoved him from the living room to the staircase and led him up to her room.

"Sola," she stared, eyes blazing, "what are you doing with that boy? I didn't know you and Derin were still friends. After all these years, shouldn't you have made new friends?"

Sola rubbed his forehead. "Mum, you don't understand, even though I've explained multiple times. We are business partners and have been working together since I got back from Poland."

"I don't have a good feeling about this boy. And I thought you would have cut ties after you left secondary school and went abroad. Has life not taught you any lessons?"

His mother's distaste for their friendship wasn't new, and although he had no way to make her see reason, her reservations were hard to argue with. When he left for university in Poland, Derin continued his schooling in Nigeria and fell into bad company, picking up a bad gambling habit, blaming it on pressures from school and the home front. Sola got wind of it and enlisted his mother's help to keep an eye on him. She stepped up to the plate, getting him to counselling and offering financial support till he graduated. Her heart might be golden, but it made her double down on her insistence that Sola stay away from Derin. Yet, whether it was because of trauma or a sense of responsibility to one another, among his group of friends, he and Derin have stayed the closest.

"Mum, I know he had a rough patch for a while, but he has picked himself back up. So far, he's been tenaciously focused on our company. He's a smart guy with a good head on his shoulders, so there's nothing to worry about."

"I know you believe that, but I don't understand it, and I don't remember him ever being a good influence. You are my priority; it's my job to protect you, and while I don't mean to upset you. Àgùtàn tó bá bá ajá rìn á jẹ ìgbẹ́, ajá tó bá bá ewúrẹ́ rìn á jẹ èpo iṣu."

A sheep that moves with dogs will eat faeces, and a dog that moves with goats will eat yam peelings.

"We reflect the company we keep," she added for good measure, "and you were reckless all those years ago, partly thanks to him. Don't make the same mistake."

"Mother hen," he pinched her cheeks. "I hear you, but I'm an adult, and a lot has changed between then and now. So, trust me, and don't worry about anything, okay?"

"Mo ti gbo. If you say so, but I'll be praying for you."

"Okay, if that helps ease your worry. Can I go eat now? I'm hungry."

"Eh, wait, there's one more thing." She bit her lip, sat beside him on the bed, and pulled his hand, placing it on her lap. "Ọkọ mi, you know I love you more than life itself, but with each passing day, I'm growing older and won't be here with you forever." She paused and sighed dramatically. "I have only one desire before I return to my maker, and that's to have both my sons sit at the same table with me and your father as one family before God."

He pursed his lips, guessing what was coming next.

"Sola, so many years have passed by, and I don't know how much pain my heart can take from seeing you and your father separate, unforgiving, and refusing to see each other."

"Mum ..."

"Sola jọ ... go see your father. It's been long enough."

"I have to go," he snapped.

"Don't be like this. Doesn't it count that I'm asking?"

"It does, but it doesn't match your husband's will and request to never lay his eyes on me again. You were a witness, so why do you act like you've forgotten? He doesn't want to think of me as a son, so I don't think of him as a father, but you keep pleading and asking when he's the one who made his wish clearly known."

"Sola ... don't forget the Bible says you should honour your father and mother. What you're doing is far from that."

"But it also says fathers shouldn't vex their sons. Tell that to your husband," he retorted bitterly.

"Ha!"

He tenderly held his mother's shoulders and kissed her forehead. "I love you very much, and I will always be here when you need me, but you need to throw out that prayer, dream, wishful thinking, or whatever you call it because the table that will take both me and your husband doesn't exist." He turned and walked away briskly so he wouldn't see her cry.

"Derin, let's go!" he yelled, walking into the living room, but it was empty. "Derin!" he called again.

No response.

Yewande came in then to tell him that Derin stepped outside to take a call.

He headed out, but his mother stopped him.

"At least take the soups that Yewande prepared," she said.

He nodded, then pulled his mother into his arms. She felt smaller than he remembered. "Thank you for the food," he said softly. "I'm sorry I can't give you what you want."

"It's okay but take the things I've said to heart. My spirit isn't comfortable with that young man hanging around."

"Yes, Ma."

Sola stacked four covered bowls in his arms and carried them outside. At the entrance, he found Derin talking on the phone. When the door clicked shut, he startled and turned around.

"It's just me," Sola said, squinting at Derin.

"Of course, I knew that." Derin chuckled nervously. "I'll call you back shortly," he said to whoever was on the phone.

"I'm ready to leave."

"Cool." He looked to Sola's mum. "Thanks for the meal, Ma."

As they descended the stairs, he turned and added. "My regards to Daddy."

three

GLIMPSES

Rebecca walked briskly to the reception area, glancing furtively behind her to confirm that Imade was still in the meeting room. Then she dialled her mother. The call connected on the second ring.

"Hello, Mummy. How are you?" Rebecca said, pressing the phone against her ear to make out her mother's voice in a sea of noise and lively chatter.

"Nwa m nwanyi, I'm fine!" her mother shouted above the clamour. "I'm in the market! You're at work, right? Did you collect the load?"

"Yes, Mummy, I'm at work but waiting for my boss. I got the bale, thank you, but please, the next one should be on a Friday," Rebecca whined. "It's not easy picking up on Monday, and you know these Imo state drivers can be troublesome if you come to the park late."

"Ehn, I understand. Don't be angry. It was because the sellers didn't open new bales till Saturday, and I wanted to pick the best ones and send them as soon as possible. Hope you liked them and selected some nice ones for yourself and your friends?"

"I haven't gone through them yet."

"No problem, I know you'll like them. Promise not to write off some of the old designs. Style them as you usually do and post them on your social media so your followers will see them. Let them decide if it's old school or not. You can call them vintage, retro rustic, or one of those fancy names you give the clothes."

"Alright, Mummy," Rebecca responded with a chuckle at her mother's endearing attempt to keep up with trendy fashion language. "How is Chimezie?" she asked, referring to her adopted brother, her late uncle's son whom her mother had taken in upon his demise.

"He's fine. He's gone to school, but I'll see him at the shop later. He's been insisting on joining me at the shop lately, unlike you, who always ran away. He even brought two of his teachers to the shop last week to buy some items. One of them, a man, bought four sets of skirt suits for his wife, although he plans to pay in instalments."

Rebecca laughed. "It's a family business, so don't worry. Allow him so that he won't be bored at home. I'll send the money from the last set of orders by the weekend; just let the ones that have gone out confirm delivery."

"Okay, no problem. Remember to remove your profit and the money you paid for transport."

"Yes, Mummy, don't worry. I made good sales this month. Also, are you eating well and taking your medications? I have the doctor's number, so don't even think of lying to me."

"Your wahala is plenty, I'm doing fine, and there's no need to worry."

"Okay, if you say so. I need to go now. I only wanted to update you."

"No problem. A hụrụ m gị n'anya."

"I love you too."

She ended the call and dialled her logistics lady to find out the status of the packages she kept for pickup. The rider was en-route, held up in traffic, but was due to arrive at the location shortly.

"Okay, as I sent to you on WhatsApp, there are six parcels labelled with the recipients' names, addresses, and phone numbers, the same as the list I shared with you. The rider should call me if he has issues with any of the deliveries so I can send them a direct message."

After the call, Rebecca thought about what to eat. She was starving—and grabbing something to eat now would leave space to catch up on work and her Instagram messages during her meal. But she couldn't do that because protocol required her to wait for Imade.

Moments later, her boss stepped out of her meeting and into the reception area, beaming like a child, and waving her arm animatedly, urging Rebecca to follow her. In the front of the building, standing face-to-face, Imade let out a breathy sigh that changed to an excited squeak—at least, that's what it sounded like to Rebecca.

"We got the approval!" Imade exclaimed. "The committee head assured me we'll receive the email later today, and you can pick up the physical letter by tomorrow."

"That's amazing!" Rebecca screamed, a mix of happiness and relief washing over her. "Well done, ma'am."

"Thank you, and well done to you, too," Imade replied, immediately putting her serious face back up.

Rebecca couldn't hold back her laughter at the quick transition. Imade caught her reaction but ignored it. "Call the driver. This calls for celebration. Let's have lunch before heading to the office."

"Yes, Ma'am."

When the driver pulled up, they headed out to the restaurant of Imade's choosing called 'PISCES.' It was pretty quiet except for a group that seemed to be having a business meeting, a couple, and about three lone diners, all male.

They settled in and ordered their meals.

Sola arrived at the Pisces restaurant and met Derin who arrived earlier, while he stayed back at the office, cleaning up the presentation.

"Hey, man."

They shared a bro hug, and Sola sat. As he reached for a spring roll on the appetizer tray, he felt Derin give him a cursory look. He instinctively knew it was about his outfit—black jeans, an unbuttoned shirt over a white T-shirt, a gold necklace, and bracelets.

"You could have at least worn a jacket," Derin said.

"Don't give me grief. You saw what I was wearing when we left the house. Besides, every suited-up man needs a sidekick in a T-shirt." Derin shook his head. "I wish you'd take these meetings more seriously and show that in your outfit choices."

Sola scoffed. "I don't need a suit for that. You already exude enough seriousness for both of us, so I'll do the rest with my talking and presentation." Sola frowned. Derin's demeanour had changed from when they were together earlier. "What's gotten into you? Why are you so uptight?"

"I'm not uptight, just nervous. We've been chasing these guys for months, I really want us to land this."

"I want the same thing but chill out. We do our best work relaxed, not stressed out."

Derin nodded, then jumped up with a nervous smile, looking toward the door. "Here they are."

Sola looked in the direction of their guests.

The chief was a buff but agile man of average height. The restaurant lightning cast soft highlights on his full and healthy all-white hair. His strides were slow but purposeful, commanding attention. Then a striking young woman emerged from behind and walked beside him.

Tiffany.

She was dressed in a striking green pantsuit that hugged her generous and curvy silhouette beautifully. Her gold and brown curly braids framed her face and hung off her shoulders, accentuating her dark complexion.

She spotted them, smiled, and walked toward them with an energy that made her the room's focal point. Confidence oozed from her every step, mirroring her father's, literally the proverbial chip off the old block. They were a powerful duo, and Derin was right—he was woefully underdressed.

Derin stepped forward, planted himself in front of him, and stretched his hand out to their guests for a shake. "Good afternoon, Chief Cearo. It's a pleasure to meet you. We're thrilled you could make it. And Ms Tiffany." He turned to her. "It's our pleasure to host you. This is my business partner and co-founder." He gestured to Sola, who moved forward to shake their hands.

"We've met, but it's still a pleasure," Tiffany smiled invitingly, her hands disappearing into Sola's in a soft but firm grasp.

The air around him filled with a delightful mix of floral and spicy scents, gently nipping at his senses. "Yeah." He coughed to clear his sudden breathlessness. "My apologies once again for my impetuousness." He swallowed hard, remembering their first encounter at a tech conference and exhibition for retailers.

He'd taken what was supposed to be a quick break from their booth to stretch his legs. Instead, he wandered the hall, listening to other product pitches. He ran into Tiffany at her booth and asked her about her product. To be fair, she was dressed casually, and when they met, she was picking up a leaflet from the floor, so he assumed she was an exhibitor. She stared at him in confusion and tried to explain that she didn't know much about the product. Still, he launched into a coaching session on pitch and the importance of understanding one's product. The final cap was when he gave her their card and asked that she visit their booth to see an example of an exhibition done right. She thanked him with an amused smile, and he left to visit other stalls.

When he eventually circled back to theirs, he met an excited Derin with another staff member who shared that they got a visit from the Managing Director of Tabano Group, who wanted to hear their pitch. A quick Google search brought up her picture on the first page. Mortified, he searched for her in futility after that, not finding her.

"It's alright, your partner and the other lady I met at the exhibition delivered a brilliant pitch, so here we are to do business."

Derin sent him a puzzled look. Sola pulled himself together and cleared his throat again.

"Thank you. We are so happy to have you. Please have a seat." He meant every word. Tabano was the sixth big business they had pitched their product to. Many of their onboarded customers were small businesses and supermarkets with less than two outlets, so getting this meeting was a huge win.

Tiffany picked a chair. Her father pulled it out for her and only sat after she was comfortable.

"Also, congratulations on your award," Sola continued, "I followed the ceremony online and saw that Dr Cearo received a business excellence honour. It's a testament to the incredible legacy you've built with Tabano as the biggest retail chain in the country. It's no easy feat, especially in this challenging business climate."

"Thank you, Sola," Dr Cearo replied gruffly, "but much of the credit goes to my daughter," he said, beaming with pride. "She does most of the work managing the business, while I enjoy the farm-cosy life with my wife in our hometown."

"That's incredible," Derin chimed.

"I started the business with my wife as a supermarket outlet in Enugu many years ago. Now we have over fifty outlets nationwide. We based the headquarters in Abuja, where Tiffany now resides. We've been looking to fine-tune our payment process and reduce losses, so Tiffany convinced me to consider your solution. So, what do you young men have for us?"

Derin went ahead with the presentation, showing them a demo and an overview of their operations, workforce, and services.

"What do you think?" Dr Cearo asked, turning to Tiffany.

"It sounds like a great solution, but I must admit that it isn't unique or much different from the other products out there. Also, the payment solution we are currently using works fine, so why fix what's broken if it's not with something better and more innovative? Still, I won't throw it out completely if you can promise that there is an opportunity for some updates to be made."

"What updates would you like to see?" Derin asked.

"A backend view showing outlet volume of daily transactions, with average basket size. I see a weekly total reconciliation, which cannot work for a business of our size and spread. Leakages are a major pain point, and your tool's insight doesn't help me solve it any better than our current solutions."

"We understand, but our solution has a more efficient user interface, dedicated customer service, and redeemable loyalty rewards for users. We are also rolling out a book-in-advance/pay-in-tranches feature, which considers the country's economic condition and the recurring feedback theme from user surveys and immersion sessions. We have about five retailers currently using this solution, and we show a demo. In addition, we can give you a free trial period. Let us know your preferred time slot, and we'll meet you at your office or anywhere else you prefer with our head of innovation. If you're satisfied, we can then talk terms," Derin explained.

Sola noticed that her hands were wrapped around her purse. She wasn't convinced.

"We can make the upgrade you need. This isn't the final iteration of the product, and we can definitely add the feature you described, especially to suit you better as a big business. If that's fine with you, we would need a little more time to have our developers work on it," Sola said.

Tiffany looked at her father and shrugged. "I like the product; I don't love it, but if you can show us a differentiation point, we can consider it further."

Chief leaned in. "You heard her. While intrigued, I have another appointment. We can continue this conversation later. We have a lot to do in two days."

"Thank you so much for taking the time to speak with us," Derin said.

They all get up and exchange handshakes. Tiffany smiled softly at Sola as she left with her father. He gave an awkward wave in return.

Sola and Derin both let out massive sighs of relief.

Sola spoke first, "I think that went well."

Derin didn't look satisfied. "I think Chief Cearo was impressed, but the princess has too high expectations," he scoffed.

They watched through the restaurant's transparent glass as Chief and Tiffany climbed into the jeep that has pulled up.

"Cheer up, Derin, look on the bright side. We had a meeting—which was great— and they were interested enough to give us constructive feedback. This only means that our work is cut out for us. We were thinking about our features for small businesses, but we need to improve them, so I'll round up the product team and get it done. We can check in with them in a few weeks after we test and iterate. For now, finish your drink." He gestured to the waiter, who brought the bill over.

Derin was still staring outside. "Man, did you see his ride? He should have covered the bill, not us."

Sola cackled. "Take it easy. We are the beggars in this equation."

"Nah, I'm nobody's beggar, especially not to people like the dynasty princess that have had everything handed to them and can't understand the struggle from the bottom."

Sola shot Derin a scathing look. "What's up with you? That's an extreme and unfair take. Like I said, take it easy."

Derin shrugged. "Whatever. I need to get back to work. I'll catch up with you later."

Rebecca and Imade had a nice chat over their meal.

The day has turned around for the better, she thought, basking in the moment. As she finished her meal, her phone rang. It was Kemi from the dispatch company. She excused herself and went to the washroom.

Rebecca returned just in time to see Imade heading out the door.

"Welp! That didn't last." She made a beeline for their table, grabbed her bag and the takeout meal for the driver, and ran out.

After Sola paid the waiter, he spotted a well-dressed lady rushing from her table, leaving a phone behind.

"Hello, hello!" he called out

She looked back with a slightly annoyed expression.

Her eyes connected with his, and it felt like a lightning bolt struck his bones with an intensity that halted him in his tracks.

"Yes, what is it?" she asked impatiently.

He blinked and shook off the trance.

"You dropped your phone," he said, stretching the device toward her.

"Oh, thank you so much. You're a lifesaver," the lady exclaimed, her face breaking into a lovely gap-toothed smile that reached her radiant brown eyes.

The familiarity of those eyes punched him in the pit of his stomach, but before he could say another word, she turned and disappeared through the door. A car pulled to a stop at the entrance, and she slipped inside, leaving him stuck in place for a minute. He saw only her eyes and nothing else, his brain desperately searching for a connection in a memory that was just out of reach.

He breathed deeply, shaking off the lingering sensation, and looked back at Derin, who was on a call speaking feverishly. As the weight of the encounter eased, he decided to head out.

four

CONVERSATIONS

Scoop, pick, pour.

The rattling sound and repeated motion permeated the room as Rebecca picked through a tray of beans. The soft hum of an audio Bible playing in the evening air, provided a much-needed distraction from her thoughts as the tough conversation she had with Imade when they returned to the office the day before fluttered around her head. A gentle breeze blew through the balcony, tickling her skin, providing welcome relief from the oppressive heat inside the house.

The familiar squeak of the gate swinging open cut through the ambience and she looked up to see Muyiwa stepping in, his face drawn.

"Hey!" she called out. He glanced her way and trudged over. "You look tired," she added, noting the dark circles under his eyes as she set her tray of beans down on the floor.

"Don't I know it," he replied, gesturing to the plastic chair beside her. "May I sit?"

Rebecca quickly swept aside the bits of chaff that had collected on the chair, wiping it down before he settled into it with a relieved grunt, the chair responding in kind with a creak.

"Long day?" she asked.

"Long week. It's tax season," he replied wearily.

Rebecca nodded in understanding. "I'll get you some water," she said, retreating into the house.

"Thanks," he called after her. When she returned with a glass, he wiped the sweat from his brow as she handed it to him.

"Would you like something to eat? I have some soup," she offered.

"Thanks, but I'm good, I got takeout," he said, pointing to a crumpled bag he'd tossed on the floor. He unfastened his jacket with practised ease and unwrapped his meal. "Join me?"

Rebecca shook her head, amused as she watched him dig into his food.

"I hope you don't mind me eating here. If I go home, I'll just get immersed in work until late," he admitted.

She tilted her head. "That bad, huh? Don't worry about it, take your time. I'm staying out here too—the heat inside is stilting."

"Stifling," he corrected, his mouth half-full.

"Pardon?"

He swallowed and smiled sheepishly. "You said the heat is 'stilting,' meaning to elevate something off the ground. I think you meant to say 'stifling,' as in uncomfortable or very hot."

"Oh, right. The latter one. Thanks, sensei." She grinned, returning to her beans.

His eyes widened, and he appeared a bit embarrassed. "Gosh, I'm sorry. I didn't mean to correct you—it's just instinct."

"It's fine. Teacher mode is second nature for you. That reminds me, Anita stopped by earlier. She wanted me to ask you about the kids' weekend lessons. No, she actually begged me to persuade you to resume them."

"Yeah. I owe them an apology." Muyiwa sighed, running a hand over his head. "My work has taken over my weekends for the next month, so I had to cancel."

"Take it easy, okay?" Rebecca said softly, drawn in by his vulnerability. "Speaking of which, have you ever thought about teaching full-time?"

He paused, carefully weighing her question, a thoughtful expression on his face.

"Once. But it wasn't practical. A consulting opportunity came along—safer and more financially rewarding—so I took it. Then my dad had that health scare, and it shook me. It made me realize that life should be more than just survival; it should be rich with heart, meaning, legacy, and purpose. I still have the desire to teach. That's why I started the weekend sessions with the kids. But on days like today, when work feels overwhelming and soulless, I find myself wishing I had the courage to make the leap into teaching full-time."

"Don't we all wish for courage? I could use a dose of it myself."

"Care to share?" he asked.

Rebecca hesitated for a moment, then continued, feeling a connection in their honesty.

"My boss has been giving me a hard time about putting myself out there. She really laid it on thick yesterday, telling me that just doing the work isn't enough. I need to own my successes and be proactive about sharing my wins with stakeholders, including her. I want to believe she has a point, and that's why I'm not progressing at work. But part of me feels like she is punishing me for not taking her advice and is trying to prove her point by holding me back."

"That sounds like a stretch."

"Maybe. But sometimes it feels easier to think that than to face the disappointment in myself. I also started looking for jobs externally, but I always freeze up at the interviews. I know what to say, but I get so anxious that I choke. It's been so frustrating. So, I'm forced to try to work on my boss's feedback. And honestly … I'll admit it. I'm afraid to put myself out there. I do good work—and sometimes I think, heck, I do great work. Why can't it just speak for itself? But when I think about it, I feel like my best work isn't good enough. So, if I share, it'll open me up to scrutiny, and maybe someone would uncover that I'm a fluke. All this talk of visibility, image, and reputation only makes me want to hide. What if I do all that and still don't get ahead?"

As she spoke, she found herself wrapping her arms around herself like a security blanket.

"I understand why you may feel that way, but if you reframe it, you'd be surprised at the difference. For example, you could say that your boss pushing you to share your work is an indirect vote of confidence. She's seen the quality and is aware that any work that goes out from her department reflects on her. I don't believe that she'll set herself up just to make a public example of you. So, trust her, and more than that, trust God, believe in yourself, and don't be afraid to take the leap of faith."

"For God has not given us a spirit of fear, but of power, love, and a sound mind." Her phone chimed loudly, the sudden noise catching their attention.

Muyiwa nodded knowingly. "Timely verse."

"Be strong and courageous; do not be afraid, for the Lord will be with you wherever you go," Rebecca added.

"Yes. But it's easier said than done," Muyiwa mused.

"But faith demands action," Rebecca countered gently. "We can't just recite Bible verses and think that's enough. We need to let them inspire us to act. Something for both of us to think about, right?"

"You're right," he agreed. "Well, it's time to call it a night," Muyiwa announced, slapping his thighs and sitting up straight. "It's gotten late, and I've hogged enough of your evening," he added teasingly. "You have a way of pulling me out of whatever rut I'm in, and I appreciate you letting me unburden myself—it was unplanned yet refreshing."

"I'll send you the invoice for my services," she joked, laughing as he playfully bowed before heading back to his flat.

Rebecca quickly picked up her phone and added teaching keywords to her job search board, humming as she remembered her first run-in with Muyiwa three years ago.

It had been a week since the running water had stopped, despite the landlord's promise to send a plumber. Thankfully, she had stored up some water for emergencies, but that day, she was facing the real possibility of running dry.

"This is no way to live," she groaned.

She was faced with three unpleasant options: Buying water, trekking two streets over to fetch from a public tap, or confronting the landlord about the delay. For the first option, she had been keeping every drop of savings for a car, and after calculating that the balance for monthly upkeep in her account would just about cover transport and feeding for the month, spending more money wasn't going to fly. The second was physically unappealing, and the third? Rebecca shrank at the thought of facing the man. But she had no other choice.

After bathing and dressing, she straightened her shoulders and, like a woman with a mission, stomped over, bag in hand, to the landlord's flat, rehearsing her rage. She knocked three times on the metal door with vehemence but was met with silence.

Playing closer attention, she heard muffled voices inside. Shifting from foot to foot, irritation grew with each second that passed. Just as she prepared to knock again, the door swung open, and she stumbled backward. Standing before her was an incredibly handsome stranger, likely in his late twenties or early thirties, his expression a scowl.

"Yes?" he asked, his tone surprising her.

Regaining her composure, Rebecca crossed her arms tightly and planted her feet defiantly. "I'm looking for the landlord."

"He's unavailable, but I can take a message," his firm voice was oddly soothing, which eased some of her resolve.

Still, she shot him a glare, unwilling to let her frustration dissipate. "Unavailable? Meanwhile, we, his tenants, are suffering like we're living in the dark ages! I don't know who you are but tell him this treatment is unfair. How can we live without water? It's a basic human right!"

"Young lady, you don't have to shout. I'm right here and can hear you clearly."

"Young lady?" she spluttered. The term and his patronizing tone rasped against her nerves, but his distracting good looks made it hard to sustain her ire. "Whatever! I have the right to express my frustration!" she snapped back, voice rising.

"Fine," he said, then shut the door firmly in her face.

Rebecca stood frozen for several heartbeats, her mouth agape. Should she knock again or turn back to work? She was still contemplating when the door opened again, and he peeked out.

"The plumber will come today to fix the issue."

Before she could respond, he shut the door once more. Clenching her jaw, she swallowed the angry remarks bubbling up inside her and stormed away with a huff.

As she reached the gate, her newly acquainted neighbour at the time, Anita, was waiting with her young daughter, who was dressed for school.

"I see you met the landlord's son, bro Muyiwa," Anita said, amusement in her eyes.

"Oh, that's who he is? No wonder he's acting like there's a stick up his butt."

"He has already charmed you," Anita teased sarcastically.

"Yeah, right," Rebecca replied, rolling her eyes.

"Anyway, did he give you an update on the water situation?"

"Yeah," she said, opening the gate. "He claims the plumber will fix it today. Fingers crossed it actually happens."

"Well, thanks for taking the bullet for all of us. I have to go now, so this little madam won't be late for school."

Rebecca nodded and, since she was ready to leave for work, walked with them to the road before they parted ways to follow their different routes.

Later that day, after work, Rebecca was sprawled on her couch, scrolling through her phone and editing a caption for social media when she heard footsteps approach her door. It halted, but no knock followed. She lowered her phone and listened. The person remained still, so she swung her legs off the couch and tiptoed to the window. There he was—the landlord's son—alternating between studying her door and glancing back the way he came, his brow furrowed. He sighed, then turned to leave, but she dashed toward the door and flung it open.

"Why are you standing at my door like I owe you money? Can I help you with something?" she queried, hands on her hips.

His face darkened with a frown. "Do you have water now?"

"Yes."

He nodded, seemingly satisfied. "Okay. That's what I came to confirm." He turned to leave.

"Stop right there, young man!" she called out.

"What?" he turned around, annoyance evident in his tone.

In a swift motion, Rebecca slammed the door shut, breath catching in her throat. She rushed to the window, satisfaction washing over her as she watched him stand there, mouth agape, mirroring the shocked look she'd worn earlier.

"That felt good," she murmured to herself, a smile creeping across her face as she returned to her couch.

Barely two weeks after the encounter with Muyiwa, and exactly a week since she swore to make her boyfriend, Felix, sweat for going incommunicado after an argument, she was standing at the entrance of her compound, after a disastrous outing, a broken heeled shoe in hand, in a haze of dust that Felix's car raised as he sped off to an "urgent appointment." When Felix came begging the day before, and promising heaven and earth if she allowed him to take her out for lunch to make up for his misbehaviour, she said yes. It wasn't until the bill came and he'd forgotten his wallet—again—leaving her to pick up the bill that she regretted the decision.

Awkwardly balanced on one foot, one hand pressed against the gate, she tugged on the other shoe, struggling to get it off.

"What is in the air that is making guys act like jerks lately?" She thought as she tried to understand not just Felix's behaviour but Muyiwa's.

At that moment, the gate swung open, and she stumbled forward, falling into someone who broke her fall.

"Oh my God! Thank you ..." She breathed, straightening up and realising that the subject of her last thought had materialised before her. "Are you stalking me now?" she exclaimed, shaking a shoe in Muyiwa's face.

"Of course not," he replied, raising his arms defensively as he took a step back. "How was I to know you were on the other side, turning a public entrance into a dressing room?"

She narrowed her eyes. "You know what? You're extremely rude to people you don't even know for no reason."

"*Rude?* You're the one who yelled at me the first time we met and have been combative ever since. I don't know who you are either!" he shot back, exasperated.

"You don't have to know me to be polite!" she retorted.

He let out a deep sigh and took a step closer, visibly trying to defuse the tension. His shoulders relaxed, making him appear less intimidating.

"Look, I understand that when we first me, you were frustrated about the water issue, but that's fixed now, right?" he said gently.

Rebecca stared at him, her expression still cold, her nose turned up.

"Fine! I'm sorry," he conceded. "I could have been more understanding and acted better."

"And?" she pressed, crossing her arms.

"And ... for shutting the door on you?"

"What else?"

He furrowed his brow. "I'm not sure what else."

"Fine, I'll take what you've given," she said with a wave of her hand. "And I'm sorry too."

"Cool." A barely-there smile crossed his face, and though his lips remained straight, his eyes lit up. "Seeing as we got off on the wrong foot, let's start over. I'm Muyiwa," he said, extending his hand toward her.

Taking his hand with her free one, she replied, "Rebecca."

"Pleased to meet you."

"The pleasure's all mine," she said, feeling the tension dissolve just a bit.

He moved to the side, allowing her to enter the compound while he stepped out to go his own way.

As she wobbled toward her door, her neighbour Anita appeared like a ninja out of the wind.

"Sisi Rebecca! I see you and bro Muyiwa are playing nice now," she chirped.

Rebecca pursed her lips, trying to avoid encouraging the conversation. "We were just talking about the water issue," she replied.

Anita fell into step beside her. "I'm sure you'll have plenty of time to discuss other issues since you'll be seeing him more often."

"What does that mean?" Rebecca asked, her curiosity piqued.

"Haven't you heard? He's moving into his parents' house permanently to help monitor the landlord as he recovers from a stroke. His mum can't handle it on her own; she has her own issues," Anita explained.

Rebecca paused in front of her door, her heart sinking as the words registered. "Landlord had a stroke?" she whispered, wishing she could take her foot out of her mouth. She'd been harsh to the poor guy when his father was ill?

"Anyway ..." Anita continued. "I just wanted to confirm if you'd heard. I hope he doesn't raise our rent, though—you know how all these young people behave."

Rebecca rummaged through her bag for her keys, managing to smile at Anita.

"Thanks for letting me know. I really need to rest now."

"Of course. I also need to help my daughter with her assignment."

But Anita lingered, making no move to leave until Rebecca got inside, gently shut the door behind her, locking it in a slow, deliberate motion.

five

FRIENDSHIPS

Soft music played from a random speaker in the open plan work space that was Luna Pay's office. Sola and Derin encouraged staff to make the space theirs, and they owned it in some unexpected ways—vibrant potted plants in stalls, miniature robots from every era in animation and car model collections jostled for space with personal pictures. Someone even had a bicycle model from the 1920s hanging from a wall.

He had arrived early to brief the team on the projects to be completed and to assign tasks. Although they ran a flexible work environment where most people worked from home, briefings and ideation sessions happened physically. Everyone understood the brief and had been fully present.

Well, not everyone.

He looked at his watch. It was 10:30 AM, but Derin had yet to arrive. He casually shrugged off the concern, chalking it up to the multiple operational tasks and vendor management Derin had on his plate.

After he dismissed the team, Sola settled into one of the cubicles. He noticed Ada, an eager finance intern, walking around a few times, shifting nervously, cradling a few papers to her chest. The hesitant way she scanned the office and tried to covertly look his way made him call out to her.

"Ada, what's up? Do you need anything?"

"Not exactly," she replied as she approached him. "I'm actually looking for Mr Dee."

"He's not in yet. Is it urgent?"

She pulled back and chuckled nervously. "It's not urgent, but I need some clarity from him before we proceed with processing the due vendor invoices. Although he approved the payments, I want to double-check."

"Got it. He should be in at some point today. But you can call him. It doesn't sound like a big problem, so don't worry.

She nodded and left.

Sola worked for another hour, typing notes on his laptop screen when his focus was interrupted by his phone lighting up with an incoming call. The caller ID read Chude, one of his long-time friends from secondary school.

"Mazi Chude!"

"Guy, how far?" Chude boomed enthusiastically down the line.

"I dey. How your side?"

"Cool, cool. I'm thinking of gathering the boys for celebratory drinks at Line Beach tomorrow night. You go show?"

"Tomorrow? What's the occasion?"

"Well...it looks like your guy got bumped up the career ladder, so I wanted to celebrate with you guys."

Sola felt genuine happiness at the news.

"That's awesome, man. Congratulations. I wouldn't miss it. I'll be there."

After the call ended, Sola leaned back in his chair and thought about the way their lives had turned out. He and Derin were doing well in the wild ride that was the startup world, but he sometimes wondered if the corporate 9-5 life would have suited him better. Sola had tasted that life during his brief work stint in Poland after completing his studies, but it had felt monotonous. He craved the thrill of exploring new ideas and building things he could call his own from the ground up, so he resigned after a few years, launched his startup, and moved back to Nigeria. Yet, a nagging voice of doubt lingered in his mind. His current life was exciting, but precarious. As his friends seemed to be moving smoothly along clear and satisfying life trajectories, he wondered if he was genuinely succeeding.

Sola shook off the descending blues and encouraged himself. This work was something he was passionate about, he was building something that not only belonged to him and Derin fully, but something that could make a real change to businesses. Not only that, he got to flex his intellect and rub shoulders with some of the smartest people he'd ever met. At any point in his life, he could pivot into anything else whenever he was ready. He had a good experience; any good company would pay him well.

Returning to his laptop, he continued his work, mentally mapping out his itinerary—a working session with the assigned project lead, a quick lunch, more work, and then heading to dinner with Derin and a prospective client.

Rebecca flipped from her side to her tummy beneath the covers, trying desperately to hold onto the last strands of sleep that the banging outside was pulling away from her.

"Why's there so much noise? Why won't it stop?" she moaned, squeezing her eyes shut, wishing the noise would fade.

Just as she began to drift back to sleep, a new sound startled her fully awake. It was a relentless rattling of her doorknob.

She sat up.

Someone was at her door, trying to get in. Without thinking, she jumped out of the bed in a panic. The cold tiled floor sent a shiver up her spine as she tiptoed barefoot toward the living room. In the dim light, she barely registered the clothes strewn across the floor and tripped on them, stumbling forward. Rebecca fell face-first to the ground with a thud, the impact knocking the breath from her lungs.

Suddenly, the frantic shaking of the doorknob stopped.

"Rebecca?" a familiar female voice called from outside her apartment. "Rebecca, are you there? Is everything okay? It's me, Hauwa. I've been knocking and calling you for a while."

Rebecca rubbed her eyes. She had totally forgotten that her friend was supposed to visit in the morning. "Yeah, I'll be right there," she croaked groggily and unlocked the door.

"What's going on?" Hauwa said as she walked in and saw how messy the room was, scrunching up her eyebrows in concern.

"Nothing a little tidying up can't fix," Rebecca casually replied.

"Are you sure? I probably called you ten times, if not more, and all that banging didn't wake you. And now your house looks like there was a break-in." Hauwa's eyes widened with worry. "Are you sick or depressed?"

"Don't be dramatic," Rebecca retorted, sinking heavily into the couch. "My house is in order. Sort of. I had an exhausting day at work last week and didn't get to unpack the bale my mother sent. I started sorting it yesterday and was up until midnight but couldn't do it anymore. I was too tired, so I just left the clothes here."

Hauwa sat beside Rebecca and rubbed her shoulder comfortingly. "Take it easy, will you?"

"Yeah, yeah. What time is it anyway?" Rebecca asked, glancing over at the window over Hauwa's head, through which light filtered into the room.

"11:35 AM," Hauwa announced after a quick glance at her wrist.

"Wow!" Rebecca exclaimed, rubbing her eyes to clear the last trace of drowsiness. "I can't believe I slept in and missed my run. Now, I'll have to do it in the evening."

Hauwa rolled her eyes "That's your worry? That you missed a run?"

"I don't expect you to understand. You're literally God's favourite." Rebecca playfully shot back. "You wouldn't add an inch of waistline even if you ate a bucket of chicken. Some of us have to work really hard to look good."

Hauwa shook her head, a smile playing on her lips. "Even if you didn't have to, you would still work hard. It's ingrained in your DNA. Anyway, I'm here now. How can I help?"

"Coffee, please. I can barely function as it is."

"Not on my watch. You need breakfast," Hauwa said as she stood up, heading to the kitchen. "Go freshen up, while I put something together."

When Rebecca came back into the living room after a good shower, she was surprised to find a plate of steaming rice and rich, fragrant stew on the centre table.

"Smells heavenly," Rebecca mused. "Did you make this just now?" she asked Hauwa before shoving a full spoon into her mouth.

"Just the rice. I brought the stew along with me from the hotel because I know how you can be sometimes."

She smiled gratefully with her mouth full of food.

"Thank you, habibti."

While Rebecca ate, Hauwa moved the clothes on the floor to one side and then strolled over to the console, brushing her hands over the rack of mementoes: Framed pictures, personal decor items, and an award plaque. She picked up the plaque and read the label: *Best performing Analyst, West Africa.*

"Amazing! Is this new?"

Rebecca nodded. "Sort of. It was two weeks ago."

"This is incredible. I'm proud of you," Hauwa said with a big smile before setting it down to pick up a framed picture beside it.

"I still can't believe your family showed up in an eighteen-seater bus for your graduation," Hauwa remarked, grinning as she examined the photo.

Rebecca's heart swelled at the reminder. Despite being her mother's only biological child, her grandparents, uncles, and aunts had shown up in coordinated outfits with their children to celebrate her. Her mother was the jewel of the family, and Rebecca, in turn, was the prized granddaughter. But it wasn't always that way.

There was a time when disapproving whispers followed any mention of her mother—single with a child out of wedlock. But her mother stood firm, becoming the first woman in her family to finish university and succeed in civil service. Those victories helped turn any occasion tied to their name into a well-attended festival. Yet, her happiness has remained incomplete because of her father's family, whose story remains a mystery—unknown to her since before his death.

She shook away the feeling of longing, the feeling of wanting a love she never knew and tried to embrace the one she got.

"What's your plan for the week?" Rebecca said, heading over to the kitchen to drop her dish in the sink. When Rebecca came back in, they started sorting the clothes on the floor into categories.

"Before I return to Kaduna next week, I plan to meet with our volunteers and guests to prepare for the conference. I would have liked to stay longer, but it gets harder to leave the kids behind with each trip," Hauwa said as she created a neat pile of trousers beside her outstretched legs. "By the way, have you changed your mind about volunteering with us? I've been pleading for the longest time. You'll do great on our team."

"Sis, you know I love you, but I can't right now. There's too much on my plate," Rebecca replied as she made her own rather unsteady pile of blouses.

"You've been saying this for a year, but I don't believe you've given it more than a moment's thought."

Although she sounded like she was teasing her, Hauwa's words stung, because there was an element of truth to them.

She and Hauwa first met two years ago at a career fair organised by Hauwa's foundation for corporate women, the Women's Chair. It was an international platform that trained female entrepreneurs and small business owners, connecting them with sponsors, grants, digital skills, and equipment for over a decade. They only recently created programs for women early in their corporate careers, which was why Rebbeca had wanted to attend the career fair.

It was her first time attending something like that and after a few minutes walking around, she'd felt drawn to Hauwa's soft yet regal presence. She recalled how moving her closing speech was, how her gentle voice and straightforward elucidation carried encouragement and hope, which inspired Rebecca and she was sure, the hundreds of other women there.

When the event ended, Rebecca waited for her turn in a long line of women who wanted to meet Hauwa. And once they did meet and speak that day, a fierce motivation was ignited in her, leading her to volunteer at some events. Their professional mentoring relationship blossomed into a deep friendship filled with easy laughter and comfortable conversations that belied their nine-year age difference.

But as her workload grew heavier, volunteering slipped through her fingers.

"I've thought about it," she insisted. "I plan to attend the program and create some content. But that's the best I can do. Maybe after I get the promotion at work, I'll have more control over the type of work without scampering around with Imade looking over my shoulder every minute."

"Hmm...If you say so."

Rebbecca perked up. "How about this? I know you and the team are doing incredible work, so I can help with visibility. I have a lot of followers who would benefit from the program. I can't be fully involved in the planning, but I can use my network to promote. That's a compromise, right?"

Rebecca stood up and headed to her room. Over the years in her influencer side hustle, she had acquired paraphernalia of the trade. Not only did she have ring lights, clips, and other supplies, she even had a mannequin. She brought out each item much to Hauwa's amusement.

"I'll take it. Thank you," Hauwa said, scooting to the end of the couch, removing her scarf, and running her hand through her long, jet-black, back-length hair. Rebecca took in her friend's look—a colourful bubu which draped elegantly to her feet and her gold jewellery—delicate earrings and bracelets that caught the light, enhancing her fair, smooth skin.

An idea sparked in Rebecca's mind.

"Hauwa, my love," she cooed with feigned innocence.

"Oh oh. I know that look," Hauwa said, tilting her head to the side.

Rebecca scooted closer. "How about we ditch these mannequins. If we really want to switch up the content, what better way can we achieve that than to have the Convener and Executive Director of the Women's Chair styled by me in these very same dresses I've been promoting?"

Hauwa chortled. "You want me to wear these clothes? I'm no model and I am way too old for any of this"

"Says who? Have you looked in the mirror lately? You are stunning."

Amid protests, Rebecca completed the setup, transforming the living room into a mini photo area. For a final touch, she hung a backdrop behind the couch and turned on upbeat music. By this point, Hauwa had loosened up a little. They took turns trying the clothes on, tucking in oversized samples with pegs as they joked and shared innuendo.

Afterwards, they fell on the couch laughing. Hauwa reached over to her bag and pulled out a box and handed it over to her.

"A little gift from me to you."

Rebecca's eyes widened. "Really?" she flung her arms around her friend. "What did I ever do to deserve you as a friend?"

Hauwa smiled. "Who else has the capacity to make me play like a kid or make me feel as good in my own skin as you do?" she said, gesturing to the living room where they just had a forty-five-minute photo session.

As she looked at the delicate jewellery set in the box, Rebecca sighed. "You have given me something so beautiful but all I did for you all day was make you model my clothes."

"You know you can get models and take photos of all these items for your page. I can link you with this great guy I know."

"Great guy for the shoot or great guy for my love life," Rebecca said with a grin and a waggle of her eyebrows.

"How about both? No harm killing two birds with one stone."

Rebecca winced. "I take it back, biko. I'm still recovering from Felix. My heart isn't ready for another heartbreak."

Hauwa leaned her head back and burst into laughter.

"Yeah, yeah, I'm glad to laugh about it, but being beaten by my bobo's main chick in broad daylight isn't a flex. Lagos is a jungle, and I was prey. Chai. I don't even want to think about it."

Rebecca shuddered at the memory of the lady's generous buttocks sitting on her chest as she gasped for breath, warning Rebecca to leave her man alone.

Hauwa rubbed her back affectionately, still laughing.

"Imagine an achalugo like me settling to be a man's side chic? When that woman appeared at my doorstep and dragged me out by my hair, shouting that I was dating her man, I wanted to die. Imagine if my story had ended up on social media. What would my life have become?"

"Did you eventually get an apology out of him?"

"Never. He even had the audacity to look me in the eye, tell me we were in an open relationship, and never promised me exclusivity."

"Ha!"

"My dear," she slapped her palms together. "I've never been played like that. The worst part was that he expected us to continue the relationship because I was the one he wanted to marry, he said he was just playing with the other babe. It was befuddling that someone could think like that, much less say it to someone else. The humiliation was too much to bear. I didn't come out of the house for days. Even when I eventually started getting out, I had to avoid my neighbours out of shame. I'm sure they still whisper behind me. In fact, my neighbour, Anita, offered to match me with her distant cousin looking for a wife. Can you imagine!"

"Look on the bright side. At least you're no longer in a relationship with a liar, right?"

"Honestly," Rebecca paused, "While we were together, he wasn't so bad, and even when he acted off, I never suspected him of double dating because he was mostly so good to me. Instead of relief, I actually wanted him to come back to me at one point," Rebecca hid her face in her palms briefly before continuing, "My mum always says that God makes everything beautiful in its time, but it feels ugly because right for a while, my mind and heart did not agree on this at all."

Hauwa pulled her into a comforting embrace. "Keep your head up and take as much time as necessary to allow the ache to fade. I promise it will, and you'll find your own person. Okay?"

"Maybe, but I am not ready for any of that right now."

"Who knows, that handsome neighbour of yours could surprise you. He seems nice enough every time I have run into him."

"Ha, bro Muyiwa? Mba!"

"You want to use bro to finish the guy, meanwhile he doesn't look much older than you."

"Yeah, but that's what everyone calls him. Besides, I can't date my landlord's son. Although we are friends and he really does seem like a decent person, that's all there will ever be to it."

"In what world is being a landlord's son an automatic red flag?"

Rebecca covered her face and groaned. "Don't question my logic, okay? I know it is a flimsy excuse, but I honestly don't want to get into anything messy. If we break up, does that mean I have to move? This is literally his father's house."

Hauwa wagged a finger. "Let's talk about the first part. You think he's a good guy, meaning you like him?"

"I dunno. He's easy on the eyes, eloquent, and responsible."

"And?"

"He's down to earth, loves kids, and the kids love him right back," she added dreamily.

"He sounds like a spec."

"Did I mention his voice and laugh? There's something about the way he focuses on you and speaks so tenderly that it makes you feel like you're the only one who matters in the world. I honestly could get used to it."

Hauwa leaned back and looked at her with scepticism. "I don't know about those defences of yours, but it seems like you're already gone."

"No, no. Nope." Rebecca waved her hands in front of her. "I'm not gone. I can admire God's work and acknowledge what's good. After all, I'm not blind.

But sometimes, he seems too good to be true."

Or maybe just too good for me.

Hauwa shook her head.

"I won't bother to advise you because I am sure it will go in one ear and come out through another. But if he's asking you out and you like him this much, I don't get why you won't give it a chance. Don't assume a bad ending before you even get a beautiful beginning."

Rebecca let out a weary sigh.

"He's a fine boy, sha."

"And you're a coward," Hauwa teased. "That reminds me, what's all this you have been saying about your boss? What's the core of the issue between you two?"

"I just feel like she's disappointed in me, no matter how hard I try to meet up to her expectations."

"Has she given you any specific feedback?"

"Well ..."

"Rebecca?"

Rebecca rolled her eyes. "Fine, yeah, she asked me to come up with a development plan for the year to capture skills I want to gain, the trainings linked to them, mentors that I want to build a relationship with, and projects I can take up as a practical form of learning."

"And this is a problem for you. Why?"

"I think it's just a way for her to give me more work and micro-manage me without any additional reward. Then she's been hounding me about sharing my work with broader teams outside our immediate unit. Because my projects deal with new capabilities that we are trying to upskill the sales team across regions to adopt, she wants me to keep the organisation updated."

"That's solid direction from a manager's point of view."

"I thought you were on my side," Rebecca mumbled.

"I am," Hauwa declared. "And I agree that Imade could do with some kindness, but that's out of your control. Here's what you can control: take the good, which is this great direction she's provided you, and make it yours. Lean on your strengths; your plan should capture how to maximize your already great areas and then add two to three other opportunities for growth. As for the visibility, you don't have to be the loudest in the room for your voice to be heard. Instead, own your space, believe in yourself, and show up confidently. Be creative about it and think of a unique but engaging way to share the progress you're making on your projects, then negotiate with your boss on the basis of that. You can't go to her with nothing and expect that she'll just lay off you."

"I understand," Rebecca grudgingly acquiesced.

"Good. I know it's tough, but you're a go-getter and I believe in you."

"Yeah, yeah ... now you're bribing me with sweet words."

Hauwa pulled her into an encouraging hug, heading back to her hotel just before 3 P.M, leaving Rebecca in a pile of happy exhaustion.

six

TRIPPING

Sola slid into the front passenger seat of his Uber, glancing out the window as they wove through the evening traffic. He spotted a lone hawker, wearing a woven hat, sitting curb side with his wares, detached from the hustle around him. The traffic was heavy, and other hawkers ran along to catch up with cars and sell their goods, but this man was focused on his own world. Intrigued, Sola pulled out his phone, and as the vehicle slowed down over a road bump, he clicked a shot.

He admired the picture, relating to its reflection of his inner conflict—to do as others or follow his own path. Typically, Sola would chat up taxi drivers, but today, he felt the need to listen to the voice in his head and relish the few moments of peace. So, they drove on in silence until the glimmering lights of the beach came into view.

As the Uber pulled to a stop, Sola took in the buzz of visitors, flexed his arm, and rubbed his palms together in anticipation. He was looking forward to having some fun tonight. He deserved it after the busy week he has had.

He quickly registered at the reception and then walked the length of the entrance, its walls covered in vibrant graffiti. Chude had opted for one of the beach arenas instead of the outdoor tents. It was easy to spot by the eclectic blue neon-lit signage that read *THE ATLANTIS*, a blinking invitation to drop reality outside its walls.

Stepping in, Sola was hit with a pulsating afrobeat rhythm. It was just what the doctor ordered. He began to move to the music's thumping bass, navigating through the interior—a blend of luxury, glam, and sophisticated ambience. He squinted against the flashing lights and scanned the room to find his friends among the different groups lounging on plush couches, lost in their own worlds. His eyes finally settled on the raucous cluster sat at the far end, but close enough to the polished bar lined with bottles of wine and premium spirits.

As he approached, a friend caught sight of him and waved him over, starting a cheer at his arrival.

Sola greeted each of his friends with hearty hugs and playful pats on the back. Derin was already there, and from the look of things, was having his fill of drinks. The hailing grew louder as someone else walked in.

Teju.

Sola frowned. He wasn't expecting his brother to show up here. Although the numerous calls he had ignored before today might have been a clue.

He sent a cautious nod toward Teju, who gave an indifferent acknowledgement as he sat.

"Now that all the rich lads are here," Chude announced with a grin, "we can celebrate properly. I'll start off the night with the big announcement."

Sola leaned forward as he and others shifted their attention entirely to Chude.

"I am sure you're all here because of the gist that I have been promoted at work."

"Hear, hear!" Derin cheered.

"Now wait a minute," Chude continued. "While that is true, it is also an extreme understatement. I didn't just get promoted. I, Chude, am the latest owner of Lithium PLC. My dad chose early retirement and passed the baton of the family business to me. Mic drop!" he proclaimed with dramatic flair.

"Odogwu!" Derin shouted, and the others followed, cheering loudly with celebratory whoops and congratulations.

"That's huge, man!" Sola exclaimed with genuine pride. "Well-deserved! It was always clear that you would do great things, not only because your papa sabi," he added with a jocular tone, "but because you put in the work and deserve every credit."

His words elicited agreement noises from the group and the clinking of glasses as they raised their drinks to toast to Chude. A waiter came over to take his order, and Sola hesitated briefly before asking for a soda.

"Come on, man." Chude jabbed at him light-heartedly. "Don't tell me you're still on this no-drinking journey. Chill out, it's a celebration. Have a whiskey or two."

Sola merely shook his head.

As the lively exchange progressed, his mother's recent plea played in his mind, moving him. Sola thought about his strained relationship with his father. He could easily be Chude right now. His father's backing would have smoothed out his life remarkably—whether as a sponsor of his start-up or even as an employee working directly in his company. But this is the path Sola has chosen, to work his life out himself. The building years have been tough, but they were shaping him into the man he needed to be.

Distracting himself, he glanced briefly at his brother sitting in a corner, talking to one of the guys. But, really, why was he here? These were his friends, and Teju always considered himself superior to and better than his crowd.

"Nice watch," Chude said to Derin.

Sola looked at Derin's wrist, only now noticing the new sleek luxury timepiece his friend is wearing.

Derin shrugged off the compliment.

"It must have cost an arm. You and Sola are partners, right? I take it that business is doing well?" Chude probed.

Derin downed another shot of whiskey, ignoring Chude's question.

"Help me out here, guys," Chude addressed the gathering. "Why would anyone return to Nigeria from a life of comfort abroad when most people are hustling to leave? And you, Derin, you joined Sola's delusionally ambitious business. Couldn't you advise him to go bow to his baba with his real estate business empire instead of this grassroots hustle?"

"Hey, Chude, lay off him," Bode, another friend, chimed in defensively.

Chude smirked, unyielding.

"I mean, I'm proud of your work, but guys, explain how this makes sense. Take a leaf from Teju's playbook."

"Chude..."

"Hear me out, okay? I know you two have your rivalry thing going on, but we've been hanging out, and he's a smart guy. He's working with this international cybersecurity firm, but he still supports your dad's company, helping him integrate tech into the business. Which is great in my books. Derin, talk to your friend."

"Bro," Derin gulped the finger of liquid in his glass then dramatically placed his arm around Sola's shoulder, turning to Chude. "I've tried to talk to Sola, but he's hard headed. There's only so much I can say because he partnered with me and I couldn't do this without him. At the end of the day, his choice is his choice. Although, if I were in the same shoes? Y'all wouldn't have to tell me twice. Passion no dey pay rent," he laughed.

His response lightened the mood, but their words only reinforced the nagging doubts Sola had been wrestling with since Chude called him about the 'promotion.'

Just then, Sola felt a tap on his shoulder. He looked up to see Teju by his side, signalling for them to go outside.

"We need to talk."

"No, thank you," Sola said, unmoving.

"Now," Teju insisted in a low voice.

Sola took a long swig of his Coke. Then he excused himself and followed his brother to one of the private cubicles a distance away.

"You always act like the main character in every situation." Teju scoffed, looking at him the way he always did. Like he found his presence nauseating. Which was funny because Sola had spent his whole life steering clear of his own brother. What reason did he have to be so irritated by him? "Chude invited me. I initially turned him down, but Derin told me you'd be here. If I knew you were going to be like this, I wouldn't have bothered to come."

"Whatever," Sola replied. "You are here now and have my attention, so just tell me what you want."

Teju pinched his lips together, forcing his words out with barely contained venom.

"I don't *want* anything, but your family does. You've been back in Nigeria for a while, and despite everything Dad has done for you, you continue to act like an ungrateful, entitled, spoiled, and unrepentant brat. Even after you almost ruined everything he worked for."

Here we go again.

"Did he not ensure that I was punished and paid my dues? What else does he want from me? As a matter of fact, what do *you* want from me?" Sola snapped. "Why don't you continue to pretend like I'm still in exile, because me being in Nigeria has nothing to do with you or your father."

Teju looked at him with pure disdain.

"You think being sent abroad for a fully funded education was a punishment? If you weren't so caught up in your own self-righteousness, you would repay *our* father for his magnanimity towards you. This I-want-to-be-my-own-man act is childish, not to mention disappointing."

"Well, join the queue of people disappointed by me. It's a long line." Sola said calmly. He had heard a variation of the same words since he was fifteen. By this point, Teju's words were like water off a duck's back. He knew he had let everyone down. Even God was disappointed in him.

But his older brother wasn't done doing the concerned big brother act.

"And what about Mum? She has been on my neck, and I'm sure she's been talking to you, too."

Sola crossed his arms. Where was all this coming from? And why was Teju chosen as the ambassador of this mission?

"How does that concern you? Can't I have a night of peace without Dad, this or Dad, that? It's been years, yet I'm still paying for my mistake. I don't understand your insistence on me going to see him. He doesn't see me as his son, so why should I try? Also, aren't you the golden child, the heir to the dynasty?" Sola sneered. "You won it all. Why isn't that enough to keep you happy and out of my hair?!" he spat.

Without warning, Teju's fist connected with Sola's face. He staggered, barely having the chance to register what had just happened. His brother, taller and wirier, stepped closer to where he leaned on the frame of a couch.

"Grow up. And stop being ungrateful. If you won't listen to Mum's pleas, maybe this will make you more rational."

Sola clenched his fists by his side, tasting blood. His eyes clouded from anger and pain.

"It's infuriating enough that you claim to want nothing to do with him but have no qualms about collecting money from Mum. Are you pretending like that's not the same thing? Also, next time I call you, pick up your damn phone."

Sola chuckled gravely. "Don't think I am not retaliating because I can't throw a punch, egbon. Just because you are a jealous and angry man, violence is all you can resort to. You can act out all you want, but nobody can make me do or be who I don't want to."

Teju leaned in, coming within inches of his face.

"I don't care who you think you are, I have only one message for you: call Dad or go see him to apologise." Teju drew back and made for the door before he glanced back at Sola. "Give my regards to the guys for me, will you? I have other places to be."

Teju might be the golden child, the venerated older brother to Sola's rebellious persona, but he wasn't the teenager Teju used to order around. He's was now man at the helm of his own life, and no one, not even the man who gave him life, can take that away from him.

Sola groaned as he stood up, his jawline smarting as he headed for the bar.

Rebecca repeatedly tapped her fingers on the table at the Atlantis bar, scanning the crowd for Hauwa. When she arrived five minutes ago, she was confused. This didn't seem like a place her hijab wearing bestie would suggest for a meet-up. Three calls to Hauwa's line later, she got no response, so she decided to wait another ten minutes.

Tapping her legs against the floor in rhythm with the pulsing music, partly to mask her awkwardness, she typed out a quick message to her, asking where she was and what was going on.

Around her, the music grew louder, and the waiters in their black shirt and trousers uniform gave way to hostesses in dazzling short dresses that sparkled under the lights.

"Nah." She shook her head. "I'm *definitely* in the wrong place."

After ten minutes with no response from Hauwa, Rebecca decided to leave. She headed toward the entrance, glancing at her phone again to check for new messages. In that distracted moment, she collided with a solid body, her phone slipping from her grasp and clattering to the floor.

"Watch it, will you!" she exclaimed, diving for the phone and hoping the screen hadn't shattered.

"You should have been looking where you were going," an angry male voice boomed back.

She picked up her phone and sighed with relief to see it was okay. Then she looked up with a scowl.

"You bumped into me and should be apolo—"

Her eyes met an unexpected gaze, a young man with a pinched expression staring strangely at her. His eyes were bloodshot, but his glare softened as he considered her.

"Why are you looking at me like that?"

The man's face spread into a wide smile. "We meet again," he said. The switch was so sudden that it made her head spin. She stepped back gingerly.

"Not sure who you are and what's going on, but I'm trying to head out that way," she pointed. He was standing right in her path.

"My bad," he said, running a hand through his tousled locs. "I'm actually excited that I bumped into you again."

"Again?" She looked him over. "Aahh," she softly gasped, recalling his face from the restaurant run-in two weeks ago. He looked charming in the light, but the swollen bruise on his cheek and red eye made her wary. He was probably drunk. Yet, she didn't smell any alcohol on him. "You look like bad news and trouble."

He winced. "Do I?"

"I'm sorry, did I say that out loud?"

"Yeah, you did, but I don't blame you. To be honest, I've had a terrible evening, but seeing you made it much better." He lifted his eyebrows invitingly. "Are you in a hurry? Or do you have time to have one drink with me?"

Despite every bone in her body screaming no, her curiosity overpowered her better judgment, and she consented, deciding to wait a little longer for Hauwa with him.

"I'll give you fifteen minutes."

He smiled a charming, grateful smile and they found a secluded table for two away from the bustling groups. He ordered a Coke on the rocks while she opted for a glass of Chapman. As they settled in, Rebecca broached the subject of his injury.

"That looks fresh and painful. Did you fall or something? And shouldn't you have it checked before it swells more than it already has?"

He grinned, but with a tinge of pain, before responding. "It's fresh, alright. My brother and I don't always see eye to eye. No pun intended." He looked amused at his little pun. "But yeah, I'm here to celebrate a friend," he gestured toward a table of guys laughing over drinks. "My brother and I went out for what was to be a chat, but he ended up punching me."

"Why? Did you say something to him?"

He raised an eyebrow and took a sip of his drink. "Are you victim-blaming now?" he teased.

She couldn't help the smile that spread over her face. "I'm sorry, I didn't mean to do that" she paused, "I don't even know your name."

"My bad. Sola, and yours?"

"Rebecca."

"Rebecca," he repeated softly as if tasting the sound on his tongue. "It's a beautiful name."

"Thanks. So back to your story ..." she urged.

Sola leaned back into his chair and sighed loudly. "Well, my brother, his name is Teju, by the way, has always been the perfect child. I grew up with my parents saying, 'Be more like Teju, can't you see how your brother behaves? Follow his example and the whole ten yards of comparisons,'" he recounted. "But along the line, something switched. How our parents treated me started to make him think that I was their favourite, despite all evidence pointing to the opposite."

"Why do you say that?" Rebecca prompted.

"It's been obvious over the years. Teju was always the best at everything. I walked and lived in his shadow; my actions were always measured against his standards. His life was basically a benchmark for mine. This strained my relationship with my parents, and ultimately, when I made a massive mistake, it led to a falling out with my dad. My family has been putting pressure on me to contact him in the past few months, but I just can't. You'd think my brother would be happy to keep me away, but it's quite the opposite; he's furious that I'm ignoring our father." He waved his hands in befuddlement, his words hanging in the air.

"What if your father is dying?" Rebecca said softly.

Sola spat his drink out all over the table.

"I'm so sorry." Rebecca gushed. "That's such a morbid thought, and I don't know where it came from. I'm pretty sure he's not dying! There are so many other possibilities—he could just miss you or maybe want to give you an inheritance or something! Anything else other than death."

Sola chuckled and dabbed at his shirt with a tissue. Before he can respond, Rebecca's phone vibrated against the table, lighting up with a call. It was Hauwa.

"Thank goodness. Excuse me, please, I need to take this," she said, standing up.

Hauwa had been running late due to a prior engagement. And as Rebecca suspected, she was in the wrong place. The right location was a spot just opposite the bar. After ending the call, she turned her attention back to Sola.

"It's been nice chatting and hearing about your interesting life, but I must go now. My friend is waiting for me."

"I'm sad to hear that." He leaned back in his seat. "It already feels like you're a long-time friend, so I'm heartbroken. But you know, we can continue this later. You just give me your number and I'll call you," he said, half teasing, half serious.

Rebecca mulled it over. She wasn't keen on handing her number to a red-eyed guy she met in a bar. But honestly, she hadn't had anything exciting happen to her recently and she found him intriguing. So, she decided to do the next best thing.

"I can't give you my number—He started to protest. "But we can connect on social media."

He pouted. "I'm not really active on social media."

"But you have an Instagram account, right? Everyone has one."

"Yeah, but I hardly use it," he shrugged.

"Give me your phone."

Sola handed it over.

She found the app, searched for her username and sent a follow request. She returned his phone and went through the process on her own device. "There you go, we are connected now. That should do."

Sola started to object, but Rebecca jumped up and sped toward the exit.

"Byeeeee," she called over her shoulder to the weird stranger who was surprisingly comfortable sharing his personal life story with her.

The rest of the night passed quickly. It's almost midnight when Derin stood up to leave, unsteady on his feet. Sola shot up and followed him to the parking lot.

"Derin stop. Hand over your car keys," Sola said firmly.

Derin rolled his eyes but didn't argue. He threw the key fob and Sola caught it, following closely as Derin led to where he'd parked.

"I'm not driving all the way to your place tonight," Sola told him as he pulled onto the road. "We'll go to mine and you can find your way in the morning. A lush Derin was slumped in the passenger seat, barely propped upright by the fastened seatbelt. He smelled like he took a long dip in a distillery.

"I hate this," Derin slurred. "I'm happy for Chude, but man, when would it be my turn to celebrate something good?"

Sola glanced at him again, this time in surprise.

"You're tipsy. You'll feel better about yourself in the morning."

"Maybe, but I'm speaking my truth right now. I have to make it in this life, man. This hustle can't be forever."

"Guy, anyone listening to you speak will think we're struggling. You aren't doing bad at all, but you complain all the time. Would it hurt you to be grateful for what you have and be happy for someone else without spiralling?"

Derin snorted. "Doing well because I have a nice ride and a couple shiny accessories? It's not the same as what you guys have. I mean the generational wealth type shii... It's different. Nights like tonight when I hang around all of you at the same time make it more obvious. I'm pretty sure they look at me differently."

Eighteen years after he was teased for being the scholarship kid from a less affluent background and it seemed like no amount of wealth or success could erase that feeling from Derin's bones.

"We've all been friends for a long time, and they celebrate with us just as we do with them. Yeah, our paths are different but that's normal. Success comes in different shades."

"You don't get it but I sha understand what I'm saying. My dreams aren't basic. I must make it in this life," Derin insisted.

"I hear you. You will make it," Sola reassured him with a light chuckle, but the only response from the passenger side of the car was Derin's snoring.

seven

PROGRESSION

Sola's head was pounding when he woke up the next morning. As he shunted Derin out of his house following a night on the living room couch, he jokingly blamed the fumes from the alcohol on his breath for making him feel hungover. He knew his body ached after Teju's assault, but he had decided not to tell Derin about it. Derin didn't do him any favours by not informing him about Teju's presence in the first place.

Later, as he idled by the kitchen counter, his gym bag resting on the floor and a water bottle beside him, he got sidetracked by the lure of Instagram rather than lacing up his sneakers and heading out. Scrolling through his feed, he landed on Rebecca's profile. With an impressive following and vibrant posts showcasing high quality and creativity, he realised that she's not a causal user of the app but a social media fashion influencer.

He admired her keen eye for fashion and style, and her ability to showcase various businesses and brands with her *Get Ready with Me* videos that effortlessly showed how to mix and match stylish outfits. If he had a girlfriend, he would add most of her curated looks to his cart without a second thought. He was bemused by how she was more corporate than creative when they first met, and again, he wondered why he felt such a strong connection—an aching sense of familiarity that he can't quite place. It was as if they were linked by an invisible thread; he felt an instinctive yet fierce urge to stand by her side and protect her. It was a powerful feeling, somewhere between attraction and the loyalty of a sibling.

Before long, he liked about twelve videos without thinking about it. Acting like a stalker was a good way to get blocked, and he didn't want that. Sola looked at his own profile, empty of his own pictures but filled with places and random pictures he'd captured—a tree, a coastal view, a city skyline, his hiking boots on a mountain, and his latest addition of the hawker by the roadside. None offered a glimpse of his face, making it likely that Rebecca might not even know it was him. He quickly navigated to his profile settings and then to his device's photo roll, selecting a corporate headshot that he took at Derin's insistence, and he completed an upload. He took a chug of water and closed the app.

That's enough social media for one day.

As he laced his sneakers, his phone dinged, lighting up with a new notification. He grabbed his bag and water, scrolling through the alert as he stepped outside.

It was an email from Tiffany. He paused and started reading. The message's tone was urgent, and Tiffany wanted an immediate response. She wanted to schedule a follow-up meeting before she left the country, and had included her mobile number in the email, requesting a call back.

He dialled her number as he walked to the car and she picked up on the first ring.

"Hello, Ms Tiffany, this is Sola. I just received your email. I hope that you're doing well."

"Hello," she replied in a sultry voice.

"Err...is this...Ms Tiffany?" he asked, thinking he might have dialled the wrong number.

"Yes, Sola, it's me! Thanks for calling back," she said.

"I'm sorry for calling so abruptly, your message seemed urgent. Thank you for getting back to me regarding our discussion," he replied, keeping his tone professional.

"Yes. So, after our last meeting, my dad returned to Enugu, but I decided to remain in Lagos for a bit. I will be heading to London tonight, but I decided that I wouldn't leave without seeing you first. I've been thinking about you and the pitch from our lunch meeting. I can't shake the feeling that you are a good match for us, which doesn't happen often."

"Uh, that's great news. Did you say you are travelling tonight?" he stuttered, caught off guard by the tone of the conversation.

"Yes. My flight is the last one out, so could we meet in the afternoon, say around 1 PM?"

He hesitated, glancing at his watch.

"I can make time for that, but my partner is travelling out of town later today and won't be back for two days."

"That works perfectly. You're the person I want to meet. I'll text you the address."

"Oh. Okay."

"So, we have a date then?" Sola could hear something in her voice that seemed incongruent with the reason they were supposed to be meeting.

"Uh, yes. See you there. Thanks for this opportunity."

"No, thank *you*. I can't wait."

The call ended, and Sola stared at the lock screen for a few beats entering the car and driving to the gym, wondering what his meeting with Ms Tiffany would bring.

Rebecca was looking forward to her last day of work before her long-awaited vacation. She had a lot of other work planned, including content for an award show. The advance had already been paid but she knew her break wasn't going to be much of a break at all.

We move, still.

She was early that morning and happy that her routine went off without a hitch—a good omen for the day ahead. As she rounded the corner to her workspace, she caught sight of Tariebi's bright, blond-dyed, low-cut hair. Seated at one of the desks on the open floor, Tari's eyes were glued to her laptop, her jaws moving rhythmically as she popped gum. Rebecca tapped her playfully, causing Tari to jump and let out a startled screech.

"Tari. Calm down, it's just me. Why are you so jumpy?" Rebecca grinned.

"Girl, you scared me half to death. Why'd you sneak up on me?" Tari clutched her chest, half-laughing, half-scolding.

"I didn't sneak. You were lost in your own world. I wasn't that quiet."

"My dear, it's not your fault, truly. There's a leadership meeting today, and my head is spinning. They'll start arriving soon, but I'm struggling to keep up with so many changes to the itinerary. And your boss, Imade, isn't making it easy. Have you seen the latest agenda?"

"Me?" Rebecca rolled her eyes. "Surely you jest. I may have prepared the decks and spent my entire weekend reviewing the slides, but according to Imade, actually *seeing* the agenda is above my pay grade. Maybe I'll look now that I'm here," she winked.

Tari turned her laptop toward Rebecca, who leaned over to skim through the page with the names of the visiting directors and the plan for the day.

"Hmm, I see a break by noon, so I have to be here in case Imade needs anything."

"Good catch."

Rebecca continued looking and shrieked excitedly at a familiar name that leapt off the page.

"Director Ranti is coming!"

"Yeah, do you know her?"

"Do I? What?" she asked dramatically. "Of course, I do. She's the first female head of strategy in this company. She's kind of my mentor. I've never met her, but she's so inspiring. Bold, brilliant, driven, and just...wow!"

Tari grinned as Rebecca gushed with excitement.

"That's a lot of love for someone you haven't met. Just don't show her all this and scare her off when you do."

Rebecca's phone pinged, drawing her attention to a Facebook post she was looking at before she left the house. Someone else had commented on a conversation thread that a man old enough to be in her mother's generation had started with former students of a school in Ibadan. The names and stories drew her in, connecting to stories she had heard about her father's childhood.

She distractedly navigated to the poster's profile. Her fingers hovering tentatively over the keyboard, then, pushed by a rush of impulse, she clicked and typed a simple introductory message, followed by a question.

Did he know Gabriel Oluwaloye?

"He's cute. I didn't know you were into mature men," Tari chimed, drawing her back. Rebecca hadn't noticed her stand up to peek over her shoulder.

"Very funny," Rebecca replied, rolling her eyes.

"If he's not an admirer, who is he?"

"A stranger from the streets of Facebook." Rebecca glanced back at the screen, waiting to see the delivered tick. Nothing changed. She let out a puff of frustration and turned to fully face Tari. "I've been trying to find a connection to my dad or his family. My mum won't say a word about them or help me at all. So I am reduced to stalking people online. This guy is probably the sixth person I've messaged. The last one...well, he asked me for money, and in my desperation, I actually sent it. Can you believe he ghosted me afterwards?"

Tari sucked in a breath. "Ugh, I'm sorry that happened to you. But does this new guy seem legit?"

"Yeah, he made a post, and I thought, what's the worst that could happen? It's like there's a missing puzzle piece in my life, and without it, no matter how far in life I go, I don't feel quite complete. I know it may sound strange, but the thought that my father's family is out there, possibly having answers to my many questions about him, weighs on me."

Tari gave her a sympathetic look. "I get it, but be careful, please. These sharks can sniff out desperation and take advantage of it."

"Ah, you don't have to tell me twice. I've learned my lesson—definitely not sending any more money."

"Rebecca!"

Imade's voice cut through their conversation, startling her.

"I'll see you later," she mouthed to Tari and sprinted away.

She dropped her bag in a nearby work cubicle and headed to the coffee stand, eager to get cups for herself and the boss. She prepared the cups, dropped hers at her station, and gingerly placed the other on the table in front of Imade, who was sitting with her elbows on the table, cradling her head in her palm.

"Are you alright?" Rebecca asked, concern lacing her voice. "Can I bring you anything?"

Without lifting her head, Imade waved her off.

"I'm fine, nothing coffee can't fix."

"Okay...um, if you have a minute, I'd like to talk to you about the development and org engagement plan you asked me to draw up."

Imade shot her a quick glance, looked at the watch and rubbed her forehead. "Make it quick."

"Thank you. So...I started work on the development plan, and I'm considering a bi-weekly newsletter that would highlight the latest capabilities and adoption rates. It would spotlight an individual or team that's making use of the learnings in practical ways. I would also like to include a contest where people take pictures of themselves in the field or of their workspaces, showing them interacting with the tools we've provided, and a league table for teams with the best completion and engagement records. I've created a draft design for the table that I can share with you later. We could then reward them with shopping vouchers or other gift items to incentivize increased adoption rates each month. What do you think?"

Imade was quiet for a few seconds.

"Doesn't sound bad, but I'd like to hear more details. Put something down and do some checks with random sales team members and their managers. You'll get additional ideas that way. We can run a pilot and fine-tune as we go," Imade said, her voice strained.

"I'll get right on that. Thank you," Rebecca hopped excitedly.

"Yeah, yeah," Imade waved her off again, still pressing her hand against her forehead.

"It looks like you have a headache...should you really be drinking coffee? Maybe I should order you a sandwich; the presentation doesn't start for another—"she checked her watch "—thirty minutes."

"Whatever," Imade mumbled.

"I'll be right back."

Rebecca exited Imade's office and hurriedly grabbed her phone to order food.

"Delivery in thirty-five minutes?" she exclaimed. "No way!"

She sprinted down the stairs and out of the building to the parking lot, where she found Imade's driver.

"Good morning, Mr Patrick. Please, I need to quickly get to a restaurant nearby to grab food for Imade," she anxiously announced.

En route to the closest cafe, she obsessively checked her watch. Dashing into the restaurant, she placed the order, and, within moments, raced back to the office with the food.

When she burst into the open plan space, the atmosphere immediately felt different. There was commotion, and a uniformed figure raced past, clutching a first aid kit tightly while another man barrelled toward the exit.

Rebecca's hands began to tremble.

"What's going on?" she called out, sprinting into the main area and toward Tariebi, who was stacking water bottles on a table.

"I've been looking everywhere for you. It's Imade. She fainted as they were heading to the meeting," Tari said.

"What?! I just got her food."

"Yeah, that can wait. She's been rushed to the hospital."

Rebecca's eyes widened with alarm.

"I have to go. I'll have her driver take me."

She bolted toward the parking lot, breathless from all the running. Within moments, she was back in the car, her heartbeat echoing as they pulled away from the office.

Rebecca rocked back and forth, her heart racing as she waited anxiously for news about Imade. The smell of antiseptic, stark white walls, and sterilized floors of the hospital felt suffocating. She hated this place, its lingering tension dragging her back to a time she wanted to forget, memories she doesn't want to confront. With every passing minute, her breathing grew lighter and faster, her mind struggling to keep the buried emotions at bay.

A colleague's voice cut through her thoughts as tears threatened to spill from her eyes.

"Rebecca, enough people are with her, you can head back to the office. The responders called her next of kin, so we'll keep you updated," he said softly.

Reluctantly, although somewhat relieved, Rebecca returned to the office. Still slightly shaken from the rush of emotions, she's thankful to escape the tension of the hospital.

"Did you have breakfast?" Tari asked as she walked in.

"Not yet, but I packed something to eat."

"Okay, you should try and eat it now. It may be a long day for you."

Nodding, Rebecca headed to the cafeteria and ate quickly, her mind still swirling in concern for Imade. Wanting time alone to catch her breath, she slipped into the break area, staring mindlessly at the TV playing silently on the wall.

An advertisement for dishwashing soap bounced across the screen—bubbles shimmering before their brand tagline flashed across, promising effortless kitchen cleanup. It ended and switched to a roundtable interview with three people speaking on prevailing national issues, including the presenter. The camera panned around the room, then closed in on the guest, a man sitting confidently to the left, and Rebecca's breath hitched in her throat. Time seemed to freeze as she recognised him, the man she had seen in the hospital the night her father passed away. A name-graphic flashed:

Chief Adesesan.

Her heart rapidly palpitated, and a guttural sound escaped her throat. Tears sprang to her eyes and rolled down her face.

No, please, not now!

But the floodgates opened, and her memories played in a harrowing loop.

"Rebecca! Rebecca!" Tari's frantic voice broke her trance, pulling her back to the present, where she could hear herself wailing.

"Come with me," Tari urged, grabbing Rebecca's arm and pulling gently toward the washroom.

Rebecca held on to Tari like a lifeline. Once inside, she swiped at her tears, breathing in shaky gasps and heaves.

"Breathe," Tari crooned soothingly. "Take it easy, Made is going to be okay. We just got word that she's out of danger for now. She's fully awake, and they are only monitoring her tonight. She should be discharged by tomorrow."

Rebecca's shoulders sagged with relief, but guilt bubbled underneath.

"Thank God you were all there. I can't believe I didn't quickly notice how sick she was."

"It's not your fault; we all need to care for ourselves," Tari reassured her. "I was searching for you to share the update on her condition. I didn't realise how upset you were."

"What exactly happened?"

"Low blood pressure and anaemia coupled with not eating properly. I guess the pressure of the visit got to her head, she stopped eating, and her body crashed. She thought it was just stress and kept putting off going to the hospital to get checked. But the scare is behind us now, so don't worry."

Tari pulled her into a comforting hug, putting a balm over the real wound underneath her concern for Imade.

"Thanks. I needed that," she said, holding onto the embrace just a moment longer.

Tari smiled softly. "I understand. But eh..." her tone switches to being upbeat, "Anyone who sees you right now would be so confused. We all could have sworn that you and Made were bitter enemies."

Rebecca snorted a laugh and shrugged.

"At the end of the day, she's still human, right?"

"Whatever you say," Tari said, flicking her colourful nails in jest. "Ahh, before I forget, you need to take the presentation in her absence. The leadership team is supposed to be on the first flight out tomorrow morning, and they still want the opportunity to go over it. Made insisted you be the one who takes it."

Rebecca leapt back like she had been struck. "Please tell me you're joking? I can't do that," Rebecca trembled. "I'm not prepared; do I look like I can give a presentation in this state?" Her eyes darted to the mirror beside them.

"Well, you're dressed well enough, except for this." Tari waved at Rebecca's face. "Which we can fix with a little make-up."

"No, please," Rebecca pleaded. "I can't do it. Can you come up with an excuse? I'm not in the right state of mind, and I was even thinking of leaving the office for the day. My leave starts tomorrow," Rebecca added.

"Fine. Let me see what I can do. Don't go anywhere, I'll be right back," Tari headed out of the washroom. As soon as the door clicked shut, a wave of nausea hit Rebecca and sent her rushing into one of the stalls. Her stomach lurched violently and she doubled over as everything she had eaten earlier rushed out into the toilet. After the discomfort passed, she cleaned herself up and splashed cold water on her face to regain some composure.

When Tari stepped in moments later, she looked gleeful.

"Great news! I didn't even have to say anything. The leaders have already decided that a few of them would extend their trip until next week. We'll rework the agenda to ensure a productive week for them. The presentation will happen in two days. Others will join the session online."

Rebecca felt dizzy with relief.

"Thank you."

"Here's your bag. You can leave if you want. I'll cover for you."

"You're a lifesaver." Rebecca gratefully nodded as she collected the bag. With one last glance at the mirror, she raced out of the washroom, made a beeline to the car park, and slipped out unnoticed.

eight

MEMORY LANE

DECEMBER 2009

Nine-year-old Rebecca carefully hid the bowl of boiled Ube and corn her grandma had secretly given her. Her cousins milled about, running around together on the large, grass-covered field they'd converted into a playground for the day. Perching on a nearby ledge, she scarfed the snack down quickly.

It was Christmas, and the whole family had gathered at her grandparents' house for the week-long festivities. She paid little attention to the loud voices coming from inside the house; it was typical for the festive crowd to be rambunctious.

Just then, she was jolted by the sound of her mother's angry voice. Spinning around, she stretched to see who the target of the ire was. As usual it was her aunt—her mother's immediate younger sister. The sisters often bickered, arguing while the rest of the family watched without interference. The subject of the fight was predictable: her aunt would complain about being left to care for her four children, from two different fathers, accusing Angel; Rebecca's mum of not helping enough given that she only had just one child. They would exchange words until Angel finally relented, promising to increase the allowance she sent each month. This time, however, Angel wasn't backing down.

"What have you done with the money I've sent you all these years to take care of your children and do business?" Angel pressed. "You take my money and shamelessly use it to feed all these useless men that flock around you!"

Rebecca ignored the ruckus and licked her fingers. She didn't notice her aunt's loud voice drawing near until an angry arm swatted the plate from her hands, prompting a sharp cry as she watched her precious Ube roll on the dirty ground.

"Will you stand up!" her aunt's razor-sharp voice cut through her cries. "You useless child, just like your mother!"

"Ah! Aunty, what did I do?" she cried out. Her aunt turned and stormed toward the field. Grabbing the shirt tails of her two youngest boys, she dragged them off as her older son and daughter ran after them. "Let's leave these selfish people and their wickedness behind." She scoffed, casting a disdainful look at Rebecca.

"See her?" her aunt pointed mockingly. "Bastard child of my useless sister! You're the reason no man has come near her. Even your own father saw you and ran away! Your mother is jealous of me, so she says that the men surrounding me are shameless!" Making a dramatic show of turning around to flaunt her body, she rattled on "If it's easy, she should go to the market to purchase a man for herself!" With that, she stormed off, her children trailing behind her obediently.

Rebecca's mother soon came over, swooped down and gathered Rebecca up into her arms.

"Don't mind her. She's just bitter," her mother whispered. But the attempt to comfort her fell flat. It was too late; her aunt's cruel words had latched onto her fragile mind. The stares, the quiet whispers of the adults, and the pointed fingers—along with the ridicule of children—ensured that those words took root. For many nights after their bedtime prayers, Rebecca would recall her aunt's words and, in the silence, pray that God would bring her father back."

God answered her prayers a year later.

Lingering by the doorway, Rebecca watched as her mother danced around the room, singing gleefully, *"Chineke idinma o, idinma, idinma ooo, idinma o, idinma e."* The familiar chorus of thanksgiving fluttered from her lips as she carefully packed their things into woven bags and colourful suitcases. A small part of Rebecca wanted to join in, but her lips trembled nervously, keeping her rooted in the shadows. For so long, she wanted to see her mother's eyes light up with joy and silence the taunts of her classmates. Her father returned a month ago, and their daily evening strolls hand in hand felt like a dream. But now, their impending move to Ibadan was hanging overhead.

The change was fast and overwhelming. Why did his return mean leaving their home? He should be coming back to them, not uprooting the very life they had built in his absence.

She sneezed suddenly, unable to stop her itchy nose from responding to the dust that had been raised from her mother's earlier sweeping. It drew her mother's attention, and she called out lovingly,

"Nkem, why are you hiding by the door? Come here."

Hanging her head, Rebecca walked forward, climbing onto the tall bedframe, her legs swinging like a pendulum. "Mummy, why are you so happy?"

Her mother sighed softly, placing a neatly folded wrapper into a bag before settling beside Rebecca. "It's the day the Lord has made, my dear. I'll rejoice and be glad in it."

"Because my father is back?"

"Yes, because God has taken my shame and given me laughter," her mother explained. "People laughed at us, some with smiles that hid their true feelings, while I bore the weight of their whispers. But now, God has turned their words into silence."

"But..." Rebecca paused. "Wasn't he the one who gave you shame by leaving us?" she whined, not seeing the sense of the situation. "And now you're just welcoming him back happily?"

"Nwa m nwanyi, there are things a child won't understand," her mother said, brushing her fingers gently through Rebecca's hair. "The years have been tough, but you've shown a strength that matches your mama's. Trust me, this is our reward. Your father's return is a wonderful gift."

"But, Mummy, you're packing everything to follow him. You've closed the shop, left your work? What about my friends at school and church?"

"Don't worry. You'll make new friends, and we'll always return for Christmas and other holidays to visit your cousins. Now, we walk with our heads held high, for our naysayers have been silenced. So, give me a smile, Ada nna."

With a reluctant nod, Rebecca allowed herself to believe her mother's words.

"Oya, sing with me!" Her mother said, pulling her off the bed and twirling her around. Giggling, Rebecca surrendered to the joy, and together they sang and danced until the loud creak of the living room door made them pause.

"That must be your father!" her mother exclaimed. "Go greet him. Tell him I'll be out shortly. I still have much to do."

Rebecca dashed into the living room.

"My beautiful little angel!" her father sang, lifting her into his arms. She squealed with delight, squirming to see what he had in the other arm.

He set her down gently and handed her a bag filled with an assortment of sweets and chocolates. She rummaged through it, selected one in gold foil, unwrapped it quickly, and popped it into her mouth. Gasping with pleasure as the flavor melted in her mouth, she licked her hands and quickly grabbed another.

"Make sure you leave some to share with your friends, okay?" Her father chuckled.

She nodded half-heartedly, shoving two more into her mouth.

"Where's your mother?" he asked, glancing toward the bedroom

Rebecca pointed, her doubts and her mother's message already abandoned for the treats in her hands and mouth.

With her father headed to find her mother, she dashed outside, bursting to brag to her friends, but not before stashing some sweets on the table, just for herself. After all, her father had said to share, but not everything, right?

The days flew by quickly in preparation for their move. On the morning of their travel, Rebecca fell ill, with a high fever which lulled her into heavy sleep. Even as they travelled to Ibadan, she slept on, sheltered in her mother's arms. When she finally awoke, it was to her mother's trembling voice and cold hands.

"Nkem, wake up. We have to go to the hospital now."

Tears streamed down her mother's face, mirroring Rebecca's own as her heart broke into a million pieces at the words that followed. "Your father was in an accident."

After the dreadful night at the hospital and the news of her father's passing, Rebecca expected a barrage of visitors at the house where they were staying.

That was how it happened when Mr Festus, her neighbour from back home, passed away peacefully in his sleep. Visitors, including her mother, went in day and night, bringing food and condolences. But here, the house was silent. The wailing that Rebecca heard at the hospital—which had turned her mother's face red and swollen—had suddenly stopped. Her mother was now slumped in a chair in the living room, her shoulders rising and falling with deep, heavy sighs. She stared blankly into space, lost in her thoughts. Rebecca lost track of how long she remained there.

Eventually, Rebecca fell asleep at her mother's feet, only to wake up and find her still sitting there—a ghostly figure with two white lines across her face, the remnants of dried tears.

"Mama?" Rebecca whispered, but there was no response. "Mama, I'm hungry," she said softly, tapping her mother's feet.

Her mother let out another heavy sigh. The silence settled back in until a knock broke the quiet.

Her mother didn't move. The knock came again, louder this time, and Rebecca glanced anxiously between her mother and the door. A man's voice called out.

"Good afternoon. Is anyone home?"

Finally, her mother stood up, tying her loose wrapper around her waist. She led Rebecca into the bedroom, instructing her to stay put. Then she went to answer the door.

I hope they brought food, Rebecca thought, turning her nose up, hoping to catch a whiff of something delicious. She strained to hear the conversation, but their voices were low and muffled.

Gently, she slid off the bed and tiptoed toward the door. She was skilled at being unnoticed—a hack borne from years of avoiding the relentless teasing from other children and the bullying she faced for being born out of wedlock. Peeking through the small crack in the door, she saw a man and a woman seated across from her mother. She could finally catch snippets of their conversation. Through their lengthy words, they expressed their sorrow for her family's loss and spoke of wanting to do right by her mother.

What did that mean? Why did they feel the need to do anything? They were strangers, and it seemed like her mother was only just meeting them.

Her mother spoke very few words, mostly shaking her head, sniffling, and wiping tears with the edge of her wrapper. Before long, they left, and a man arrived with food that Rebecca devoured hungrily while her mother sat unchanged, not touching a single morsel. Soon after, another set of visitors knocked—a pair of women, one older and one younger, who bore a striking resemblance to her father. Her mother sent Rebecca back into her room, but Rebecca snuck back into her peeping position.

This time, instead of sympathy, the women unleashed a storm of insults, shouting and berating her mother.

"Witch!" the younger woman screamed. "You tricked him! That's the only way he could have fallen for someone like you."

"You used him!" the older woman added. "We thought he had escaped your grasp, but ten years later, he chose to come back to you and that child, disowning me, his own mother, because of my disapproval. I knew you did something to him, and now my only son is dead!"

Rebecca gasped, drawing her mother's attention, who rushed over to close the door, shielding her from the rest of the conversation.

The next day, they left Ibadan and returned home. News of their tragedy spread quickly, and visitors poured through their doors. The scorn and bullying were replaced with soft sighs and pitying looks. This was, to Rebecca, the worst fate. The children left her alone, and the adults whispered their condolences. When she returned home each day to narrate her experiences, her mother, who once had an encouraging quip, now simply sighed.

"But, Mummy, someone laughed at me today!" Rebecca cried one evening.

"Let them laugh. Even the heavens are laughing at me. What do I care about children?" her mother replied. The protector, her strong and guiding figure, seemed to be losing her will to live.

So, Rebecca did what she knew best—she fell back into their routines. Each night, she prayed alone. On Sundays, she walked to church by herself, kicked stones along the way, picked up her Bible, and recited memory verses. During the week, she studied diligently at school, hoping that if she did everything perfectly, her mother would awaken from this haze. But the light in her mother's eyes had dimmed, and nothing Rebecca did brought it back.

nine

TWISTS

Sola arrived at the hotel lobby at 1:01 P.M. Soft music filled the air, accompanied by a low buzz of conversation from guests lounging around the elegant space, oblivious to the drizzling rain.

He swept his gaze over the area as he dialled Tiffany's number. She answered on the first ring to tell him that she was already waiting for him, giving a detailed description of where she was seating. Striding purposefully toward the other side of the restaurant, he found her quietly sitting alone under a cabana overlooking a swimming pool, water sparkling with the gentle patter of rainfall. She was dressed in a stylish bathing suit paired with a flowing kimono, exuding a relaxed sophistication that caught him off guard. A sun hat rested on the table beside her, along with a dog-eared novel and a cocktail. She was typing on her phone and looked up when she sensed him looking at her.

Their eyes met and her face lit up with a dazzling smile that revealed perfectly defined dimples. She stood up and opened her arms wide, inviting him into an affectionate hug that felt intimate yet genuine, something one would typically reserve for the closest of persons—a sharp contrast to the professional coolness of their first meeting. The sweet, heavenly scent of her perfume enveloped but he quickly pulled away. His eyes roamed her bare-faced yet glowing beauty.

This was no ordinary business meeting, Sola thought.

"Good afternoon, Ms Tiffany." He smiled tentatively as they settled into their seats.

"Please call me Tiff," she replied, typing into her phone and taking a sip of what looked like a Mojito. "I think business is just a starting point for many amazing relationships. Do you agree?"

"Of course," he replied. He retrieved his laptop from the bag and placed it on the table between them, eager to impress her with how much work he had put into the UX of the software. "You'll be happy to see that I updated our last presentation based on your and the Chief's feedback. I've also included our team's improvements so far with the products and services we showed you."

Looking over his head, Tiffany called a waiter over, ordered him a drink, then turned again to her bedazzled phone. As her fingers danced across the screen Sola looked on, noting the rapid shifts in her expression—each one more animated than the last, mirroring the exchange she's having with someone on the other end.

"Just a second," Tiffany announced, then tossed her phone aside with a flourish. "There. Done."

"I hope everything's okay," Sola asked.

She let out a sparkling laugh. "With me? I'm perfect. Can't say the same for the rando whose fingers decided to write a check that his sorry self can't cash. Can you believe the audacity of some men? Spewing trash at women online like it's an Olympic sport!"

"Sorry?" Sola squinted, confused.

She leaned in.

"I was scrolling through my feed when I saw a post from a friend on vacation. We were all hyping her up in the comments until I spotted a vile comment. Someone shaming her for being plus-size and throwing around vulgar, dehumanizing terms. There's no way I'll stand for that. I don't play with my girls, and I always have time to spare, so I fired back."

"Ah, I see." Sola slowly nodded.

"It's all good. The cretin has crawled back into his hole. Let's get down to business."

Sola steadied himself and started his pitch, talking her through their new service ideas and improved interface for a couple of minutes that seemed like forever before she interrupted him.

"Let's look at this part over here." Tiffany pursed her lips. "This page should have a tutorial, but in an engaging way that doesn't make the user want to log out. You can use small pop-ups to show what each icon is for and how to navigate the features on the page. For each prompt that the user follows, show a celebratory icon or something similar that provides positive reinforcement that they are doing the right thing. I don't want my staff to find it too complicated, so lower the barrier of usage to encourage curiosity. If not, they'll shut it down the first time they use it."

Sola nodded enthusiastically, noting her comments and paying close attention to the other input she provided over the course of the remaining presentation. As he wrapped up, he had a sense that she was assessing him and offered a silent prayer that he had impressed her enough to convert their account.

"In terms of next steps," Sola started tentatively. "We would create an account for you and assign a hands-on account manager to guide you and your staff through the demo period, providing immediate support for any issues that arise."

"Sounds interesting," Tiff said, leaning away. "With so many services from businesses who would kill to onboard us, I'm sure you can understand why I need to weigh our options carefully."

A knot tightened in his stomach. This was the same feedback she had given him before, in more or less the same words. His mind scrambled for a way to convey the importance of the opportunity to Luna Pay.

"I understand, but..."

She held up a finger. "You have one thing working in your favour. I'm interested in more than just your idea," she said with a glint in her eye. "I'm fascinated by you and can't help wanting to know what makes you tick"

Sola blinked, taken aback. Her words swirled around his head before settling into a warm feeling in his belly. She continued speaking, her voice low but filled with a quiet conviction.

"I see myself in you: Intelligent, curious, innovative, driven to succeed. I admire that. And while this solution can bring our business value, I also want to support your success. So, I'll speak with my dad and get back to you with a decision."

Sola played it cool, internally overjoyed by the small victory. He packed away his laptop and mustered as much sincerity into his voice as possible.

"Thank you so much for your time."

Tiff glanced at her phone and let out an exasperated hiss.

"This degenerate is back with more slurs. But for every low blow he dishes out, I can go lower," as she spewed, her fingers poised over the screen. "Tell me why some men resort to such pathetic tactics, unprovoked. It's like every beautiful, accomplished woman is seen as someone who's just lucky enough to have a glucose guardian."

"A what?"

"Sugar daddy." A smirk tugged at her lips.

"Ah."

"It used to irk me," Tiffany continued. "As a woman, I felt the need to prove myself twice as much, to earn my place at the table. Even the smallest mistake, a poorly timed comment, could tarnish my image. But a man? He could bulldoze into a meeting, mumble nonsense, and still be seen as strong and confident. Even more infuriating is that a man can hurl a slur at you, and that label can cling, no matter how hard you fight against it. Then one day, I realised that their cruel words say far more about their own smallness than they do about me. So, I stopped explaining myself, defending my hard work, or shrinking to fit their narrative. Instead, I took up space—unapologetically. I carved out room for myself where there was none, daring anyone in my way to either move or be moved. Yet, when I see these petty attacks on my girls, it still boils my blood."

"Looks like that guy met his match today," Sola observed, a small smile on his face.

"Of course. I may lean into diplomacy in the boardroom, but on these streets? I'm petty."

She furiously typed out a message, then returned her focus to him, playfully leaning closer.

"I'll let you in on a secret."

"Yeah?"

"One of the reasons why I went looking for your booth at the conference was because of how you spoke to me before even knowing who I was. You were self-assured but offered correction with what struck me as genuine concern and desire to teach. It was non-condescending, yet impactful. Then, when the lunch rolled around and you knew my name, you still had that down-to-earth vibe, curious about how we could connect our perspectives. Today also felt like a conversation where we both learned from each other, it wasn't a one-sided lecture being shoved down my throat. I like that kind of energy around me, so keep doing that."

"Uh, thanks for saying that because to be honest, I was shaking in my boots, so I'm relieved you enjoyed it."

Tiff let out a playful laugh. "The shaking was obvious too ... and I may have enjoyed that part just as much! By the way, you haven't touched your drink," Tiffany noted.

"Sorry?"

"The hard part is over, right? No need to be tense or rush off. "

"Uh, okay."

He took a deep breath, letting his shoulders relax. While he sipped his drink, Tiffany attempted to take a selfie, changing postures and facial expressions.

Sola opened his mouth to speak, closed it, but finally said. "I can take a picture of you if you like."

"Yes, please," she exclaimed. "It's so nice of you to offer."

He took her phone, quickly adjusted some of the settings, and clicked a few shots of her in different poses before sitting back down.

"Oh my God, these are perfect. Thank you," she squealed.

"My pleasure."

"Anyway, I have to leave now if I want to make my flight."

Sola hadn't noticed when the skies dimmed. They had been together for hours. He coughed to mask his disappointment at the sudden end to the evening. Generally, he wasn't one to mix business with pleasure, Tiff was proving to be an exception. There are no downsides to enjoying a drink and conversing with a beautiful woman.

He stood as Tiffany readied herself to leave. She sent one last smile over her shoulder, waving goodbye. As he watched her walk away, he was surprised to feel a mix of hope and desire swelling in his chest.

The last woman who made him feel like this was one who he always felt he could never really have. Sammie.

The rain poured down in torrents as Rebecca drove into her estate, her headlights cutting through the deluge. She tightly gripped the steering wheel, every turn of the tires pulling her farther away from the workday chaos, as the facade of calm she'd worn around Tari crumbled.

Memories flooded her mind, their cold hands dragging her back to that hospital room. She saw herself standing there, clutching at her mother's wrapper, unable to stop the screams echoing in her ears, drowning out everything else, each cry like a knife to her heart.

"You killed my husband! Take my life too!"

When she pulled up to the estate, someone had parked carelessly, blocking the gate. Unable to muster the energy or anger to confront the situation, she parked on the side of the street and walked through the rain to her apartment, letting it wash over her, its cold droplets mingling with her trail of tears. She stepped in, soaked and shivering, stumbling forward to reach the couch. Worn out, she collapsed in a pile of tears.

Rebecca dialled her mother's number, but the call didn't connect. She flung her phone across the room, and it landed softly on the carpet.

A sudden knock on the door jolted her. Hurriedly wiping her face, she straightened her blouse.

"Who is it?" she called out; her voice shaky.

The response was muffled, but an urgency pulled her up from the floor. With a deep breath, she opened the door.

"Felix."

With a flick of her wrist, Rebecca slammed the door shut, hissing loudly in annoyance.

"Unbelievable," she muttered under her breath. "What is this idiot doing in my house? Can today get any worse?"

"Becca..."

"Go away, Felix. I don't want to see you." It had been months since she last laid eyes on him and blocked him on every platform she could think of.

"Becca, please, don't be like this. I just want to talk to you," he pleaded. "It's urgent," he said, his voice raspy with emotion.

Rolling her eyes, she opened the door to find him dripping wet on her porch.

"What do you want?" she hissed through clenched teeth.

"May I come in?" he asked, his voice soft and desperate.

"No, you may not." She scoffed in disbelief. "You're lucky I haven't poured hot water on you, but I just might if you remain here bothering me."

"No, no, please. We can talk here. I actually had to see you face-to-face." Felix reached out, extending an envelope slowly in her direction as if not to startle her.

"What's this?" Rebecca ripped it open and pulled out a wet card. The inscription on it struck her like a slap in a telenovela.

"Felix, is this a wedding invitation? *Your* wedding invitation?" Her pulse quickened. "Is this some sort of sick joke?"

"It's not a joke. I would never do that to you," he said. He took a deep breath, "After everything—the drama, the breakup—Florence pressured me to marry her. I had no choice but to give in, so we started preparing. But it all just feels so wrong. It's supposed to be you and me, us together forever. When I got the invites printed, it hit me harder than expected. I lost the greatest person in my life."

Rebecca's heart lurched painfully at his confession, but Felix continued before she could process his words.

He dropped to his knees, eyes pleading, taking hold of her legs. She nearly lost her balance as he feverishly begged.

"Becca, please! Tell me to stop. Just tell me not to go through with this wedding, and I swear I will drop everything to be yours forever."

"Are you out of your ever-loving mind!" she shrieked as blood rushed to her face.

"Becca, please, my life hasn't been the same since I lost you. I can't sleep, I can't eat, I can't be happy. It was you who made my life worth living!"

"Let me go!" She struggled against his firm grip, kicking and bracing herself against the door frame.

"I can't leave you, Becca. Please just say the words. I know you still love me, and I love you too with my entire being," his voice trembled.

"Felix, I'm warning you now. If you don't let go of me in five seconds, I'll scream," her words spilled out, sharp, commanding. The situation's absurdity drew a bitter laugh out of her. "I don't even know what to say to you, just let me go, and I'll pretend this didn't happen."

"Becca," he continued, pleading.

"*One*," she yelled, her eyes narrowing.

"Becca, please."

"Two ..."

"You're my life."

"Three ..."

"Believe me, please, I need you."

"Four ..."

"What is life without you, Becca?"

"Five ..."

Her last count hung in the air, heavy and final. Overwhelmed by a rush of pent-up emotion, she drew in a deep breath and let out a blood-curdling scream. With the rainfall down to a drizzle, her voice echoed through the space, and Felix stumbled backwards, his eyes wide in shock.

"Okay, okay, I'm sorry. I've let go," he stammered.

Rebecca's entire body was shaking, her nerves jangled by the day's turmoil. Tears blurred her vision, but she sensed someone approaching. Before she could make out who it was, warm arms and a familiar scent wrapped around her.

"Muyiwa?" she whispered.

"Yes, it's me."

She pointed at Felix, who's still kneeling on the floor, but words eluded her, lodged instead in her throat.

Muyiwa turned his gaze to Felix.

"I know this guy. Isn't this your ex? Is he hurting you?"

She nodded, and that was the cue Muyiwa needed to release her, drag Felix off the floor, and push him and his protests until he was out of the gate.

Rebecca crumbled against the doorway, wiping the tears on her face, and breathing deeply to slow her racing heart.

Muyiwa quickly returned, concern etched across his face.

"Are you okay? I saw you come in earlier, and you didn't look too good."

She managed a nod, but her lips quivered.

He quickly bent down to pick up a paper bag, which he'd dropped earlier, and then reached out his free hand to help her to her feet.

"I got you some diced fruit along with a burger and some nuggets. I was hoping to help you mark the last night before your leave began with flair. Then I heard your scream."

She wiped her eyes, touched by his kindness.

"I'm fine," her voice was barely a whisper.

"Rebecca," he urged softly, "you don't have to talk to me if you don't want to, but please take the food. I know eating is probably the last thing on your mind, but I promise it'll help."

"Okay," she said, reaching for the package with trembling hands. Her forced smile quickly crumbled into a sob.

Muyiwa stepped forward but halted as if unsure how to approach her. "Is there anything else you need? I can leave, but I can also stay if you want to talk. I'll just listen. Are you sure you're good?"

Unable to hold back, Rebecca found herself looking into Muyiwa's eyes.

"No, I'm not okay. It's been a terrible day, then that buffoon showed up, and it felt like the world was mocking me," she said bitterly. "But still, I would rather just be alone right now, okay?"

"I understand," he calmly replied, slowly backing away. "I'll check in on you later."

Rebecca softly closed the door, listening to Muyiwa's retreat. She stood there for a moment to catch her breath, then walked to the sitting area with the food clutched in her hands.

Sinking into her chair, she picked up her Bible, searching for familiar comfort. As she flipped the pages, the words blurred together. She tried to pray, but the prayers she'd memorised fell flat and felt hollow. In a fit of despair, she slammed the Bible shut.

She leaned instead, into the relief from the food, stuffing herself beyond comfort, and afterwards fell into a fitful sleep.

ten

RECALL

SEPTEMBER 2013

When he saw Sammie again, Sola was in the middle of a record-breaking streak. Not the kind that earned applause or made parents beam with pride. No. He was on track to be the most summoned student at the Dean of Student Affairs' office. His journey had already taken him through the offices of counsellors, his faculty head, and his course adviser, but their warnings and scolding had slipped right past him, unheard and unheeded.

The dance was easy—feign regret about the accusations, plead for mercy, and more often than not, they would grant him a reprieve. Then, he'd lie low for a spell before diving right back in.

But what was the actual crime in helping his fellow students succeed? After all, he was just filling the gaps left by their overwhelmed lecturers, offering extra classes to those struggling with their studies and providing a little side assistance on assignments. They should be thankful, not angry.

His self-satisfied thoughts were interrupted by the secretary's voice ringing out in the waiting area.

"The dean will see you now."

Sola swallowed hard. Twice was two times too many to be called in for misconduct. As he stood up, he rubbed his clammy palms against his trousers and tried to shake off the feeling of his legs turning to rubber.

"Please, take a seat," the dean said, bypassing formalities.

This was serious.

"Mr Adesesan," the dean began. "It has come to our attention that you impersonated two students during the last round of examinations. Just four months ago, you received a documented warning about your low attendance, but we showed leniency because of your otherwise excellent track record throughout your two-plus years here, as well as your proof of conducting extracurricular lessons."

The dean paused, removed his glasses and wiped them clean. Then, with the glasses resting on his nose bridge, he leaned back in his chair.

"You have so much potential. You're one of the brightest students to walk through this office. But instead of taking our warning seriously, you decided to plumb to new depths, offering paid assignment help, then impersonation. That's quite a leap, even for you."

"Sir, I can explain—"

"Be quiet!" The dean raised a finger, silencing him. "I heard you out last time you came to my office. I even extended an invitation for you to meet if you needed any support. The entire faculty has been rooting for you to succeed, but you chose this path instead. You'll be facing the disciplinary committee in a week, so I will see you then."

God, no.

His mum was going to kill him if she heard about this. He opened his mouth to plead, but the dean wasn't listening. He slumped out of the office and took the documents from the secretary, who rattled off instructions and reminded him to check his student email for more information.

As he left the Dean's office, Sola pictured the next phone call with his mum. He hadn't told her about the initial warning; how could he possibly explain a disciplinary meeting that could very well end in suspension? What if, God forbid, they brought up expulsion? He shuddered at the thought.

He felt a light tap on his shoulder. When he turned around, he saw a familiar pair of bright eyes practically bouncing with excitement. His jaw dropped, and he struggled to hold back a shout from the joy that bubbled in his body.

"Sammie? I don't believe it. What are you doing here?" he exclaimed, opening his arms for a hug, which she welcomed with enthusiasm.

"I go here, silly."

"Wow. How did I not know this? It's my third year here, and I had no idea. It's so good to see you!"

"Well, you sort of vanished after our final exams. The last time I saw you was at...um..." She paused, tapping a finger against her chin. "Ah, yes. It was

Meks' party."

Sola's entire body went cold with discomfort at the memory, and Samira caught on.

"Are you still upset about that night?" Samira's eyes widened. "We were just kids."

"Of course not. That was ages ago. I'm genuinely happy to see you."

"Me too! But, um, it's not just a random happy coincidence. I actually came here looking for you."

"You did?" Sola jerked his head back. "How did you know I was here?"

"I've been searching for some study help, and it turns out one of my roommates is your classmate. She recommended a brilliant geek who could completely turn my academic life around. I followed her to your department this morning, only to find out you were in trouble with the Dean, so here I am."

"Oh, that? It's no big deal."

Samira didn't look convinced.

"I hear what you're saying, but your face says otherwise. I have some time today; we could grab lunch, and you can spill the beans."

"I already had lunch," he countered, not ready to dive into a grilling by Sammie.

But she persisted, and he eventually gave in.

"I started my first year in Uni back in Nigeria, but when my parents finalised their messy divorce, my mum decided to leave everything—except me—behind and move here to stay with her sister. I had to start over when I got admission into Data Science, so I'm a year behind. Maybe that's why our paths haven't crossed, even though we're in the same faculty."

Sola leaned back in his chair, surrounded by beeping registers and snippets of conversations, as he listened closely to Sammie.

"I see. I'm sorry to hear about your parents," Sola said softly. "But also, congratulations, I guess?"

"Right back at you," Sammie replied and leaned forward. "Third year,

Computer Science. Impressive. But what brought you here?"

"I didn't have much choice either." A dry chuckle escaped his lips. "My father wanted me as far away from him as possible. This was his compromise with my mum."

"Why?" Sammie paused. "Was it because of the accident? We heard rumours about it, but nobody knew the details. Your friends only mentioned that you got hurt but recovered well. Is it related to your dad's decision?"

Sola gave a sharp nod. "Yeah, but I'd rather not talk about it." He kept his other thoughts to himself—his father and Derin had sworn him to secrecy.

"I hear you. But Sola, you seem different. When my roommate mentioned your name, I couldn't believe it."

"How do you mean?"

"Well, the part about your smarts and being a great study coach was easy to believe, but that you were a wild card? That's hard to picture," she said with a laugh.

Sola shrugged. "You're different too, you know."

"In what way?"

"For one, you're drop-dead gorgeous," he said, earning a playful roll of her eyes. "But seriously, you have this mature vibe about you. Now that I say that out loud, I realise it's not new. You've always carried yourself like you're that girl. And you are."

"Thanks," she whispered.

"So, about that help you wanted ... Are you sure you want to be associated with the likes of me? I'm facing the disciplinary committee next week," he blurted.

Sammie's mouth fell open. "Disciplinary committee? Whatever you did can't be that serious."

Sola had braced himself for disappointment but was met with genuine concern in her eyes. It had been ages since anyone looked at him like that.

"I guess I'm actually irresponsible." He swallowed, his indifference slipping under her gentle stare.

"No, that isn't who you are," she insisted, shaking her head. "Maybe you're going through a phase or something, but this isn't the real you, Sola."

Something about how she said those words made him want to believe her. But after almost three years of burdening guilt and unmet expectations, trusting that feeling was hard.

"Let's not make this about me, okay?" He held his palms up. "You're not my therapist, so let's focus on you."

A hurt look crossed her face.

"Fine," she said tightly before sharing her academic concerns with him. After listening, Sola agreed to help her set up a schedule in the coming days.

"You may not believe it," she said as she prepared to leave, "but I'm very happy to see you again."

A week later, Sola received the verdict from the disciplinary committee. A six-month suspension.

The dreaded phone call with his mum followed. At first, he attempted to lie, but she caught him effortlessly. Her response was a wail of genuine sorrow that echoed through the phone, making everything even more conflicting for him.

When his father first sent him to Poland to avoid the family's shame, Sola had vowed that the disgrace he brought would reach far and wide, that no distance would shield his father from his actions. But his mum's constant check-ins, prayers, and loving scolding had kept him mostly on the straight and narrow. Now that the consequences of his carelessness had come home to roost, he had broken her heart. She had always stood by his side, and he couldn't bear the thought of letting her down.

And as if that wasn't enough, Derin called with news that struck Sola like a physical blow. He had lost his scholarship.

"I got into a fight," Derin's voice was so low that Sola struggled to make out his words.

"Unbelievable! What kind of fight was worth your scholarship?" he spat angrily.

"I don't know what came over me! Derin replied, trembling. I was in a tight spot. I owed some guy money for my younger siblings' school fees. You know how hard my mum's been struggling since dad lost his job, so I tried to help out. But when I couldn't pay the guy back in time, he confronted me in class, and things got out of hand. Before I knew it, I punched the guy. It was self-defence, but the department wasn't having it."

"What were you thinking? You're not earning an income, so you shouldn't have taken that risk in the first place."

"That's easy for you to say. Taking risks is the only option I have without your kind of privilege," Derin's voice suddenly rose. Sola felt his ire relent.

"I didn't mean it like that. It's just…ugh…everything is a mess. You could have talked to me."

"I wish I had, but I didn't want to stress you."

Sola immediately got the sense that Derin wasn't telling him everything.

"What are you leaving out? I can't help you if you're hiding stuff."

Derin hesitated but finally spilled. It wasn't just my sister. Some guys in my faculty were organising a trip and invited me. I had to save face and say yes, but it was expensive. I couldn't have come to you for something like that."

"What are you going to do now? You still have a year of fees left to pay."

"Yeah, and that's why I'm calling. I desperately need your help. Can you lend me the tuition? I promise to pay you back. I've picked up some odd jobs around campus and in town, trying to save, but it won't be enough by the time classes start."

Sola paused, searching his mind for the right words to turn down the request without sending Derin into a fit.

"Guy, I know I'm asking a lot here," Derin pleaded, "but please, you have to help me."

"I don't have it," Sola finally admitted. "My mum manages my allowance, and it's just enough for necessities. There's nothing left for extras."

"But if you ask her, she'd probably front you something, right?"

"I'm walking a tightrope right now, so I don't know how she'd react."

"Please, Sola. I swear I'll pay you back."

Sola promised to talk to his mum, but he would need a good reason to explain why he needed more money than usual and was at a complete loss for a cover story.

"Penny for your thoughts?"

He looked away from his now blank phone screen at Sammie. She had gone over to order their food at the café they had agreed to meet at while he talked to Derin.

"Penny? Maybe a cargo of pennies," he joked, bracing himself for another round of grilling, as she placed a cup of steaming hot chocolate in front of him. She settled onto a bean chair, looking cozy as she sank into the soft fabric. Sola had chosen a low chair, but Sammie patted the comfy bean bag next to her.

"Trust me, you'll love it," she said, as she spread her books out. Sola made himself comfortable beside her.

"I heard you got suspended," she said, cutting straight to the point.

"Wow, going right for the jugular."

"There's no point in skirting around it. It is what it is. What's your plan?"

"I don't have one."

"Exactly." Sammie took a sip of her coffee and shook her head disapprovingly. "We can't have that. You need a plan otherwise you will fall behind."

Sola could see the spark of an idea form in her eyes.

"What are you thinking?"

"You should do an internship. It'll boost your resume and give you real-world experience. Plus, it's a chance for you to gain new skills."

He blinked. "I hadn't thought about that."

"You're welcome," she winked. "I'll let you sort out the logistics of that, but I need all the help I can get right now, so let's focus on me like we talked about.

And focus on her, they did. As they parted ways that afternoon, Sola couldn't shake the thought that if he had even a fraction of Sammie's passion to succeed, his life might look entirely different.

The suspension, Derin's troubles, his mother's tears, and Sammie's enthusiasm were all working together to override his desire to stick it to his dad. Was throwing away his own chances at success worth it just to defy his father? Or should he have been trying instead to succeed, despite his father's shadow?

JULY 2024

The sting of hunger was just as strong as the energy high from Sola's workout, but as he set his bag down to head for the kitchen, his phone rang. It was Tiffany.

"I have news for you, and I'm sure you'll love it," she said excitedly.

His heart raced. "Yes?"

"Congratulations! My dad and I have decided to buy your product and extend it across all our stores. We like your progress, and although it isn't at a hundred percent yet, we are sure your updates will reflect that. My dad likes your spirit, and you guys seem honest."

Sola stands speechless with disbelief for a few moments before responding.

"Wow, this is amazing news. Thank you so much for taking the leap with us. I promise you won't regret it."

"I hope I don't," she replied, a hint of humour lacing her voice.

Sola's mind ran through the next steps; they needed to leap into action immediately.

"Uh, well, we'll pull up the contract and email you before the end of this week. I hope that's fine?"

"No, it's not." Tiffany responded. "We want to add a training requirement to the contract, so you'll need to onboard representatives from different outlets on how to use the product. We'll sort out its logistics. I assume that's easy?"

"Sure," he replied quickly, nodding even though she can't see him. "Yes, it is."

"Okay, then. See you in Abuja next week. Before we roll out, we'll sign the physical contract and conduct the first training session with the test stores."

"Uh, you want us to be physically in Abuja?"

"Of course. Hold on, were you planning to sign an account as big as ours via email? It's an opportunity for you to get pictures and do some PR. That'll benefit your business reputation, don't you think?"

"Uh, sure. I'm sorry I didn't think about that," he replied, embarrassed that it was Tiff considering his business's image. "I'll discuss it with Derin and my team and get right back to you. Thanks again for the opportunity."

"You're very welcome," Tiffany's enthusiasm remained palpable through the phone. "I look forward to seeing you, okay?"

"Sure thing, Ms Tiffany—I mean, Tiff. I look forward to it as well. Take care."

He ended the call, pumped his fist in the air, and exclaimed, "Yes!" He turned around, drummed his fingers on the table, and immediately dialled

Derin.

Derin erupted in joyful disbelief.

"Bag secured, Man. This is incredible. Don't worry about the contract. I'll take care of it with our lawyer."

Rebecca was the first to arrive at work. She found solace in the quiet office until a familiar voice cut through her thoughts.

"Rebecca!"

Startled, she jumped at the sound of her name and the sound of popping gum.

"Tari! Why scare me like this? I didn't hear you approach."

"Good morning," Tari said in a sing-song voice. "Revenge is best served cold and on a morning like this, don't you think?"

"Morning," Rebecca replied, her voice low and distant.

Tari paused, studying her.

"Is it because you had to come in during your leave? I almost didn't recognise you from afar. This is probably the first time I have seen you in a pair of jeans and a T-shirt early in the week. And sandals? Did you forget that you're presenting today? Where are your heels?"

"In the car. I just don't feel like wearing them right now," Rebecca admitted, shrugging.

"Okay, that's a first. Are you sick? Did Made somehow pass her ailments onto you?"

"No. I'm just not feeling like myself, but it'll pass." Rebecca smiled weakly. "Don't worry about me. I'll go get my heels."

"Hold on," Tari stopped her. "I've been worried about you. The other day in the bathroom, I thought you were stressed about Made, but it felt like something more. It was unusual for you to throw such a fit, especially after we had gotten good news from the hospital. Especially over Made that we all know."

Tari's switch from serious to snarky lightened the mood, and Rebecca chuckled.

"My sweet Rebecca, if you need to talk, I'm all ears," Tari continued.

Rebecca took a deep breath and confessed.

"When I was ten, my father was killed in a car accident, and I saw a man from the hospital on that interview show that aired on TV that day. It sent me spiralling, but I think I'm better now."

"Dear Lord. That's rough." Tari grabbed a chair. "Was the man responsible for the accident?"

"No, I don't think so, but he's related to the person responsible somehow."

"That's a heavy thing to have carried for so long."

"That's not the end of it. When I got home, my ex showed up at my doorstep."

"Ha! Felix?" Tari's eyes widened in disbelief.

"In the flesh," Rebecca replied, rolling her eyes.

"But was he lost? What does he want with you after all this—"

Their conversation was interrupted by a security guard approaching with a beautifully wrapped package.

"Good morning, Miss Rebecca. We just got these delivered to the gate. They were addressed to you," he announced.

"Thanks, Ola. Please drop them on the table."

He gently placed the stunning bouquet of flowers and box of chocolates on the table and left.

Tari squeaked excitedly. "What is this? Who are they from? You didn't tell me you now have a man in your life! Ah ahn, it's not only the sad stuff we get to talk about, you know?" she whined.

"Calm down. I don't even know who sent these."

Tari was practically bouncing on her feet. "So, what are you waiting for? Check the card."

Rebecca carefully opened the attached card, and her smile widened.

"Read it out loud," Tari urged, now breathing over her shoulder.

"*To Rebecca, the girl whom Jesus loves. I hope these add a little colour to your day. I'm a call away if you need any pick-me-ups.*" She looked at the end of the note, where a heart was signed simply as *From Muyiwa*.

"Ha! And there's a heart emoji after his name! Please, who is Muyiwa? And is it just Jesus who loves you?" she asked, delightful mischief in her tone.

"Muyiwa is just a neighbour ..."

"And...?"

"A very sweet neighbour."

"Is that it?" Tari huffed. "No wahala. Looks like you'd rather keep this close to your chest. But it's only a matter of time. I'll get the full gist eventually, that's a promise."

Rebecca nodded, knowing Tari would do whatever she could to uphold that promise.

"Anyway, back to our previous conversation before this delightful interruption," Tari continued. "You said there was a man in the hospital?"

"Yeah, I remember seeing that same man the night my father died. He also came to our guesthouse before we left Ibadan. My mum has never talked about the incident in all these years, she prefers to tell stories about meeting my father versus losing him, so I only have my memories to rely on."

"Nobody got the police involved? Did they share anything with you about who the culprit was?"

"Yes, with my mum, but everything resolved quickly, and we left Ibadan for Abia after the accident. Now I want to find the person responsible for my father's death."

A tense silence hung between them. It was the first time Rebecca had ever spoken those words out loud and it felt powerful and dizzying to utter them.

"Why do you want to find him, and why now? Won't that just bring back the pain that your mother seems to have put behind her?" Tari asked gently.

"It feels unfair that their lives just continued without any justice, leaving us to pick up the fragments of our lives back then. My mum may have made peace with it, but she was cornered and had no choice. Right now, I don't know how to make peace with it. How did I go all these years without questioning everything? I was fine until just last week. And now ... not knowing means there's a question mark over how my father died. I can't accept that."

"Fair enough. Maybe I can help," Tari offered.

"Don't be ridiculous. I don't have a name or a face to go with? Besides, fourteen years have already passed, they won't look the same. I'm yet to connect with my father's family despite my best efforts."

"Yeah, but we can start with the identity of the man you saw." Tari was unfazed. "Talk to your mother for more details about what happened."

Excitement sparkled in Tari's eyes, contrasting sharply with Rebecca's lack of optimism.

"Treat this like you do your job. Prepare a plan, research, and gather details about the hospital, the accident—names, dates, anything. Then dive into your father's known relatives, friends, work, anything you know that will help."

Pursing her lips, Rebecca scribbled three names. A pitiful list.

"My father's family never reached out to us."

"For now, focus on your presentation prep. After work hours today, we will get the ball rolling."

"Sure," Rebecca replied as Tari headed to her workstation, even though she was anything but certain.

eleven

PRECIPICE

Abuja's sprawling landscape came into view as Sola and Derin excitedly chatted about their upcoming visit to the Tabano group. When they landed, they were pleasantly surprised when Tiff offered to cover their travel and accommodations for this trip.

The Tabano office was on the top floor of a bustling three-story shopping centre. They were ushered to the polished boardroom, surrounded by some of the company's top executives. The walls were adorned with stunning landscape photography, a map of Nigeria, and painted artwork that spoke to Nigeria's and the brand's rich heritage. They lightly chattered with the staff as they eagerly awaited Tiffany's arrival.

When she glided in, she was like a vision, attired in an ankle-length black dress and heels. The room fell silent, all eyes glued on her as she took her seat. But the atmosphere soon changed when she cheerfully began to greet them all.

"Daddy Ibeji," she gestured to the man sitting across from Sola. "We're happy to have you back from your paternity leave. How are your wife and the twins doing?"

She similarly greeted the others, then introduced Sola and Derin to the team, before handing over to them. Derin demoed the new interface they'd developed to test run with the Tabano team, informing them that Operations had already kicked off the software installations over the weekend.

"After this meeting, we'll be visiting the stores over the course of the week. The schedule has been sent to your email, and we look forward to your support and feedback as we commence. Thank you once again for the trust."

As discussions wrapped up and the contract was signed by both parties, Tiffany turned to one of her staff.

"Mr Tokunbo, please ask the photographer to come in."

"Photographer?" Sola echoed.

"Yes. We want to capture this meeting for a press release. I'm sure you want to announce this partnership," she said. "I'll be more than pleased to provide a statement."

"Great idea," Sola said, turning to Derin, who nodded his approval. Sola had an aversion to having an online footprint, so he turned back to Tiff. "Derin will take this. He can represent us for the picture. I need to use the washroom quickly. I may have had too much tea."

"That's fine. We can wait," Tiffany assured him.

"No, no. I don't want to be a bother or delay the process. Derin is a better muse for the camera anyway," Sola joked, trying to ease the mood. With that, he hurriedly slipped out of the boardroom and found the nearest washroom.

He relieved himself and started a mental countdown as he waited, giving sufficient time for the picture session to end—trusting Derin to handle it smoothly. As he walked back, he noticed staff members exiting, and relief washed over him at the thought of the meeting's success.

Entering the boardroom, he was surprised to find Tiffany still there, seated gracefully and completely engrossed in her phone. Her eyes were glued to the screen, and she didn't notice his arrival at first. Suddenly, a loud cackle erupted from her, clearly delighted by whatever she was watching. Sola couldn't help but laugh in response.

Tiffany looked up, startled. "You're back."

He nodded and took a few steps toward her.

"Hey, I thought everyone had left," he said.

"I was waiting for you," she replied, her smile brightening the room. "Have you seen this trending video?" Tiffany practically thrusted her phone into his face. On the screen, a clip of cats misjudging their jumps played, each failure more hilarious than the last. Sola felt a grin spread across his lips.

"I'm a dog person, but cats are hilarious," Tiffany admitted as she collected her phone, still chuckling to herself. He glanced around the room, realising it's almost bare—nothing but his and Tiffany's things are on the table.

"Have you seen Derin?"

Silence.

"Tiff?"

"Huh? Sorry, bad habit. What did you say?" she replied, snapping back to the moment.

"Do you know where Derin is?" he repeated.

"I believe he said something about another appointment."

"Understandable, that's Derin for you, always hustling."

"Here I thought that your trip to Abuja was solely for us," she said with a note of disappointment. "Seems like we're not that important."

"Uh, I'm so sorry about that," he apologised, heat flooding his face. "I promise you it's not at all like that. Derin and I are thrilled about this partnership."

"There's no need to apologise, but you owe me a photo," she said as she pulled Sola closer. Their faces nearly brushing against each other.

"Smile!" she commanded, lifting the phone for a quick shot and looking it over. "Perfect! This works." His chest swelled at the stamp of approval.

In that moment, the world around them faded, leaving just the two of them. She smelled intoxicatingly divine, and Sola was momentarily breathless. But the moment passed quickly as Tiffany pulled away and began to pack her laptop.

"I'm heading to a friend's birthday party later, but I need a date. Will you join me? It'll be fun, with karaoke too. Plus, it'll be a perfect way to make up for you rushing off at the end of the meeting."

"I thought the selfie already did that."

"Nope," she replied, grinning eagerly for his answer.

"Alright, I don't see why not," he said, unable to resist her charm.

"Fantastic!" she squealed, "I'll pick you up at your hotel then. Is that okay?"

"I'll be waiting."

"See ya." She grabbed her things and gracefully glided out of the room.

"I brought snacks," Tari announced as she entered the private room they had chosen for their after-hours research.

"You're the best. I'm starving. I skipped lunch because of my nerves, so I'll take whatever I can get," she said, grabbing a parfait and taking a big scoop, savouring its coolness. The day was a whirlwind of nerves, and her presentation had mostly gone smoothly—until she stumbled over answering a question from one of the executives. In that instant, she caught a senior colleague, Eric, smirking at the blunder. Thankfully, director Jimi had bailed her out, but the temporary manager filling in for Imade sat quietly, offering no support.

Despite this, the feedback from the leadership was both constructive and overwhelming, with a demand for more coordination from her teammates to churn out updated work by week's end.

"So where do we start?" Tari prompted, biting into a slice of pizza.

"I think my dad had a friend who worked with him," she said, picking up a pizza slice.

"Okay, I'll look up your father's engineering firm and his friends' details; you can focus on his family."

As they settled into research mode, a wave of laughter filtered into the room from the corridor, making Rebecca pause.

"I thought the office was empty. That laugh sounds like Moji," she noted, tilting her head.

"Yeah, a few people are hanging around. I saw your teammates in Wing B. It looked like they were debriefing about the earlier meeting."

"That's strange."

"Maybe." Tari shrugged, focusing on the screen before her.

"I'll check in with them quickly. Be right back."

Rebecca found the group of four huddled together in Wing B as Tari described. As she approached, their laughter faded and was replaced with a silence that sent a chill down her spine.

"Hi guys, what's up?" she forced her voice to remain casual despite their odd expressions.

Moji avoided her gaze, staring intently at the floor while the others showed disinterest. Only Eric met her eyes; irritation evident in them.

"What are you doing here?"

"Just hanging out. And you guys?"

"Working on the feedback from earlier," Eric sharply shot back.

"Okay, I didn't know a meeting was happening. We're supposed to work on it together, right?"

"We have it covered and don't need your input," disdain dripped from his voice.

Rebecca was taken aback by the hostility. "But I worked on that presentation with Imade," she protested. "The executives expect us to collaborate, and I was hoping that you guys would share feedback on the capability project."

"Right. The chosen one needs our help," Adonai interjected mockingly.

"What does that mean?"

"It means you're Imade's pet," Eric sneered. "We are your seniors, yet she delegated the presentation to you, but we're supposed to help you on this and other projects? Dream on, sweetie."

"Wow. I had no clue you felt this way, considering that I support you all on your projects. Wasn't it just last week that I was translating reports for you, Adonai? And you, Moji, you've been on the team for only six months—do you share the same opinion? Are you also not going to help me?"

"I don't have much choice," Moji mumbled.

"This isn't a guilt fest," Adonai taunted and Rebecca threw her hands up in exasperation before turning away, rage that she couldn't put into words pulsing through her.

Rebecca stormed back to the room, slamming the door behind her, startling Tari, who jumped.

"What happened?"

"Can you believe it? They hate me and don't want to let me input on the presentation, nor do they want to help me on my project," Rebecca ranted.

Tari's expression softened. "This isn't news unfortunately, but I didn't say anything so that you won't feel bad."

"It's so unfair."

"Yeah, but it's also a projection of how they feel about Made."

"How?"

"It's a long gist, jare."

"Well, seems like I'm the only one in the dark, so I'm all ears."

"Okay then." Tari sighed. "Several candidates were vying for her role before Made returned to Nigeria. The competition was fierce, and the politicking got downright nasty. Many people didn't even consider Made because she was abroad and she left partly because of the harassment and discrimination she'd faced back home."

Rebecca's eyes widened. "I had no idea."

"It was awful. When Made was eventually offered the role and returned, many people were furious because they felt entitled to the position."

"But she was qualified for it."

"Exactly," Tari affirmed. "And considering the sensitive nature of her work and the types of projects that role would lead, the president had to select someone competent. I heard it took a lot of persuasion to get her to come back. Some of those who harassed her before were let go after an investigation, but some of their allies are still here, eager to see her fail."

Rebecca's frown deepened. "What does this have to do with me and my team, though?"

"Someone senior must have promised them something—a reward for undermining Made, and well, you aren't making it easy since you're almost like her assistant despite how you both bicker."

"That's insane," Rebecca exclaimed.

"Yeah, well, now you know that there's a target on both your backs, especially since she became your biggest advocate. You may not know this, but she sings your praise the loudest, especially when you aren't there. She even nominated you for the analyst award."

"I didn't know that. She's usually so mean," she said introspectively. "I admit that she can be tough, but she knows her stuff and holds us accountable for our work."

Tari shrugged. "Well, the way you stick it to the others is to continue to do a great job. Made delegated to you, so take the lead confidently. On her end, Made is a big girl and can take care of herself."

"You're right," Rebecca said thoughtfully. "But what about Director Jimi? Is he involved in all of this? There always seems to be some friction between them."

"Nah." Tari chuckled. "He's sweet on her and has always had her back. There were whispers that they were more than friends, but he was clearly hurt when she decided to leave. Their drama is a love story, so don't mind those two."

Rebecca laughed. "I get it now. It makes sense why they act like overgrown kids around each other."

"Right? Nobody can put mouth in their matter o. We can only watch," Tari replied. "But enough of Made's gist. Are we going to tackle your situation or what?"

"Sorry, I felt bad for her, but you're right. I have my own problems. Let's focus."

They spent the rest of the evening searching the worldwide web for clues and pieces of Rebecca's past.

twelve

UNCERTAINTIES

AUGUST 2019

Sammie's house was alive with laughter and chatter of her friends, but Sola slipped away to the kitchen for a moment alone. He was lost in thought when Sammie's voice broke through the silence.

"Earth to you, baby," she teased, wrapping her arms around his waist from behind. Her head rested softly against his back. He turned to face her, enveloping her in his arms, pulling her close to his chest, and planting a gentle kiss on the top of her head.

A loud shout erupted from the living room, followed by fits of chaotic laughter that hinted at the mayhem of their charades game. They both turned their heads toward the commotion.

"Looks like everyone is having the best time out there. Even your mum and aunt are vibing with our friends," Sola noted with a grin.

"You bet. When I told them I was hosting a game night, they insisted on joining, claiming they're cool kids too. Can't argue with that."

"Mmm hmmm," Sola mumbled, leaning down to bury his face in the crook of her neck, inhaling her sweet scent. "You smell nice." He tightened his grip around her, feeling her softness meld against him.

"That's off-topic," she giggled, playfully nudging his chest.

"You can never be off-topic," he replied, trailing soft kisses along her collarbone.

"Uh, babe. My mum is right behind this wall," she protested, though a smile danced on her lips.

"Who cares?" he countered cheekily.

"I do." Sammie laughed, pulling away just enough to look up at him but remaining in his arms. "And don't think I'm falling for your trick."

His eyebrow arched in playful defiance.

"You were deep in thought when I walked in. You've been in your head a lot lately. What's going on?" Sammie pressed.

He shrugged.

"Don't just shrug it away like it's nothing," she insisted. "You promised to talk to me whenever you were worried about something."

"I'm good," he reassured her.

"Fine, don't talk." She took a step back but was still within his reach. "I'll go back out there."

"No, wait. You're right, and I'm sorry I didn't say anything sooner."

"Is it about what we discussed after Antoine's wedding? I told you, we don't have to rush into marriage until we're both ready. Our lives are just now coming together. You've got your loans and career to think about. Let's give ourselves time to secure a solid financial footing before we dive into that."

"No, it's not that," Sola interrupted, his voice firm yet gentle. "Sammie, I love you. I want to spend the rest of my life with you. There's nothing I'm more certain of. The loans, the career; they don't matter as long as I wake up next to you every day. I don't mind whether we have a big wedding or elope. Although your mom might have a heart attack if we elope. But when the time is right, I'll be here."

"Then what's troubling you?" Her eyes searched his.

Sola took a deep breath.

"I've been thinking about travelling to Nigeria."

"Sounds great. We can plan a trip for Christmas," she replied, looking relieved.

"No, baby. I want to move back permanently. And I'd like you to come with me."

Sammie blinked rapidly, and her shoulders tensed as his words sank in.

"You just said you're right here. How does that mean moving to Nigeria?"

Sola raised his hands in a calming gesture.

"It's just a thought. I didn't want to bring it up because I didn't want to worry you. But I've been unhappy here. I feel like a stranger, wandering without purpose."

"And you think moving to Nigeria will solve that?" she asked, her voice strained.

"I don't think Nigeria alone will fix anything," he admitted. "But who knows what life could bring?"

He watched as different emotions crossed her face: confusion, sadness, and finally, her shoulders sagged.

"Will it ever end?" she asked.

"What do you mean?"

"Th—this pattern. Every time life changes, we have this same conversation. You finished college, but it wasn't enough, so you went for your Master's. You started a job but left because it wasn't fulfilling. You threw yourself into photography, landing big gigs, then ditched it for that app you built. Now, Poland is the problem? Or is it the thought of marrying me?" she said, her voice rising.

"Baby ... please," he said softly.

"The problem isn't these things," she pressed on fiercely. "You can't accept good things happening to you. God keeps blessing you and showing you favour, yet you keep throwing them all away because of one bad thing hanging over you. How long are we going to stay stuck?"

Her words struck him deeply, echoing the insecurities he struggled to voice. Before he responded, she turned away in a decisive move that felt like she was finally leaving him behind.

AUGUST 2024

Sola was already waiting in the hotel lobby by 5:30 PM, and true to her word, Tiffany arrived thirty minutes later to pick him up for the party. The venue was an exclusive restaurant, and the entire floor was reserved for their group.

As soon as they stepped inside, Tiffany was in high spirits, her energy contagious as she greeted her friends with squeals and kisses. She held Sola's hand firmly during greetings and introduced him to everyone. She then led him to the celebrant, Kasiemobi, standing by a table close to the centre stage, beaming and chatting animatedly with some guests. When Kasiemobi saw Tiffany approaching, both ladies let out a screech, their laughter drowning out other conversations. Sola watched with a smile as they embraced and air kissed.

"You look absolutely dashing in that dress! I should steal it after tonight," Tiffany teased, admiring her friend, who was dressed in a glistening black knee-length dress with dramatic pink roses for sleeves. Kasiemobi's makeup was radiant, featuring glittery eyeshadow on her eyelids, completing her look with metallic jewellery.

"Thank you. I made sure no one could upstage me tonight, but girl, you're giving me a run for my money! I'm this close to throwing you out for being too beautiful," Kasiemobi teased back.

With a twirl, Tiffany exclaimed, "I couldn't very well make it easy for you, now could I?"

"That's right. I love it." Kasiemobi then turned her gaze toward Sola, her curious eyes openly inspecting him. He felt severely underdressed in his simple pants and a green T-shirt. He tried to style his outfit by adding a jacket and gold necklace, replacing sneakers with polished black dress shoes, and allowing his neat locs to fall to his face.

"And who is this dashing young man?" Kasiemobi said, touching his shoulder lightly.

Tiffany slipped her hand onto Sola's elbow, nudging him closer to Kasiemobi.

"This is Sola, a new friend of mine." Tiff winked. "Sola, meet Kasie, my best friend from way back."

Sola extended his hand to Kasiemobi, feeling her warmth as she took it with a coquettish smile.

"It's a pleasure to meet you, Kasie. Happy birthday."

"Hi, Sola, our new friend, charmed to meet you, too. Tiff rarely makes new friends, so I hope you both have a good time tonight. Make yourself at home."

"Sure thing. Your party looks fantastic, and you are the shining highlight," Sola replied.

Kasiemobi smacked her lips together and turned to Tiffany. "Keep an eye on this one, eh? He has a sweet mouth. I like it."

Another friend cut in, pulling Kasiemobi away.

The rest of the night unfolded with an exciting mix of games and laughter at the MCs' masterful jokes, music, and Kasiemobi's antics that kept everyone entertained.

When it was time for karaoke, Tiffany, with her usual enthusiasm, volunteered them for a duet. Sola shook his head in protest, but the cheers and hoots from the other guests pulled him into a playful performance.

They selected a classic song by Lagbaja, which brought back fond memories. Soon, they were singing their hearts out, their voices rolling like waves on a beach, creating a harmonious melody that filled the room. It was as though they were the only two people in the world as Tiffany's hands wrapped around his neck, bringing her face close to his as she sang. Her playfulness elicited laughter from the audience. The guests joined in, and he pulled her gently around the waist, turning her around and singing like long-time lovers separated for years.

"You're always on my mind ..."

The room erupted into applause and whistled as they sang the last note.

Tiffany lingered in his arms, her breath tickling his ear as she whispered, "I believe we put on a splendid show. Let's bow and get some air."

They bowed dramatically, and cheers followed them as they left the stage and slipped out into the cool night air, still giggling uncontrollably.

"That was so much fun. I didn't know you could sing like that," she exclaimed with infectious happiness.

"Happy to impress," he quipped with another exaggerated bow. They found two chairs and sat across from each other. The music floating into the outdoor area set a dreamlike backdrop for their conversation.

"You must have had a beautiful childhood with the way to allow yourself to express joy," Sola said wistfully. "You don't find that just anywhere, especially with how tough the country's situation is."

"You could say that. My parents didn't joke with education and academic success, but they also made sure that I had fun experiences. Although I've experienced both struggle and loss, my family always pushed through," she admitted with fondness. "They sacrificed so much, holding onto faith even when things seemed uncertain, and that has shaped how I see the world."

"Would you say you carried on with that faith?"

Tiffany nodded. "Wholeheartedly, and personally for myself. It wasn't about carrying on something handed over. I'm a Jesus girl through and through."

"I like that you're non-apologetic about it," Sola remarked with a smile that reached his eyes.

"Ahh, yes. I don't joke about my faith in Christ. I'm grateful for everything, success, provision, all of it. Yet, I know how fleeting it can be. Money, beauty, influence, the people you think you can trust, they can fade away. But God? He's constant," her voice was sharp and filled with conviction. "In every season, He's faithful and true to His word. I've faced my share of curveballs and experienced life both with and without Jesus. I choose to walk with Him." A low laugh escapes her lips as she continues. "I've come near death, and that could have torn my family apart, but for God's grace. In both the highs and the lows, He's kept me. I've felt His love and tasted His goodness. I'm nothing without Him, so yes, I'm unapologetic about my faith."

She leaned forward.

"What about you? What's your story?"

Sola cleared his throat, fiddling with the stack of bracelets on his wrists. "I share your faith," he began, glancing down momentarily as he searched for the right words. "Though sometimes, it feels like I fall short of God's standards, you know? But I try."

Tiffany's smile was warm and understanding. "Looks like there's a lot to unpack in that, but I'll let you off the hook tonight," she said gently. "And your family—are you close?"

Sola took a deep breath and chose his words carefully.

"I have a great relationship with my mum, but I'm not that close to my dad or my brother," he admitted.

"Why not?"

His mind goes to her likeness to Sammie and how he could never escape her interrogations.

"We just drifted apart as I grew up. My father was strict, and when I tasted a bit of independence, I didn't look back," Sola explained, skipping over the ugly details.

"That's sad," she whispered, her eyes revealing her understanding of something deeper, and her choice to let it go.

"So, tell me, is there a woman in your life?"

He chuckled. "That's direct."

"I'm not one to beat around the bush. So, is there?"

He momentarily considered her question before he replied. "No, there isn't."

The pleasure on her face was unmistakable.

"That's a great response but now I'm curious—why isn't there one? Aren't you interested in love, or are you one of those players who toy with hearts?" She squinted at him. "You do look like a heartbreaker."

"Not even close," he laughed. "I've had a few serious relationships, but they ended for different reasons."

"Why did your last relationship end?"

"Uh..." He paused. "We couldn't handle the pressure of a long-distance relationship, so we mutually decided to end things," he lied.

"Hmm. And that ..." She leaned over and pulled gently at one of the bracelets on his wrists "This one with the angel inscription on it, is it from her?"

"Uh, no. It's from another time. A different story," he said, hoping she won't press. She didn't, and they shared a moment in silence, the music filling the space between them. A waiter nearby approached with some small chops and soft drinks.

"Thank you," Tiffany cooed, taking a sip before fixing her gaze back on him.

"Aren't you going to ask me if there's a man in my life?"

"Uh, I'm sorry. Do you have a man in your life?" He picked up a ball of puff puff, trying to match her light-hearted tone.

"You don't sound curious enough, so you don't deserve an answer," she pouted.

Amused, he leaned forward. "Okay, please tell me. Pardon my impertinence. I really want to know your answer."

Her smile spread, and his heart skipped a beat.

"Yes, there is—" she shrugged "—and he's the best thing to ever happen to me. He's handsome and kind, a handful on some days, but I haven't found a companion like him yet."

Sola shook his head. "I'm confused."

Tiff burst into laughter, pulling out her phone. "Here he is," she trilled, revealing the picture of a cute white terrier.

Sola chuckled. "That's funny. He's cute. What's his name?"

"Mr Paws. But jokes aside, there isn't a man right now. Not for lack of interest, but I haven't found him. It's almost as if he's not trying hard enough. A couple of fellows have shot arrows in my direction, but none of them was quite right."

"What's your definition of 'right?'"

"Hmm. You?"

"*Me*? What?"

"You're my definition of 'right,'" she said with flourish.

He chuckled. "Are you sure I can compete with the little white fellow?"

"I'm being serious. I usually know what I want, especially when it's right in front of me. I don't always get it, but believe me, I try. And as of now, with you sitting here, there's no doubt in my mind that I want you."

Sola looked at her disarming smile, speechless, but pleased.

"Do with that information what you will." She winked and took another sip of her drink.

As he gathered his thoughts, a voice interrupted them.

"Tiff. There you are. We've been looking all over for you. It's time for the toast."

Tiffany nodded at the lady. "Be right there." She brushed her fingers against Sola's cheek and whispered. "To be continued."

After she headed back inside, he remained outside, holding on to the fading excitement, wishing he had said something more, chastising himself for letting Tiff be the one to shoot her shot. He stood up and headed back inside to find Tiffany on stage, mic in hand, and the audience laughing at something she must have said. He'd missed the start of her speech but listened as she continued.

"Dear Kasie, my ride or die. The personification of *ride* because you drive me nuts, while I've come close to dying multiple times due to your crazy shenanigans. But that's who you are. Lover of life who doesn't ever let me forget that life is worth living to the fullest extent. You ride hard for all your friends, and that's why we are all here for you today. You've never allowed me to entertain even for a moment that I'm not good enough. People think that I'm the confident one, but as a teenager with low self-esteem and conscious about my changing body and how different I sounded, I would cower from being teased, but Kasie would square up against anyone who said an unkind word to me or just looked at me funny. And the art of showing up when it's inconvenient? She has it locked down. Travelled from flight school to the hospital when I had surgery. You raise the bar of ambition with your adventurous spirit. I mean, guys, she flies planes for a living. Best at keeping me straight, the hype queen, and no one does it better. You're no less wild and wonderful as always. May God bless and keep you and may all the traffic lights turn green when you speed by," she raised her glass. "Cheers to 30."

The crowd echoed the cheer with the clinking of glasses, and the celebration continued.

After saying their goodbyes, Tiffany fields multiple calls as they drive back to the hotel, leaving little room for conversation. But as they arrived, Sola finally spoke up.

"Tiff. I had a great time and would love to see you again."

"I sure hope so," Tiffany replied with a smile. "Good night."

Sola inhaled her scent, holding on to the night as a promise of what is possible. She blew him a kiss, and he caught it playfully.

"Goodnight, Tiff."

As he got out of the car and watched it pull away, nothing else mattered to him except the endearing feeling slowly but surely budding in his heart.

The days flew by as Sola and Derin navigated a hectic schedule of meetings and training sessions at various Tabano outlets. Sola had hoped to see Tiff after that night, but they don't get past exchanging messages.

On the day of their return, a company car with a driver arrived to take them to the airport, and Sola's heart sank. Despite the thoughtful gesture, it was hard to shake off the disappointment of not getting to say a proper goodbye to Tiff.

As they headed down the serene roads, Sola's phone buzzed with a message from her.

"I would have loved to see you off, but I have a series of meetings lined up for this morning. Let me know when you land."

"You're unusually quiet today. Seems like this visit was more than just business for you and the princess," Derin chimed.

Sola shrugged. "It's just business."

"Come on, man. You got all the attention during this visit. You were her date to a party, and now you're grinning at your phone. She's definitely sweet on you."

"Nah, it's just how she is. This partnership is important for both our businesses, and she's making sure everything flows smoothly. What about you, though? You were MIA most of the time. What were you up to?"

"Don't change the subject. You have your interests, and I have mine," Derin said, waving his hand dismissively. "But seriously, if this relationship helps with the partnership, you have my blessing. Just don't break her heart and ruin everything, alright?"

Sola looked at his friend with irritation. "Why does everything have to be so transactional for you?"

Derin rolled his eyes. "I've said my piece. Take it or leave it. Just don't let this slip through your fingers. Remember Samira? You walked away from her at the drop of a hat. What if this princess loses her allure, too? Will you walk away?"

Sola bristled at the mention of his ex.

"You're way out of line," Sola seethed coldly.

"Chill out, man, I'm just joking," Derin responded, but there's an edge to his tone. "But, you know, I'm right. It's not just about relationships; you've flitted from one thing to another. Almost ditched your degree, jumped from job to job, then startup to startup. Luna Pay is our joint hard work and more than a business; it's my passion and sweat. So, lock in and don't self-sabotage this one."

Sola ran his hand across his face and pinched his nose to calm himself. Derin's words hit too close to home. Each jab, though wrapped in pretentious light-heartedness, was piercing. He met the curious gaze of the driver in the rearview mirror and let out an uncomfortable cough.

"This isn't the time or place for this," Sola said, his voice low and taut. "I don't know what's got you all twisted up, but there's no need to attack me like this."

"Whatever, man, sha no pour sand for my garri," Derin grinned, his tone dismissive,

Sola stared out the window, and they spent the remainder of the ride to the airport in uncomfortable silence.

II

REPAIR

thirteen

INCURSIONS

Rebecca's stomach growled loudly, reminding her of the hunger she had earlier ignored. A week back from her leave, she had been caught in a loop of updates, feedback, and revisions. To distract herself from the raging war in her mind, and as a step in faith like Muyiwa had encouraged, Rebecca spent many late nights obsessing over the plans and templates she'd promised. But she was still struggling. Imade had returned and torn apart her work, providing a deluge of technical feedback that she was swimming in. If she didn't nail this, Imade was not going to be pleased.

"But what's the point anyway?" Rebecca grumbled to herself. "Imade is *always* displeased."

Just as she was about to escape for lunch, Tari appeared.

"Come on," Tari's tone was urgent as she tugged Rebecca toward one of the vacant focus rooms.

"Have you spoken to your mother yet?"

"Not yet, but I will before the week runs out," Rebecca replied, looking at the floor. Actually, she had been dodging her mother's calls in a feeble attempt to avoid the emotions she wasn't ready to face.

Tari's gaze softened.

"Never mind that. I found something about your Dad." She excitedly pulled out her phone, handing it to Rebecca, whose heart skipped a beat.

"Already?" She looked at the screen. "What am I supposed to be looking at? It's just a Twitter post."

"Keep scrolling," Tari insisted. "I tweeted and mentioned I was looking for your father's friend based on your description. Most of the responses were just noise from trolls, but then I found this." Tari pointed to a specific comment.

Rebecca squinted at the screen, but the words didn't make sense to her.

"Yeah, I see that, but what does it mean?"

"This guy commented how weird it is that someone asked this question on his father's birthday," Tari explains. "So, I sent him a direct message. Turns out he's the son of your father's friend, Mr Subomi. We chatted for a while, he wanted to make sure I wasn't a fraud. But he eventually sent pictures and confirmed his father's connection to yours."

Tari pulled up a sepia-coloured photo of two young men on her phone.

"This is Mr Subomi on the left. Is the other man your Dad?" she asked, her eyes sparkling with hope.

Rebecca's breath caught in her throat.

"Yes, that's him," she choked out.

"They grew up and worked together," Tari continued. "He was there when your father fell for your mother. He's willing to talk to us, so we can call him if you're up to it. I got his number."

Rebecca sniffed. "No, not now, I'm not ready for this. I didn't think we'd start getting leads this soon."

"I understand. I looked Mr Subomi up. He was with an engineering firm, and he and your father were listed as directors on some old website. It seems legit. I didn't want to set up the call until I showed you, but isn't this exciting?"

Rebecca's mouth hung open.

"I don't know what to say. I can't believe how you dove into this. I always knew that you were a pro at social media stalking, but this is next level."

"Ehn... Is that an insult? Tari eyed her.

"Not at all! I actually admire you. But it's a lot to handle. Can you take the call and let me know what he says? Just...do you."

"I can't do that," Tari replied softly, placing her hand on Rebecca's shoulder. "This is your story, so take your time. We'll pick this up when you're ready."

Rebecca pulled Tari into a hug.

"Thanks, Tari."

"Anytime, boo." Together, they headed to the cafeteria, and from there on out, the day passes in a blur of reports and meetings.

On her drive home, Rebecca passes by a roadside vendor selling roasted plantains and yams. She's tempted to stop but kept her eyes mind on the salad she had prepped for dinner already. When she got home and settled to eat it, she found her appetite ruined.

Her phone rang, breaking through her thoughts. It was Hauwa.

"Hauwa. I've been trying to reach you. Are you okay?"

"Yes, I am, dear. A bit stressed from life logistics, but I'm starting to feel settled now. How are you? Hope you aren't stressing yourself."

"Life has stressed me this week, o. But I've decided to rise above and just forget about it."

"Is that healthy? What's going on?"

Rebecca could hear Hauwa's empathetic sigh through the phone as she recounted the whirlwind of her past few weeks.

"Have you spoken with your mum?"

"Not yet. We've been exchanging messages, but just casual checkups. I don't want to burden her with any of this until I have some resolution. It's hard talking about my dad and how he died. I thought it would help both of us if I could find closure, but now I'm not so sure.

"You might be right," Hauwa intoned. "Maybe she's found her peace, but what about you? Have you found yours? This could be more about you than her, and I worry you might regret walking away."

Rebecca felt her face tighten.

"I didn't think much about his killer for a long time. I just wanted to know why his family rejected us. I longed for their love, hoping it would fill the void my dad left behind. But when I saw Chief Adesesan on that screen, anger took over. I'm scared to confront it, so I want to let it go. It's okay to stop seeking closure, right?"

"I am just worried about you. What if you don't like the answers you find? But on the other hand, what if they lead you to the resolution you need? We don't know which way this would swing, but at the end of the day, I don't want you to get hurt."

"I'm already hurt, so no matter how it goes, I'll decide what to do. Just tell me you're on my side."

"My dear, I'm always on your side. Even more so now. Just be careful, okay? And let me know if you need anything."

"Thanks, Hauwa. That means a lot."

"Anytime, dear."

"When are you coming to Lagos next?"

"In a month for the Rising Women in Corporate event. Speaking of which, the flyers are ready for posting. We started the drive weeks ago, but we still need vendors to join us. I'll send the details over to you for the collaborative post. I hope it helps attract more interested parties."

"Sure, I'll put them on my page once you send them."

"Thanks, darling. Oh, and we have a new coordinator and head of operations! Her name is Sandra, and she'll be at the event too."

"That's great. Send me her profile, let me check her out. With all your travelling, it's good to have someone in town running things."

"Exactly. You'll love her. She's taking it up as a retirement gig but is passionate about the work. I'll introduce you both at the event."

"Looking forward to it. Take care. Love you, sis."

"Love you too."

A pang of hunger tightened around Rebecca's stomach after the call ends. Maybe she should walk back to the road and get those plantains after all.

I should probably also find Muyiwa, she thought, but his car was nowhere in sight when she arrived earlier.

As she approached the gate, it creaked open and Muyiwa's car pulled into the driveway. She hurried back to greet him.

"Bro Muyiwa!" she called as he stepped out of the car looking impeccable for the end of a workday.

Ever since he sent those flowers and chocolates weeks ago, the relationship between the two of them had slightly shifted. She had let her guard down a lot, feeling more comfortable expressing warmth toward him, and Muyiwa? Well, he seemed the same. Steady, reassuring.

He looked at her now with an open, bright-eyed smile. "Rebecca."

"How was your day?" she asked softly.

"Better now that you're here. Are you going somewhere?"

"The lady down the road for some roasted yam and plantain," she tapped her tummy and laughed. He joined in and shook his head.

"Should I join you?"

Her tummy fluttered at the simple request, and she swayed, glancing away.

"No...go rest. Maybe next time."

"I'll let you go now, have a nice evening.". The warmth in his voice left her heart content. She liked how being around him made everything seem right with the world.

"You too."

Weeks after their return to Lagos, Sola had settled comfortably into the routine of his day-to-day life, the city's energy coursing through him like a heartbeat. He dragged himself to the gym earlier, still half-asleep from a late-night call with Tiff that stretched well past midnight. He then woke up groggy but in a fit of laughter from a dream that had felt more like reality. His dreams lately were filled with images of Tiff, a relief from the usual tumultuous nightmare. They were looking over memes and laughing together, and when he woke up, he looked at his phone to find his notifications blinking from over ten more memes from Tiff. When she'd said she was chronically online, she'd meant it, yet he found himself looking forward to her messages. It was becoming a language between them. So he sent a few back to her.

Now, post-workout, Sola was savouring a few forkfuls of the jollof rice and goat meat he prepared the day before—edible but not quite at his mother's delicious standard.

A smile crept across his face as he typed out a birthday message to Tiff, even though he already shared well-wishes during their late-night call. Tiff was like a breath of fresh air, and he tried to shake off the nagging thought that he'd been less than honest with the stories of his past. Maybe with time, he would share more. For now, Sola hungrily soaked in her childlike wonder while plotting a little surprise for her during his next trip to Abuja. He knew he'd have to pull out all the stops to sweep her off her feet, but he's determined to give it his best shot.

After sending the message, he switched to Instagram, scrolling through his feed leisurely until a post from Rebecca caught his eye. She said she was collaborating with an organisation running a social media challenge for women in the corporate sector. The winners will receive professional headshots, makeup, and a curated selection of outfits—an open call for vendors and sponsors.

His fingers moved across the screen as he composed a message.

Hello, pretty lady, I never got that call back from you, he typed before quickly deleting it. He rephrased his words, feeling the need to be more professional in case her page was being handled by a third party.

Hi Rebecca, It's lovely to see that everything is going well with you. I came across your post and would love to offer my photography services for your giveaway. I can also arrange to use a friend's studio.

I look forward to hearing back from you.

After reading his message one final time, he hit send. Almost immediately, his phone chimed with Rebecca's response.

Hey, Sola! How's your eye? ;-) I thought about reaching out, but life got in the way. I'm so glad you did! I'd love to take you up on your offer. That's really gracious of you. I'll add you to our operations group to share updates as we prepare.

My eye, lol. I guess you'll find out when we see, he replied, rounding up their casual banter. With that message sent, he rang Suleiman to confirm the studio arrangement.

Feeling like he's done a good deed for the day, Sola headed to the sink to wash his empty dish, then settled at his workstation, focusing on the interface edit his team has been fine-tuning. He makes a mental note to check in with the commercial team in an hour about the growing interest from other retailers following the Tabano chain's deal—the news spread quickly, largely thanks to the press release backed by Tiff.

His thoughts return to her and linger—brilliant, witty, feisty, Tiff with a smile that lights up even the darkest days. He checked his phone and his eyes clouded with disappointment. She hasn't replied yet. Did the gifts not arrive, or was she just busy? Should he call to check in, or would that seem too eager? He scratched his head, feeling like a 'finished man.'

He decided to message the vendor for confirmation about the package delivery. When he received a green light, he called Tiff and she picked up on the first ring.

"Hey, how are you doing?"

"Just the voice I've been waiting to hear all day," she replied sultrily, making his heart drum in his chest.

"Well, you didn't have to wait. I was worried you didn't get my package or were upset with me."

"It didn't seem fun to call you right away," she teased. Besides, I may have assumed it was one of my many admirers who sent the gift. There was no tag."

"Uh, my bad...or the vendor's bad in this case. I wasn't trying to be mysterious and very much wanted you to know that I'm your biggest fan."

"I like the sound of that. Go on..."

"Well, happy birthday." He broke into his rendition of the *Happy Birthday* song, and her giggle echoed through the phone."

"You should have added this to the playlist you curated. The card with the barcode was brilliant. Imagine my surprise when I scanned it and it led to a personal playlist. It's so beautiful. Been listening to the songs on repeat since."

He pumped his fists in the air but only says hmm into the phone.

"But you're sneaky. I didn't know when you took the candid picture of me that you used as the playlist cover thumbnail."

"But you love it?"

"So, so much. No one's ever done that for me before. It's sweet," she crooned.

"My pleasure."

Silence stretched between them for some time before Tiff broke it.

"I need to catch up with some meetings, but thanks again for the call and the gifts. Talk later?" she asked, a hint of playfulness in her tone.

"Sure."

As the call ended with a beep, he leaned back on the chair, running his fingers through his hair, weighing his feelings. He wants to ask Tiffany out properly during his upcoming trip, but Derin's echoing voice gnaws at him. What if he messes up again, just like he had in the past?

Self-sabotage.

He leaned his elbows on the table and buried his face in his hands, feeling the sting of his friend's words.

Deep down, he knows the cycle he's trapped in. He's running, not toward something, but away from the emptiness and regret that haunts him daily—the shame of failing his father, the unshakeable sense of unworthiness that creeps over him whenever happiness touches him, and the crippling fear of ruining someone else's life. A fear that drove him not just from Poland, but which broke Sammie's heart. He didn't fight for her, and now she's gone, happily married, while he's still chasing meaning in a life that feels hollow. What looks like winging it on the outside is just a façade for a deeper question—how can he claim happiness when he ruined others' lives? How can he ever explain the crushing weight of feeling undeserving, knowing he contributed to ending a life?

But then, there's Tiff, who has sparked a new light in him, a desire to truly live. He wants to stop running from these shadows and embrace life on his own terms. If only he has a crystal ball to predict whether he will flee again if things get too good with her.

With a resolute sigh, Sola sat up.

He doesn't need a soothsayer. Tiffany likes him, and he likes her back. Yet, anxiety fluttered in his stomach, like a boy nervously stepping into a new school. He opened the chat with Tiffany and started to type:

Hey Tiff,

I've been thinking about you... like, a lot. I keep flipping through memories of our time together like they're little snapshots I can't stop revisiting, and every time I do, I end up smiling. Even just hearing your voice can turn an ordinary day into something special. And those cute, excited squeals of yours? They pull me right in and leave me smiling long after we've said goodbye.

There's just something about the way you talk that makes even our simplest conversations stick with me. Maybe it's your laugh, your eyes, or that uncanny way you always seem to know exactly what I didn't even realize I needed to hear.

I never feel like I quite have the right words to describe you. You're smart, bold, and unapologetically yourself—so genuine that people are naturally drawn to you. Your faith humbles me and challenges me in the best ways.

Anyone who knows you is lucky, and I keep finding myself wanting to know more of you, up close.

You've captivated me completely and lit a fire in me that won't burn out.

Sola stopped shy of baring his heart completely, his fingers hovering over the phone. He deleted the last line and resumed typing:

"I hope you know how much I appreciate you. Happy Birthday once again."

He clicked send, and a few minutes later, Tiff's name lit up his screen.

"I got your message, but it felt incomplete. Is there something you want to ask me?"

"So... I'm coming to Abuja soon. I wanted to know what your schedule is like so I can pick a date that works for you. We can go out if you're up to it," he spewed the words in a rush, not giving himself time to back out."

"By 'go out,' you mean ...?"

"I mean a proper date. I'd like to treat you."

A brief silence lingered, and he held his breath.

"Interesting. Let me think about it."

"Please?"

"Just kidding! I'll let you know, okay?"

"Sure." He said with a deep sigh.

"Is everything okay?" she gently probed.

"Yeah," his voice shook slightly with nerves. "Just wishing I could be there today in person, but I promise to make it up to you and more."

"I'll hold you to it."

He could hear another voice interrupting in the background.

"Sorry, Sola," she drawled, "duty calls."

"Of course, you're a busy woman. I'll let you get back to your day. Have fun."

"Don't miss me too much," she teased.

"That's not possible, my dear."

"Alright, talk later. Bye..."

"Bye," he echoed, a smile breaking on his face.

As the call disconnected, a flicker of hope lit up his heart, and he lets it.

Maybe, just maybe, this will end well.

fourteen

CROSSINGS

Rebecca moved from the changing room to the photo area amid the flurry of activity, her eyes scanning guests' well-being. The studio that Sola secured was nothing short of a dream—spacious, elegant, and perfect for the shoot. It consisted of multiple sections—a podcast studio, live recording studio, photography and cinematography studio, and content spaces. Clearly, he had connections; the fact that they got this exquisite venue for free spoke volumes about his status. The best part is that his friend, Suleiman, had offered her a complimentary session in one of the content spaces and the services of their professional team. She was already dreaming up the script to execute. The makeup rooms in the photography studio were buzzing with women, mirrors reflecting dazzling smiles as they watched their transformation. Multiple changing stalls lined the walls, providing privacy for them to slip into their attire. Despite the excitement, time was of the essence, and the entire event had to wrap up in three short hours.

Hauwa's last-minute plea for assistance had Rebecca taking over as lead coordinator for the day, no thanks to Sandra's unexpected medical emergency—something about symptoms that flared out of nowhere, landing her in emergency and later, compulsory bed rest. Rebecca was trying her best to stay ahead of the moving parts, combining giving directions with capturing content for social media. They'd also increased the winner's pick of their challenge from ten to twenty, which meant more people to cater to.

Thankfully, Sandra's teenage daughter was with the other volunteers to ensure the day ran smoothly. Nineteen-year-old Tiwa was radiant, outgoing, and charming, showering compliments like confetti while keeping a good grip on the schedule.

"Looking in control there, Rebecca!" Tiwa flashed a wide, infectious grin as she approached. "The first set of ladies will be out shortly. The makeup artists are putting their final touches, so the photographers have a few more minutes."

"I hope the clothes fit," Rebeca replied. They'd taken care to get the women's measurements and chose a stunning mix of dresses, blouses, trousers, and jackets—all varied in size, the costs covered by their sponsors.

"They're perfect. You should see the ladies in them—like little girls at a costume party!"

"Superb! I'm happy you're here. You're the perfect hype woman," Rebecca said, feeling genuinely grateful.

"I try! Trust me, I'm enjoying myself as much as they are. I'm home on break from Uni, and my mum usually thinks she's dragging me along to her events. But truth be told, I love it. Just don't tell her." Tiwa laughed with a mischievous twinkle in her eye.

"Ahhh, I got you." Rebecca nodded, chuckling at the shared secret.

They wandered toward the women, peeking into the room, thrilled that everything is unfolding beautifully.

From the corner of her eye, Rebecca noticed Sola taking a photo of her and Tiwa just before striding toward them. He's in jeans and a fitted black t-shirt, showcasing his lean frame and subtle muscles. His locs were handsomely styled in an updo, accentuated by a sleek gold chain hanging casually around his neck. He exuded an air of effortless confidence, undeniably more than just another face in the crowd. Tiwa walked away as he reached them.

"Everything's looking good here. Thanks for the opportunity to participate," he says, with a smooth voice and a smile tugging the sides of his lips.

"I should be thanking you for arranging such a magnificent studio. You're a big boy," Rebecca said.

Sola winked. "We're ready for our models now, so once they are set, I'd love for you to send them out in threes. We've set up the space for three photographers, including myself."

"Okay. Give us about five more minutes."

"I hope you'll also send yourself my way," he added, a teasing lilt in his voice.

She pointed to herself. "Me? Don't think so. Not today."

"Not acceptable. You have plenty of time to get your makeup done and change outfits. I'll wait for you," he insisted.

"That's kind of you." She giggled shyly. "I'll see what I can do."

Tiwa passed by, and Sola pursed his lips, pulling up his camera to show Rebecca his earlier shot.

"Is she your sister?"

Rebecca chuckled, amused at how often she has fielded that question today.

"You're the third person to ask!" she exclaims. But looking at the photo Sola pulled up, she understands why. "We do look alike. But no, she's actually Sandra's daughter—our coordinator who couldn't make it. We just met today."

"Wow, the resemblance is uncanny. You two should do a DNA test! You could be related."

"Anything is possible in this life, but I know everyone from my mother's family, or at least something about them. My father's side on the other hand is a blank slate."

"He doesn't talk about them?" Sola asked, scrolling distractedly through pictures.

"Well, no. I mean, he can't. He died when I was younger, in a freak car accident. A drunk driver." Rebecca's voice dropped a notch, and Sola's hands stop moving for a few seconds.

"I'm so sorry for your loss," he choked out finally, and Rebecca mouthed her thanks.

"I'll send the ladies over shortly."

Sola nodded and walked away hurriedly. It was then she noticed, for the first time, that he had a slight limp in his stride.

I wonder if he's okay, she thought, then let it linger. Aside from their banter, Sola was difficult to read, and his interest in her was hard to understand. Their encounters felt like miracles, but she wondered if he had another motive.

"He's cute," Tiwa's voice jolted her from her thoughts.

"He's not bad," she shrugged.

As Tiwa gently ushered the first set of women out, Rebecca jumped in to join her.

"I hope your mum is feeling better," Rebecca asked.

"Yeah, I called my dad a few minutes ago, and she's settled. She'll be okay," Tiwa said with a slight tremor in her voice. "She's dealt with this condition for years, but these flare-ups can be so unpredictable."

"I'm so sorry to hear that. Whatever this is...its curable, right?" Rebecca asked.

Tiwa nodded and begun to share about the history of the many doctor visits, both at home and abroad, in search of solutions. Sandra needed surgery, and complicating matters was their search for a rare donation that none of their relatives could provide.

Rebecca felt Tiwa's sadness palpably. She resolved to call Hauwa later to ask how they can help Sandra.

When the session wrapped up and after her own photoshoot, Rebecca thanked Sola effusively.

"I had such a wonderful time today!"

"My pleasure. It's not often I get to explore my creative side. But thanks to you and Suleiman, I finally did." Sola carefully slung his duffel bag of equipment over his shoulder. "I need to head out now. My friend is waiting for me outside."

"Of course. You were incredibly helpful," Rebecca acknowledged, noting some ladies giggling as they gawped at him nearby. "It seems the ladies enjoyed your company. That didn't hurt, did it?"

Sola smirked, tilting his head. "Hmm ... just them?"

"Yeah, just them," she teased back. "Oh, before you leave, won't you tell your friend to come in for some refreshments?"

"Nah, it's fine. I'll just grab some on my way out."

Rebecca leaned in. "Or is it your lady out there, and you don't want to show her off? I'd like to meet her."

"Okay, you got me there," Sola replied coyly.

Rebecca packed some snacks into a paper bag and headed outside with Sola. He leaned in to drop off his bag in the vehicle's trunk, and then his friend stepped out.

"Oh, you're a guy," Rebecca exclaimed.

The man's head popped back in confusion.

"I sure like to think I look like one."

"I'm so sorry. That came out wrong. Sola led me to believe his friend was a woman."

"No, no, no. You led yourself to believe that."

Rebecca swiped at Sola playfully.

"This is Derin, my friend and business partner, the genius behind our business," Sola introduced him and Rebecca stretched out her hand, which Derin took.

"It's a pleasure to meet you. I'm Rebecca."

"The pleasure is all mine," Derin replied.

"And thanks again, Sola, for today, and for also making me get my picture taken."

"Absolutely. I'll share the links with you so you can make an initial selection before we do the final edits."

"Sounds good. I have to get back now," Rebecca replied, waving as they pulled away and drive off.

As Rebecca walk back into the studio, she felt a twinge of longing.

It had been all work and no play for days, so an outing with Muyiwa to let her hair down wasn't such a bad idea. She'll reach out to him later and hope he's available for the weekend. A spark of excitement flickered at the thought as she joined the others to clean up.

Out in the Sunday sun, hand in hand with Muyiwa, Rebecca felt giddy about heading to the movies together. She'd devoted the afternoon to perfecting her makeup and styling her hair. It felt worth it when Muyiwa's eyes widened in admiration, and he complimented her. Now, she relished the glances from strangers as they entered the mall's long lobby toward the cinema. His hand wrapped around hers, firm and comforting.

They scanned the movie options and decided on a romantic thriller that had just started.

Finding seats near the back of the dark theatre, their arms grazed as they settled in. Neither of them moved away.

Her phone buzzed in her pocket. It's Hauwa calling. Excusing herself, Rebecca stepped into the corridor.

"Hauwa, I'm on a date," she whispered feverishly.

"That's wonderful. Sorry to bother you. I'll be quick," Hauwa replied, her tone becoming serious. "I spoke with Sandra about her condition, and it's quite bad. She's on the waiting list for a donor, but it doesn't seem promising, so all she can do is wait and manage her health. I'm coming into town next week to see her and her family. Would you like to come with me?"

"Of course, I'm free any evening next week."

"Thanks, darling. Enjoy your date and try to relax, okay? Glad you're out in the first place."

Rebecca entered the cinema and settled back beside Muyiwa, who was already eating popcorn. She uttered a silent prayer for Sandra and hoped their visit will comfort her.

Afterwards, they strolled leisurely through the mall, talking about the just-concluded movie.

"Do you mind if we check out some home decor stores?" Muyiwa asked. "My sister just moved into a new apartment, and she's made it explicitly clear that I owe her a housewarming gift."

"I don't mind, let's go," Rebecca quipped.

A cheerful attendant greeted them as they walked into a chic store. Muyiwa politely dismissed her, wanting to explore on their own.

"Is the place fully furnished? Are we looking for ornaments?" Rebecca asked, her eyes roaming over the items.

"Yeah, something like that. You know, wall art or a lamp," he muses.

Rebecca spotted a lovely, off-white ceramic table lamp and picked it up. "This looks pretty."

He took it from her, admiring it closely, "It's nice, but let's see what else is there."

"Sure," she chirped. "What about a potted plant?"

Muyiwa laughed. "A plant for Sope? Her house already looks like the Garden of Eden. Once in a while, I gift myself from her collection. She even has an Instagram page dedicated to vlogs and posts about plant care."

"That's cool. I didn't know the plant love is a shared family trait."

"Actually, it's just us two. My two elder siblings can't be bothered. Sope and I are closest in age and naturally have a closer relationship, so when she started showing interest in gardening, my parents made me join her, so I kind of picked it up as well."

They moved toward another section.

"Sope is the baby of the house that we all take care of, but I admit she does more of the caring and looking out for the rest of us. In some ways, you remind me of her."

"In that I take care of you?"

"Not like that," he laughed. "I mean, you have a nurturing way about you. It's easy to be genuinely myself with you and to be honest about things I won't admit to myself or anyone else. It's comforting. You look out for people without being asked, like when you sent me links to EdTech job listings after our conversation. You go all out with your volunteer programs to help others, all while juggling business and work. I know you must hear this a lot, but I think you have a beautiful heart."

Rebecca let out a shy chuckle as he continued.

"And that's how I know Sope would love you."

And you? Would you love me? Rebecca thought. Muyiwa locked his wide eyes with hers, as if he heard the words in her heart. He opened his mouth to speak, but then turned to a vase instead, picking it up.

"This looks nice," he said.

"It's ugly." She gently took it from him and set it down. "I'm curious," Rebecca ventured. "Your parents are hardly ever around, and you are the only one living at the house. Why's that?"

"Ah, well, the first two siblings are abroad with their families. Sope lived with our parents until she moved to the north for her NYSC three years ago. When she returned to Lagos, she wanted her own space, so she got a flat. My dad had the health scare, so I moved back to help out."

"I see," she said, her mind drifting back to that time.

"Yeah," he continued. "Thankfully, my dad bounced back, but my parents decided life's too short to stay cooped up in Lagos, so they've been exploring the world a bit. They started in our hometown because they thought the air was better there, and then they went on a few vacations. They even went to help with our brother's baby."

"Both of them went for omugwo?" she asked, finding it hard to imagine.

"Yeah." He laughed again. "Those two are inseparable. So, I'm the one managing the house while they gallivant around. They visit occasionally but never for more than a month. But it works for me, no complaints."

"Of course. I wouldn't complain either."

As they reached the end of the store, they found nothing else that captivated them. Eventually, Muyiwa bought the lamp and left a tip for the attentive attendant.

After a pleasant drive home, except for the occasional wild driver cutting them off and incessantly honking, they stepped out. Muyiwa grabbed the lamp from the back seat, and Rebecca saw his brows furrow in disappointment.

"You don't seem entirely satisfied with that lamp," Rebecca said. "I can curate a personalised gift basket for Sope if you want."

His face brightened. "Would you? That'll be great! Thank you so much!"

"Don't mention it. I'll send you my ideas on WhatsApp, and we can finalise them together."

He nodded and smiled. Cradling the lamp against his chest, he reached for Rebecca's hand with the other, intertwining their fingers.

"Thanks for a wonderful day. I had fun. Can we do this again? We can go to a game arcade or do a game night."

Her laughter rings in the cool evening air, but it's not enough to dispel the rush of dizziness brought on by his intense gaze.

"You sound like you're curating activities for an eleven-year-old."

"I apologise, but that only means you'll be in for a good time. I'll even get you ice cream."

"Tempting," she mused, a smile teasing the corners of her lips.

"But tell me if you prefer something else, maybe pottery or a classy activity where you sip wine and pretend to know what you're doing?"

"Bro Muyiwa..." She shook her head, feigning exasperation. He shook his head as if scolding her.

"Alright, fine, Muyiwa it is then. I surprisingly had a great day with you," she admitted with fondness.

"Surprisingly?" he asks, crossing his arms against his chest in feigned hurt.

"Okay, okay. But yes, I'd love to do this again, and the arcade sounds like a great idea," she conceded.

"Awesome. Next weekend?"

She scratched her forehead. "I'm working next weekend. Another time?"

"I'll pencil in a tentative date."

Muyiwa gently released her hand, leaning in closer. He whispered with a soft, feather-light kiss on her cheek, his voice husky.

"Goodnight."

She nodded, her heart fluttering a bit.

"Yeah, goodnight.'

She reluctantly walked away, suddenly feeling the chill of the night and his stare on her back as she hurried into the comfort of her house.

fifteen

LAYERS

Sola quietly hummed a tune, the rhythm carrying his good mood. His weekend in Abuja had ended better than he could have imagined—he was now Tiffany's boyfriend, his first real relationship in years.

He had shown up with his stomach in knots, worried he'd forgotten how to charm a woman. Everything needed to go right. He liked her too much for any part of his well-curated tour to falter. He'd even practiced his smile in the rearview mirror on the drive over to her place. *Could she say no if I smiled wrong?* he'd thought, half laughing at himself.

When he opened the car door and Tiffany slipped in, her dimpled smile nearly undid him. He forced a relaxed grin, gripping the wheel a little tighter than necessary to regain control. But as the evening unfolded—the candlelit dinner at the Mongolian restaurant, her delighted squeal when the leather artisan unveiled the bespoke bag embossed with her name, their easy teasing on the morning hike before church the next day—his nerves melted away. And when he finally offered her the flowers and gold bracelet, asking her to be his girlfriend, her exuberant *yes* was a worthy reward. It couldn't have gone better.

Now, he tapped away at this laptop, soaking in every minute of happiness and heartily greeting anyone who walked past. A message from Tiffany brought a grin to his face.

At work, thinking about you. What are you up to?

Nothing quite as interesting as you, he wrote back. *Catching up on my checklist for the day. Working onsite.*

After a few exchanges, Sola headed the bathroom, and bumped into Ada, walking toward him. She apologised and beat a hasty retreat, but Sola made up his mind to chat with her later.

At his desk, he bumped into Ada again, spilling her coffee onto his shirt.

Wide-eyed with shock, she stumbled over a flustered apology.

"I'm so sorry, Mr Sola. I didn't see you. I'm so clumsy and wasn't looking."

"Hey, no need for that," he replied reassuringly.

"Let me get you some tissue," she insisted, already making a beeline toward the kitchenette before he can protest. He followed her and met her at the door with a handful of tissues, which she shoved at his chest awkwardly.

"Why don't we take five minutes to breathe and chat unless you have something urgent to attend to?" He suggested, leading her to sit down.

"No, I don't," she said, shaking her head and taking a chair.

As they talked, Sola coaxed her out of her shell, inquiring about her time at the company and what she enjoys most. Soon, she's relaxed, laughing, and talking spiritedly. He cut the conversation short when a reminder beeped on his phone, notifying him about a client meeting.

"I'll let you get back to work now, but I had a great time chatting with you, so promise me you won't run away next time you see me?" He teased standing up.

"Agreed," Ada replied with a shy smile. Still, Sola caught her biting her lower lip as if she was trying to stop herself from saying something else.

"Is there something else on your mind? I still have a few minutes," he offered.

"Well, actually ..." she began. "I thought Mr Dee would be here today. I've been trying to reach him..."

"Derin is tied up with external commitments but should be back tomorrow. Have you tried calling him?"

"I did." She let out a frustrated sigh. "But he didn't pick up and hasn't replied to messages or emails.

"That's odd. I'm sure he'll reach out when he can. But is it something I can help with?"

"I'm not sure. I think I messed up some vendor payments. Mr Dee usually handles those, but some were reading as overdue, so I took the initiative to treat them," she explained, biting her lip nervously. "But there were issues."

"Like?" he prompted gently.

"We have multiple vendors listed for some projects, which isn't unusual. But for standard office supplies, there's only supposed to be one vendor. Yet there are duplications for the same payment that mirror the main vendor's transaction, with the same proof of delivery and purchase order. I didn't realise this when I authorised payment, so now we could have overpaid. Unfortunately, the issue applies to multiple expenditure items. I want to put a hold on it, but it'll affect all the due payments."

Sola leaned back.

"Got it. Do the vendors have historical payment records?"

"The main one does, but the others are relatively recent."

"Okay, that's clear. I have to go, but please email me the details of your findings and the examples you mentioned. It could be a simple error in the system, but I'll also check with Derin."

"Okay, thank you," she said, relief washing over her features.

He headed back to his station, adding her concern to his to-do list and dialled into his meeting.

Rebecca paced in her living room, her heart racing in anticipation as she glanced once again at the time on her open laptop. Awake since dawn, she scrubbed every inch of her apartment, trying to channel her nervous energy into something productive. Her footsteps echoed in the silence as she waited for Mr Subomi, her father's old friend, to dial into their scheduled online call at 7 AM.

She'd reluctantly agreed to the video call after weeks of Tari's urging, thinking it might be more personal than a phone call, especially since the man was overseas. But now, she wishes Tari were here with her.

"Hello," a voice rang through her laptop, and she rushed over.

"Good morning, Sir." She greeted him, squinting at the screen. All she can see is the lower part of a man's face with a greying stubbled beard and darkened lips that seem to curl into a smile.

"Hello, my dear. Is this camera working? Can you see me?"

"No, sir. You need to move back a bit or raise the camera. It's working, but your face isn't fully in the frame," she said, her voice high-pitched from the nerves.

"Humph. Sorry ehn, I'm not tech-savvy like you young ones. So many new things, I can't keep up with them." He chuckled, shifting back, and his face finally came into view.

"Perfect, sir!"

"Good, good," he said, peering over his glasses. "I can see you too. Good heavens! You look just like Gabriel! How is Angel doing?"

She swallowed at the mention of her father's name, trying to keep her emotions in check.

"My mum is doing well, and thank you for taking my call, Sir, especially since we've not met before now."

"It's my pleasure," he replied kindly. "There's no way to express how sorry I am that we are only meeting now and under these circumstances. When my son, Tobi, told me he had received a message about your father, I knew I had to speak with you. Your father was a good man."

"But he abandoned us," she blurted out.

"Hmm ..." He paused, leaning back to his chair, the weight of years evident on his face.

"If there's one thing life has taught me, it's that no one is perfect. Even good people make mistakes. No excuses I can offer will change that. Your father's story is a tragic one. I can only share my deepest condolences for your loss, my dear. He loved you and your mother very much."

"Thanks for your kind words, sir," she said, her voice choking with suppressed tears.

"Gabriel was like a brother to me. We grew up together in Ibadan, dreaming about the future," he continued wistfully. "But life took an unexpected turn. After the accident and your mother left, I should have sought you both out, but I gave in to his family's wishes. I regret that deeply because Gabriel would have wished otherwise. Hearing from you is like his message to do the right thing."

"So, you know his family?" Rebecca asked.

"Yes, I do. We lost touch over the years, but it's worth mentioning that his mother has passed away, his father is still in Ibadan, and his sister is in Lagos. I can help you get in contact with them."

"No, sir." She shook her head in firm refusal. "I used to want to reconnect, but now I realise that they would have made it happen if they truly wanted the same. Clearly, they want nothing to do with us, so I'll return the favour." She paused and then said quietly. "But maybe I can find the person responsible for taking his life."

"Hmm...to what end, my dear?"

"I honestly don't know," she admitted. "They took away my chance at knowing my father at all, so I deserve to know who they are."

"I understand where you're coming from. This feels like it happened ages ago and yesterday, but I promise to do anything to help. I wanted to first get to meet you, and I'm glad we were able to talk. I'll ask my son Tobi to help me set up another call later, so that we can talk in much more detail, okay?"

"Okay, sir."

After the call ended, Rebecca was swept into a web of her own nostalgic memories with her mother. A vivid image appeared in her mind.

She remembered walking in on her mother at dawn, sitting on her rocking chair, staring into space, lost in thought. Her teenage self had asked:

"Mummy, what's on your mind?"

Her mother had smiled, pain etched in her eyes, pulling her into her lap. With a gentle hug, she replied, "Love and life, Nkem."

sixteen

ORIGINS

AUGUST 1995

The air was thick with sorrow and celebration as the community gathered for the burial ceremony of one of the town's esteemed elders. These events were seen as celebrations of life, and the colourful displays truly lived up to that title. The music from beating drums and the stomping feet of dancers filled the atmosphere with energy. The crowd responded in kind, mimicking the movements and clapping along. Clad in bright-coloured wrappers and painted faces, the dancers stepped forward, young men and ladies, graceful yet powerful in presence, with a masquerade in elaborate regalia at the centre. The lead male dancer took centre stage, his body gyrating as he leapt into the air and his feet pounded the ground. His beaded headpiece shook with every movement, and the other dancers joined in following his lead.

Among them was Angel, dancing along with her group. A plastered smile hid the concentration behind her movements. Petite and delicate, she twirled and bent with otherworldly strength, ululating with a high-pitched trill. She felt the sweat trickling down her body, but the energy from the onlookers fuelled her passion. Today marked her debut as one of the three leading ladies, and there was no room for imperfection.

With a deep breath, she adjusted her smile and stepped forward to replace the male dancer. She leapt high with a twirl that earned her hearty cheers from the crowd. Her smile grew wider, and she moved her arms with slow, fluid grace like leaves in the breeze. Each sway of her hips was intense and sensual, accentuated by her beautifully woven wrapper. Coral beads jingled at every strike of her feet on the dusty earth. As the music slowed, she rocked her body gently, ending the performance on her knees, offering a heartfelt salute to the heavens as if to release the elder's spirit.

The crowd roared as she exited the stage with her group, dispersing in different directions, with most heading toward the food stall. As always, the caterer would have set aside their plates, but there was still a risk of running out of food if they delayed.

Still in costume, Angel pulled her friend along, laughing as they approached the stall. Girls looked at them in admiration, while women watched their husbands whistle in admiration. They exchanged greetings with the onlookers—at gatherings like this, the performance didn't end on the stage. Often, they received tips from the audience afterwards.

A little boy ran up to them.

"Papa said I should give you," he said, thrusting a crumpled 500 naira note into Angel's hand. She looked up to find the boy's father waving, his eyes roving too lecherously for comfort. She knelt slightly in gratitude, and turned away, quickening their pace.

Arriving at the food stall, they greeted the servers and others nearby before grabbing their food and settling in a corner with empty chairs. Soon after, a young girl approached, calling out to Angel's friend. Her chieftain father wished to introduce her to some important guests.

"Don't worry, I'll be okay. I want to stay and watch the masquerades perform," Angel waved her friend off.

"I have seen an angel!" a booming voice interrupted her solitude moments later.

Looking up from her plate, she saw the man from earlier, whose son had handed her the money. A cold feeling crept across her skin as he claimed the seat beside her, his body spilling over the plastic chair. The area was nearly empty, and the closest onlookers were too engrossed in the performances to notice them.

She forced a smile as she responded, "You flatter me, sir."

The man continued speaking, but she scanned for an escape, wishing fervently for her friend's quick return. Suddenly, his hand was on her thigh. She jumped, a nervous chuckle escaping her lips.

"Are you shy, my dear? Don't be. I just want to talk to you. I couldn't take my eyes off you while you danced," he said, his gaze lowering to her breasts.

"But what of your wife and son, sir?" she managed to ask, her voice trembling.

"Ah ahn, you're not a little girl," he waved dismissively. "You have nothing to worry about or fear. But I certainly want to see you again, ehn."

She gathered her courage and darted toward the main area. Glancing back, she saw him following, but she quickly widened the distance between them.

She spotted a family huddled nearby and approached them, greeting them cordially and hoping to draw them into conversation. Then she slid into a seat beside them and held her breath. Once he finally walked out of sight, she released loudly exhaled. She stood up to greet the family goodbye but accidentally collided with a young-looking man as she turned. Her accessories slipped from her fingers, clattering to the ground.

"Sorry, sir. It was my mistake," she exclaimed, hastily bending down to gather her items.

"No, it was my fault," he replied. "I was too excited about the shows and wasn't watching my steps. I hope you're not hurt."

"No, I'm okay, thank you," She said, looking up to find concern melting into pure excitement.

"You're the dancer," he declared, a spark of joy in his eyes.

"I dance, yes, sir."

"No, I meant that you were one of the lead dancers in that earlier performance, with the heavy bowl and that incredible flip. It was amazing."

A shy giggle escaped her lips.

"Yes, sir. Thank you for your kind words."

"I'm Gabriel," he introduced himself, extending a hand toward her. She shook it with a mix of nerves.

"I'm Angel."

"Are you teasing me because I said my name is Gabriel?" he joked.

"Oh, no, sir. My name is truly Angel."

"Well, that's a fitting name for such a beautiful lady. I hope you're not leaving because of me. I didn't think I'd get a chance to meet you. Would you mind sitting with me for a little while? If you aren't busy, of course."

She glanced around, uncertain, but the lingering memory of the man from earlier influenced her decision.

"I promise I mean no harm. My family is right here," he reassured her, and the sincerity of his smile made her heart flutter. "I wish you would say yes."

Just as she was about to nod, her friend's voice called out from across the canopy.

"Sorry, sir. I have to head home now. Thank you for your kind compliments."

"That's too bad, but I hope we get to meet again."

With a nod, she bent her knees in greeting and jogged toward her friend, leaving the encounter behind her.

It was a rainy morning when Angel arrived at the supermarket, shaking off the wetness from her dripping umbrella before entering. The store's hum came alive as she turned on the lights and machines. The other two salesgirls joined her a few minutes later, their chatter blending with rain pattering against the windows.

Angel set her study materials down at her stall, which included a well-worn JAMB past questions book and a jotter filled with her notes. As the day passed, she stole moments to study between assisting customers.

Around noon, the door chimed, and another customer entered the store. Angel's face lit up when she saw Gabriel.

"Good afternoon, sir," she greeted.

His face brightened immediately. "The dancing Angel," he exclaimed, a delightful grin breaking across his features. He began browsing the store, picking up some items, then circled back to her stall.

She rang up his items and took payment, but he lingered, clearly interested in her.

"I see you're studying for university admissions but working at the same time? Isn't that stressful?" he asked, genuine concern in his voice. "Wouldn't it be better to study full-time?"

Angel sighed. "That's a luxury I can't afford. I left secondary school two years ago, but my parents didn't have the money for the admission fees and exams. So, I've been working and saving money as a salesgirl here and as a dancer. I make more money from the performances, but those are few and far between. Being a salesgirl provides a steady income."

The part she didn't say was that she only had one chance to pass, so every chance she got, she studied. If she didn't make it, her father might make good on his threat to marry her off, get dowry, and send her to become someone's property and responsibility.

Gabriel was studying her intently as she spoke.

"What about you, sir?" Angel then asked. "I guess you're new here since I haven't seen you before yesterday."

"You're right," he replied. "I'm just in town for a few days. The late chief was my dad's longtime friend and business partner, so we came for the burial.

"Okay, but what do you do?" Angel pressed. "Are you in university?"

He laughed.

"I'm an engineer, although I'm just starting out."

"That sounds interesting. I want to study Economics," she replied.

Another customer came forward, pulling Angel back to work. But Gabriel hung around the store for another hour, patiently waiting while she attended to customers. When she was free again, he pulled close to continue their conversation.

"Have you thought about the future and how you'll pay your way through school?" he asked.

"Yes, sir, but I'll cross that bridge when I get there," she replied. "I've applied for a few scholarship programs, but I need my results to move forward."

"That's a step in the right direction," Gabriel said, pausing with a furrowed brow. "You know, my mum runs a university scholarship program you could apply for. You need to meet the minimum cut-off mark to get admission into a federal school. You'll also need to maintain a solid GPA throughout your stay. I'll put in a good word for you."

Angel's mouth dropped open.

"You'd do that for me? But why? What do you want in return?" she asked, cautiously optimistic.

"Nothing at all, I promise," he said earnestly. I believe it's important that everyone gets a good education. Plus, you're working so hard. You deserve to get what you want."

She eyed him warily. "I hope you don't think I'll marry you if you take care of my education. Some other girls do that, but I'm not interested."

"Marriage? God, no." He laughed.

She scrunched her face and pouted her lips. "Now, what does that mean? Why say it like marriage to me is a taboo?"

"Just think about my offer, okay?" he replied, leaning closer.

"Okay." She smiled, taken in by his honest eyes. "I will."

As she headed home at the end of the day, the conversation replayed in her mind. She chose to keep it to herself, knowing that sharing it with her mother would only raise false hopes. Empty promises were too common in her world, and she'd learned to take words with a pinch of salt. After all, men often changed their minds when they don't get what they want.

SEPTEMBER 1997

Two years flew by quickly for Angel. Since her university admission, her bond with Gabriel grew deeper. Each day, she whispered a prayer of gratitude for him, who believed in her potential and helped her secure the precious scholarship. But more than gratitude for him, she enjoyed his visits and looked forward to spending time together. Their friendship flourished through letters, a growing collection of stories of his work and exciting travels, contrasting her musings about classes and late-night studying.

Today felt different. Gabriel was in town, and Angel could barely sit still during the lectures as she impatiently counted down the time in a failed attempt to bridle her excitement. As her lecture wrapped up, she dashed out. He leaned against his car in the parking lot with that warm smile that made everything else fade into the background. They hopped into his car, and he drove them to the cosy guesthouse where he was staying. Inside, they share a leisurely lunch, laughing their hearts out. Sinking into the comfort of his presence, she soaked in every second, relaxing and letting go of her stress for the little time they had.

"I got you something." Gabriel pulled out two identical bracelets engraved with the words "My Angel." He placed one around her wrist and the other on his.

Angel laid her head on his shoulder as they settled, listening to him speak. His deep voice was soothing, like her favourite song.

"You're all I can think about," he confessed, "I thought you were beautiful the first time I saw you, but you've bloomed even brighter since then."

She giggled like a carefree schoolgirl. "You always say the sweetest things. I think your travels have made you delusional."

"That's a strong word. I'm totally sane. With you, everything falls into place. It makes sense for us to be together," he said.

"You shouldn't think that way," Angel said, not taking his words seriously. "You're like a big brother to me."

"Whoa. Don't put me in the dreaded friend or brother zone. That's the worst," he exclaimed.

"How about this, you're a special friend then? That's better, right?"

"Not exactly, but I'll take what I can get for now."

"I didn't think you would give up that easily, special friend Gabriel," she said mischievously.

With a soft chuckle, he lifted her chin, gently stroking her face with his fingers. Their eyes locked in silence, and she felt a rush of heat at his stare, heady from his intensity.

"I would give anything to be by your side every day," he said, his voice a low whisper sending butterflies in her stomach. "When I'm away, it's like a part of me is missing, like life is empty without you."

She swallowed hard, and his tender words pulled her in deeper as she quickly abandoned her earlier defences. The world around them faded away, leaving just the two of them in their intimate bubble. His fingers caressed her skin, sparking a fire within her that she hadn't realised was there. His lips brushed against hers softly, breaking down her inhibitions, and suddenly, the moment was theirs alone, and they lost themselves in it as their bodies melded together in pleasure.

seventeen

CLOSER

Rebecca jogged in place, warming up at the walk's starting point, her mind drifting far away from the other participants bustling around her. Beside her, Tari happily dug into a meat pie, crumbs dusting, flying, and dropping on her mismatched sports attire.

"I can't believe the year is almost over. I thought I'd be planning my wedding by now," Tari sulked.

"Help me understand," Rebecca teased. "You wanted to meet a man, fall in love, get engaged, and start planning a wedding all within one year?"

"Hm, yes. It's just October, though, so I still have faith that the falling in love part can happen. Anyway, spill the tea already! What did Mr Subomi say?" Tari urged, her mouth half-full and eyes shining with curiosity. Rebecca chuckled at her friend's enthusiasm. Earlier, she almost backed out of the walk. But Tari's insistence over the phone brought her here, promising to serve as a distraction to hear her out.

"We talked for over an hour," Rebecca began distractedly. "He shared stories about my dad growing up and how he met my mum. It was bittersweet, you know? He also confirmed my fears about the man I saw on TV. It was his teenage son and a friend who caused the accident. I wish he remembered the son's name, but I only got the father's identity. With that, we can dig deeper online."

Dusting off her shirt, Tari stood straighter, and her expression shifted to one of sympathy.

"I'm so sorry."

"Thanks," Rebecca softly replied. "He also mentioned that my dad has a living sibling here in Lagos. I asked him to hold back until I talked to my mum first. It's only fair before I open a can of worms that might affect her, too."

"Of course, it's understandable," Tari nodded. Just let me know what you find out about the son. I'll do some digging on my end, too.

"Thanks."

"Anything for you, babe. By the way, is your friend still joining us?"

Rebecca glanced at her watch and then scanned the crowd.

"Hauwa should be here by now. It's unlike her to be late. I was happily looking forward to you both getting to meet."

Hauwa was in town not just for the cancer walk but also to visit Sandra. Unfortunately, another emergency hospital visit derailed their plans to meet during the week.

A familiar, infectious laugh rang through the air. Rebecca turned toward it, waving her arms until Hauwa spotted her and jogged over. Introductions were made, and Tari and Hauwa hit it off immediately.

"I thought your bro Muyiwa was also joining?" Hauwa teased.

"Yeah, but he's nowhere to be found," she said flippantly, but still found herself looking around for the sight of him. The three ladies soon picked up a comfortable pace, occasionally stopping to hydrate from the stands lining their route. The excitement and laughter keep them going, and they cheered each other on.

In the midst of it, she saw a father-daughter duo, and the bittersweet memory of her own father's absence tugged at her, mingling with a fresh wave of anger. Lost in thought, she collided with someone at one of the stands.

Looking up, surprise and recognition flash across her face.

"Sola!"

"Rebecca!" he exclaimed, feigning exasperation, though a charming smile lights up his face. "We keep bumping into each other."

"Yeah, I didn't know you attended things like this."

"Come on now, a fitness event and in support of women and their health? Two of my favourite things. Count me in any day."

Rebecca chuckled, then asked, "How's your leg? I noticed you had a slight limp the last time we saw."

A shadow darkened his expression, but he quickly masked it with a smile that didn't quite reach his eyes.

"Uh, that! It's a lingering pain from an old accident years ago. It flares up sometimes when I'm stressed. But I'm good today. See?" he said, breaking into a light jog.

Hauwa interrupted their conversation and greeted him with a glint of mischief as Rebecca introduced them, emphasising his role in supporting their event. Less coy with her admiration, Tari chimed in as their light banter carried them toward the finish line, where a crowd waited.

Spotting Muyiwa in the throng, Rebecca shouted, "Muyiwa!" and waved at him before remembering that she was supposed to be upset. She attempted to mask her delight.

"Someone's excited! Is that your man?" Sola asked. Hauwa and Tari snickered beside her.

"No, he's just a friend."

"Hmm, but he's not looking at you like you're anything but special," Sola quipped. "And now, he's staring daggers at me, so I should probably take my leave."

"That's such an exaggeration," Rebecca rolled her eyes.

"Better safe than sorry." He responded with a wink before turning to Hauwa and Tari. "Bye, ladies. It's been a pleasure. Rebecca," he added, "see you at our next coincidence." And with that, he was gone.

Leaving the other two behind, Rebecca jogged over to Muyiwa, her heart beating in rhythm with her steps.

"What are you doing here?" Rebecca asked flatly.

"Rooting for you!" he replied, handing her a T-shirt emblazoned with the word "Superstar," but Rebecca didn't smile.

"When I didn't see you at the starting line, I thought you'd bailed on me."

"I'm sorry," Muyiwa mumbled, looking remorseful as he continued. "I had everything planned out, but I worked through the night and ended up sleeping right through my alarm. Can you please forgive me?"

"Errr, do you think you'll get off that easy? You have to earn my forgiveness a bit, don't you think?"

Muyiwa squinted at her, shook his head, and cleared his throat dramatically, channelling his inner Shakespearean actor.

"My fair maiden," he began with grand flair, "better is the end of a thing than the beginning. For though I may not have taken off at the start line alongside you, I endeavoured, and here I stand at the finish line to bid you well done and," his voice softens, "I truly am sorry."

Rebecca smirked, crossing her arms playfully.

"Oh, thank God. I wondered how long you'd keep up that act. You're terrible at it! Promise me you won't do that again, and I'll consider forgiving you."

With a hand placed dramatically onto his chest, he pledged. "I promise! And one more thing ..." He pulled out a shiny bag of sweets.

Rebecca caught sight of the bright golden wrapper of candy. "I—I can't take this," she stammered.

"My mistake," he replied "I didn't think about how sweets would be inappropriate for the end of a fitness walk. But don't worry, I'll make it up to you."

"No, it's not that ..." She paused, her throat tightening. "You know what? I'll take it." She grabbed the box eagerly. "Let's not let a beautiful day be ruined by sweets. I'll even share with you."

"How kind," Muyiwa marvelled.

"You know, you could have still joined the walk, even if it's to say you ran. Or in this case, walked after me and caught me ... a beautiful victory story," she teased.

He stuttered, momentarily caught off guard, then chuckled.

"You're right, I'm chasing after your heart, after all," he admitted, locking his gaze with hers.

Just then, Hauwa and Tari, who'd been chatting with other ladies nearby, join them. After some light-hearted conversation, the group decided to head to a cafe for lunch. He took her hand in his as they strolled home side by side.

Sola shook and rubbed his aching left leg. He was in good spirits despite the irritation pricking at him from the pain. The vibe from Rebecca's group was positive, making for an enjoyable walk. Rebecca had a way of pulling out his playful side and making him let down his guard. Yet, he's still puzzled by the magnetic draw he feels toward her. He cast the thought aside, instead reaching for his phone to video call Tiffany, eager to share his day. They were still greeting each other sweetly when he unexpectedly ran into Ada from the office.

"Hey, Ada. How have you been?" he said cheerfully, expecting her usual shy smile in return. Instead, she brushed past him without a word, her lips set in a tight line.

He stared at her in silent confusion. Tiffany, watching from the other end of the call, narrowed her eyes.

"She's like a woman scorned. What did you ever do to that lady? Break her heart?"

"Uhh … Not that I know of. She's an intern at my company, and we usually get along, so I'm surprised at her reaction. But maybe it's because I dropped the ball on an issue she reported. Give me a sec, I'll talk to her quickly and call you back."

"Okay… I also need to talk to you about some of our remittance reports, but do what you need to," Tiffany replied and ended the call.

Sola jogged after Ada.

"Ada, can you chat for a minute?" he called out to her, hoping she'll accept. She shot him an icy look but eventually excused herself from her friend.

"I can see you're upset," he cautiously began. "I want to apologise for not following up on the issue you reported. I had a lot on my plate and assumed Derin took care of it. If not, we can definitely discuss it more tomorrow." He maintained eye contact, hoping his sincerity comes through but her eyes narrowed into slits.

"I can't believe it," she hissed, her voice shaky yet fiercely loud.

"Am I missing something here?"

"Wow," she snapped. "Is this the strategy between you and your partner? He plays the bad cop while you pretend to be the aloof, cool good cop?"

"I don't understand."

"Let me spell it out for you. Mr Dee fired me two weeks ago without notice. I came to you with the issue first, and after I corrected it, he let me go. You're acting clueless like you didn't have a hand in this."

Sola's mind raced. This wasn't just a simple misunderstanding.

"I promise you, I had no idea this happened. I didn't even get to discuss it with Derin. He fired you? But why would he do that?"

"Why else?" Her voice was sharp with frustration. "The issue wasn't a mistake, obviously. I poked my nose where it didn't belong. Did you really not know about the termination and the reason why?"

Sola shook his head. "I had no clue."

Something softened in her gaze. "Well, against my better judgment, I actually believe you. But you'd better start paying more attention to your business. If not, one day, you'll wake up to chaos. I don't have much experience, but even I know that much," she scoffed.

"What does that mean?" he blurted out, but Ada continued to walk away without answering. *What just happened?*

Needing closure, he quickly texted Tiff about an urgent issue he had resolve, promising to call later, and headed home.

Sola burst into his apartment and rushed to his workstation. He flipped on his computer and searched through his inbox for the email from Ada. Diving in, what he found on the portal didn't match her detailed payment references and screenshots. More confusion set in as he spent the next couple of hours in a rabbit hole of overpayments and unaccounted vendors. Approval signatures from Derin and the finance manager, Osha, were on each document, adding to the puzzle.

How did this happen? It had to be a mistake.

The sound of his phone ringing broke his concentration. It's Tiff. He ignored it and continued his scrolling. He focused on the latest batch of payments for a familiar supplier. At first glance, nothing seemed amiss, but something felt off. He ran the numbers and noticed that the invoices were unusually high. He opened the detailed payment report.

There it was.

Two nearly identical invoices from the same vendor, same period, but paid into different accounts.

He wiped his brow. The vendor only issues one invoice per service month. The duplication meant that they had paid twice. He pulled up the payment logs and found that the second invoice had a slightly altered bank account number. Sola pulled out his phone, opened his bank app, navigated to transfer and entered the account number. He waited a second and a name appeared.

Derin.

He leaned back in his chair, staring wordlessly at the screen. This wasn't a mistake. Derin was stealing from their business.

He started to dial Derin's number, but Tiffany's call interrupted again.

"I'm sorry sweetheart, but it's not a good time."

"Are you okay?"

"Yeah, I mean..." Sola considered telling her what was going on but thought better of it. "Just some vendor issues, but I'll sort it out."

"You sure?"

"Yeah. Sorry I didn't call you back earlier. What did you want to talk about?"

Tiffany's sigh carried over the phone, catching Sola's attention. He pressed the phone against his ear as she started.

"We promised not to talk business over the weekends, but I had to break the rule. I was reviewing our sales reports ahead of our joint reviews next week and there are some inconsistencies. One of the branch managers flagged an issue a few weeks ago, so I assigned him and others to cross-check sales and remittance reports. I've been looking through them since last night."

Sola's heart started to race.

"Are you there?" Tiffany asked.

He swallowed the lump in his throat. "Yes."

"Good. I didn't want to ambush you in the meeting, but every location shows a consistent shortfall between actual sales recorded and the remittance your service sent. There's a small but consistent 1.2 percent deduction across all the payments, unaccounted for in our contract or fees. It's bleeding our margins."

Sola ran a hand through his hair and shook his head vigorously. Tiff was quiet, waiting for his response. His mouth opened.

"Uh....," but nothing else followed.

"Do you think there's a glitch on your application?" Tiffany asked.

"Yeah, yeah. Most likely, but thanks for the heads up. I'll check it with the team and have an answer by next week."

"Please do. I have to go now. I'm running late for dinner with a friend, but we'll talk later, okay?"

As the call ended, Sola immediately dialled Derin. The line rang for minutes on end, but Derin didn't respond.

eighteen

DISCOVERY

Hauwa and Rebecca were greeted by the sounds of Afro gospel music in Sandra's home, a familiar tune that Rebecca hummed along to as they entered. Tiwa welcomed them at the door, later bringing them snacks, crisps, and cool juice. Rebecca reflected on her past conversations with Tiwa and Hauwa as they settled in. Sandra was living on borrowed time, but Rebecca chose to hope for the best, clinging to the idea that a miracle was just around the corner.

Before the visit, Rebecca had spent countless hours checking out Sandra's profile, articles, and talks. Personal branding and development goals were top favourites, tackled eloquently. Knowing that Sandra was battling her demons beneath her confident face made her admire the woman more. Showing up to empower others and taking stages worldwide to inspire people takes courage. Her work was meaningful, just like Hauwa's, tirelessly pulling people together from various fields, creating a space to exchange knowledge with young people like herself and thousands of others.

Sandra walked in with a broad smile, but her sunken eyes betrayed her fragility.

"It's so nice to finally meet you. I binge-watched your videos, and they're brilliant." Rebecca gushed.

Sandra's eyes twinkled at the compliment. "I'm glad to hear that. It's lovely to meet the Rebecca that Hauwa keeps raving about. She only has glowing things to say about you. Thank you for standing in for me at the last event; Tiwa testified to how great it turned out."

"Oh, it was nothing. Glad I could help."

"I'd love for you to get more involved with us directly as I coordinate Lagos. Your experience would help us greatly."

Rebecca shifted in her seat. "I'll miss Hauwa's visits, but I'm happy she has you taking over. I'm set on becoming a commercial manager soon, so full-time non-profit work isn't part of my immediate plan. Although," she added, "I do enjoy being involved whenever I can."

"I know you didn't come here to hear a pitch," Sandra said. "But think about it, please. Being here could open doors to executives who are aligned with your goals. You have so much potential."

"Thanks for the vote of confidence," Rebecca replied, feeling flattered.

Hauwa cleared her throat gently and redirected the conversation, "I love that we are talking about careers, but we came to check on your health, Sandra," she said softly, concern etched on her face."

Rebecca nodded in agreement.

"Thank you for coming. The worst of it has passed for now," Sandra said with a tone that carried heartfelt gratitude. "Having you both here has lifted my spirits more than I can express."

"I've been worried about you. Has the doctor given any updates on the donor?" Hauwa asked.

A weak smile crossed Sandra's face.

"Nothing new. For now, I'm managing with medication. My best hope for a match was within my family, but sadly, neither my husband nor Tiwa qualify."

"What about your siblings or parents?"

Sandra's smile faltered. "My mum is late, but my father isn't a match either."

Rebecca felt her heart tighten with compassion. She listened as Hauwa asked more questions, and Sandra explained the donor conditions and process.

"We'll be praying along with you," Hauwa assured her.

"Thank you," Sandra replied. "It's been an overwhelming, long journey with glimpses of hope here and there. Sometimes I feel I don't have the strength to keep holding on." A teardrop falls down her face, and she wiped it away. "But I have faith that all will be well," she continues, her voice steadier now. "There's so much that goes into picking myself up, but God and my family have been my strength through this."

Rebecca struggled to hold back her own tears, wrestling with the unfairness of it all.

Why does such a good person have to endure such pain?

Sandra gestured for help to stand, and Hauwa moved to assist her.

"I just need a minute to pull myself together. I don't want the visit to be all moody, okay? I'll be right back." She headed inside, leaving the three ladies alone.

Sandra's husband walked in then, and he teasingly remarked on Rebecca's uncanny resemblance to Tiwa.

"Let me show you how she looked as a baby," he said, bringing out family albums for them to look at.

"No, Dad!" Tiwa squealed in protest. "No one needs to see all of that."

Ignoring her, he dropped the albums onto the centre table and returned to check on his wife. Laughter filled the room as they flipped through the pages. Tiwa turned to her mother's graduation pictures, and Rebecca's heart stopped. There, standing next to Sandra, was an eerily familiar young man grinning broadly at the camera.

"Who is that?" Rebecca asked with a shudder.

"My mum's twin brother. He's late now," Tiwa replied.

"Twin brother?" Rebecca's body started to tremble. "Did he die in a car accident?"

"Yeah, how did you know? Mum doesn't like to talk about it much. It was quite hard on her."

"That's my dad," Rebecca choked. Hauwa let out a stunned breath, and Tiwa simply gaped at her.

"Are you sure?" Hauwa pressed, extending a hand to Rebecca. Rebecca snapped out of her daze and rummaged through her bag. She pulled out her wallet, found a photograph, and dropped it onto the table. Tiwa picked it up and placed it next to the graduation picture.

"It's the same person." Tiwa gasped.

"That's a picture my mum and dad took," Rebecca stammered.

Sandra and her husband walked back into the room and slowly took in the scene. Rebecca was a mess, rocking back and forth in Hauwa's arms, tears streaming down her face. Tiwa remained rooted to the spot, staring blankly at the table.

"What's going on?" Sandra's husband asked, glancing between them.

Sandra snatched up the photograph, and her face turned ashen.

"How do you have this picture of my brother? Who is this woman? What's going on? Someone say something."

Hauwa quickly explained the situation, and Rebecca added, between tears.

"You can't be my family, the same one that abandoned my mum and me?" Her voice rose, "You treated her like she had a disease all these years! It was you!"

"Take it easy, Rebecca." Hauwa tried to calm her down.

Sandra was frozen in shock, her husband holding her up as she processed the news.

"Mum, is this true?" Tiwa demanded. "Did you know your brother had a child?"

With tears in her eyes, Sandra nodded.

"I just want to leave," Rebecca said, her voice quiet and filled with pain.

"I'm sorry, Rebecca. I c—I can explain. It's been so long. But we searched for you and your mother, but after your mum changed addresses, it was hard. I had no idea that you were within reach."

Rebecca considered her, wanting to believe they cared, but nothing prepared her for the words that followed.

"I knew that you being my brother's child meant that you could be a match to me, and here you are, standing right in front of me." Sandra choked on her tears. "If this is true, you might be the miracle we've been praying for."

Rebecca's eyes narrowed. "You only looked for me because of your health? You must be crazy if you expect me to donate to you." Rebecca shot to her feet and shouted in a fit of rage. "Over my dead body!"

Hauwa swiftly grabbed their bags and guided Rebecca out to the car.

They were quiet for a few minutes as Hauwa allowed Rebecca to gather her thoughts. Suddenly, there was a tap on the driver's side window. It was Sandra's husband, searching for Rebecca. Hauwa rolled down the window to hear him.

"We can't ask anything of you at this time," he said gently, "but Sandra wanted me to give you these." He produced a bundle of letters. "Your parents consolidated their letters to each other when they reunited. The bundle was in your father's possession in his family's house."

Hauwa collected them, and they drove off.

The usual calming music playing in the background belied the tension in Sola's stomach. He and Teju were hunched over multiple screens in one of the private rooms in his office. The staff were going about their business, oblivious to the crisis he was trying to avert.

They've combed through all internal documents and Tabano's spreadsheets, which were sent by Tiffany's representative. Tiffany herself has been hard to reach.

He had narrowly prevented the Tabano review meeting from turning into a trainwreck when it began as a heated discussion. Although the meeting was initially planned to be virtual, he travelled to Abuja, hoping to handle the situation better in person. He explained the issue as an error, then offered a refund and a discount on their standard commission rate for the rest of the year. The team seemed satisfied, but he still received cold stares throughout his branch visits that day.

Tiffany had turned down his dinner invitation, and they hadn't spoken since. Derin didn't attend the meeting and continued to ignore his calls.

Sola returned to Lagos the next day, promising to look for Derin at home, but he had instead called Teju, hoping to lean on his cybersecurity expertise. Initially, Teju hadn't answered Sola's calls, but after Sola sent a message explaining the situation, Teju quickly arranged a morning meeting. Sola arrived early, even skipping his usual gym session, half-expecting Teju not to show. When Teju arrived, Sola profusely thanked him, but Teju ignored the small talk and got straight to business.

The hidden commissions from Tabano matched almost perfectly with the same stretch of weeks as the doubled invoices.

"Have you spoken with Derin about this?" Teju asked.

"No. Not for lack of trying. I hope he's alright, but he's been AWOL. He isn't picking up calls, has missed multiple meetings, and hasn't shown up at the office," Sola responded.

"Don't contact him anymore. When you're being robbed from the inside like this, you never tip your hand. You finish investigating or anything suspicious might disappear." Teju squinted, then scrolled back to an earlier page on the screen. "There—right before the extra commissions started hitting, a new integration and a rushed system update was made to the settlement module. The timing is too specific to be a coincidence."

"I'm aware of the system update. I signed off on it, but we didn't touch the fees table or vendor master after sign-off," Sola insisted.

"And only you and Derin have access to change these?"

"Yeah."

"Okay. I can't touch this because if this goes legal or regulatory, anything I do personally will look biased. You need an external team who handles incident response and systems audits. CISA-level experts."

"Ugh!" Sola placed his face in his palm. "I don't want to turn this into a circus. I just need answers."

"That's exactly why you get professionals. They'll pull every log, version history, user access record—stuff you probably don't even know you're keeping. If someone added those extra commission rules or tampered with vendor banking details, they'll find the fingerprints. I'll connect you with a firm I trust. They know payment platforms inside out and where to start digging."

"Okay"

Teju stood up and faced Sola.

"Don't warn your Derin until the team has had a chance to look."

"I want to give him a chance to explain."

Teju lets out an exasperated sigh. "Your priority is to protect your merchants and your company. If it's an honest mistake, Derin is protected. If it's not, you're going to need that external report when this blows up."

Sola nodded. "Alright. Make the introduction."

"I've sent a message. You should get an email in the next hour."

"Thanks again for helping me with this. I'll walk you out."

"It's no big deal," Teju snorted, packing up his laptop and bag before they both left the room.

Sola showed up at the fashion show hoping to escape his endless thoughts, but his mind refused to cooperate. When Suleiman offered him a free backstage pass with the media crew, he grabbed his camera and blended right in, snapping stunning photos alongside the official team even though he wasn't technically one of them.

"Tiff would love this," he muttered. He adjusted his camera, zooming in on a model strutting down the runway, captured the shot, then checked his phone. Nothing from Tiffany. He'd been sending her pictures all afternoon; especially outfits she might like. The show added an online pre-order with a month's delivery window for certain designer pieces. He had already bought two for her, picturing her in them as soon as they arrived.

He groaned. He'd found someone amazing, fallen for her, and in less than three months, managed to wreck it all at once, hurting both her credibility and her business. He got why she was keeping her distance, even if he wished they could talk it through.

He has tried everything—messages, voice notes, emails—asking how he can fix what he broke. Her replies come in short, three-word bursts that made sense but left him desperate for more. He carried on for another hour. A male model stepped into the spotlight, and Sola lined up his next shot.

Suddenly, his phone buzzed in his pocket. His heart jumped when he sees Tiff's name on the screen.

"Thank God," he breathed, weaving through the crowd of camera operators, stylists, and assistants until he finally found an exit and stepped into the heat.

"No, no." The call had already ended by the time the setting sun hit his face. He tapped his foot, hoping she didn't think he was ignoring her, and wondered if she would answer if he called back.

Before he can decide, the phone rang again. He steadied himself and picked up immediately.

"Tiff, you called," he said, breathless.

"What the hell!" Tiffany was yelling. She'd never raised her voice at him.

"I'm so sorry, Tiff. I didn't mean to embarrass you, especially not in front of your staff," Sola said, hoping his sincerity would calm her down.

"Don't play with me!" Her voice was still loud, but it was now tremulous.

Sola looked at the phone screen for a second, at a loss for words at how angry she sounded.

"Hold on, sweetie." His attempt to pacify her fell flat, but he continued. "I know you're upset, but I'm here. We can talk."

"Don't sweetie me right now!" she shot back. "Just tell me what in God's name I'm looking at and why you're mixed up in it!"

"I don't understand," he said, sitting up to pay better attention.

"Check your WhatsApp," she snapped. "I sent you pictures close to an hour ago, and you just ignored them."

He quickly set the phone on speaker as he navigated to his messages.

"Okay, I'm checking now. I didn't mean to ignore you. I lost track of time and must've missed my phone's vibration. I was checking my phone just before them. I'd have called you immediately if I saw them."

"Whatever Sola. Fraud, Money laundering, wrongful termination! And you're at the centre of it?" Tiff said acidly.

His stomach dropped as he took in the barrage of screenshots of his company's financial records, damning messages, and more.

"How...how did you get this?" he stammered.

"Is that what you're asking? I trusted you! I could have handled all the snide remarks that I received all of last week about running my father's business to the ground because of a man, if it was a mistake. But you lied to my face and said the extra commission on our account was an error, but all of this points to deliberate theft."

"I can explain, please."

"No. That ship has sailed. I stuck out my neck with my dad, and now our company is associated with yours in public! Do you have any idea how much trouble this could cause us? And our relationship, is that all a lie, too? Are you using me to cover all your illegal activities?"

"I had nothing to do with this," he pleaded, growing desperate. "I should have been upfront with you, but I didn't have all the answers. The intern I met that Saturday had raised some issues that I didn't take seriously, but our run-in made me look deeper. I spent the entire weekend digging through payment files, before traveling for our meeting. I'd just picked it up again especially in light of your own discoveries. Yes, I found a lot of inconsistencies, but I'm still investigating. I even hired an external audit team."

"That's downright irresponsible! I came to you with my discoveries, the least you could have offered was truth. Now, everything I sent you is sitting on a journalist's desk. The only reason you aren't reading it on the news is that he is an old friend who gave me a heads-up. He's holding off for forty-eight hours before he releases it."

"Thanks, Tiff," he managed to utter. "You've done me a huge favour, and I'm so sorry for dragging you into this. Let me fix this. I promise not to let it hurt you."

"You already have," she said flatly. "There's a recording of Derin bragging about how you landed our account by using my attraction to you. In his words, I stood no chance against your charms."

"What?" he groaned in disbelief. "You know I'd never say that."

"We've been together only a few months, and you already pulled this stunt. So, it's hard to believe anything coming from you right now," she ended the call.

"Damn it!" Sola stomped his foot against the ground, immediately wincing as sharp pain shot up his leg. He steadied himself and took one deep breath after another to release the tightening in his chest.

He laughed bitterly at the irony of the situation. If it were three to four years ago, he would have shrugged off the situation as merely inconvenient and left it up to chance or taken it as a sign to move on to something else. But not now.

He wants this. He'd found purpose in his work…and with Tiff. His life was beginning to have meaning. There is no way he would let things fall apart again. And most definitely not by Derin's hands.

He dialled Derin, but the call went unanswered. He quickly headed back into the venue, said something to Suleiman about a personal emergency, grabbed his gear and the rest of his things, jumped into his car to start driving, not stopping until he arrived in front of Derin's house.

She hadn't meant to lose control, not like that, and especially not in the presence of the very people who hurt her.

Rebecca sat alone on the floor days after her visit to Sandra's house, the dim light of a lamp casting shadows around her, time seems still. The bundle of letters are her only company, but she's unable to bring herself to open them.

I can't do this alone.

In desperation, she dialled Muyiwa's number, but there's no response. So, she sent him a text:

I need some company, please come.

As she waited, the minutes turn into hours, and she dozed off in exhaustion. When she woke up, the room had grown darker. Her phone blinked with notifications—three missed calls from Hauwa, but there's still no reply from Muyiwa. Still groggy from sleep and no longer in the mood for a conversation, she reached for the bundle of letters, her hands trembling as she began to unwrap them.

The words danced before her tired eyes as she read.

The first few letters overflowed with declarations of love between two starry-eyed lovers and ordinary updates about their lives apart. But then it shifted—becoming darker, heavier. She moved through the letters quickly at first, but one in particular caught her attention. She slowed her pace, absorbing the words, stirring feelings and awakening emotions that were far beyond her physical exhaustion.

DECEMBER 1998

My Dearest Angel,

There's no easy way to begin this letter, but I need you to know how truly sorry I am for the pain I've caused you. When you first shared the news of your pregnancy, I was grateful that your school session ended and the long holiday started during your first trimester. I witnessed firsthand the toll it took on you, especially while you arranged and participated in the introductions between our families and the traditional ceremonies. That's why I thought it was best for you to stay at my family home in Ibadan, where my mother and sister could provide the care and support you needed. I was overjoyed when you agreed.

But then, work called me away sooner than I'd planned. Yet, I took comfort in knowing you were in good hands. However, when I returned, my heart sank to learn that you had gone back to your town due to your declining health. It tears me apart knowing that you felt so compelled to escape, and hearing from my friend Subomi about your tearful insistence only deepened my regret. The idea that my mother could treat you poorly is unfathomable to me, and I'm still at a loss trying to understand her actions. I genuinely believed that she would welcome you, my fiancée, and the mother of our child. It's cruel that instead of offering you warmth and safety, I left you vulnerable.

I completely understand if you want to distance yourself from my family. I regret the sadness my choices and absence have brought you. But I ask you, from the depths of my heart, for your forgiveness. I pray for you and our little one every day, wishing for your health and happiness.

Please extend my gratitude to your family for their kindness in this difficult time, and especially to your father, who has shown me such grace. I am committed to making things right. As we finish the project I'm currently involved with, I plan to return home in the next quarter. After that, I want us to focus on our civil wedding. The thought of calling you my wife and holding you and our baby close fills me with hope and joy.

With all my Love,
Gabriel

Obim,

As I sit here, feeling the cool wind on my skin, my heart is thankful for the incredible blessing that we've been given, our very own miracle. At the same time, I find myself fighting feelings of regret about us and the path we took together. From the first day we met, you believed in my dreams and aspirations, and your love made me feel so special that I allowed myself to become vulnerable, carried away, which clouded my judgment.

I often asked myself if I would choose differently if I could go back in time. But then, I feel our little one kick in my belly, and the rhythm of her heartbeat against mine, and realize that I can't give regret the space meant for love. I've embraced this precious gift of life and accepted the great responsibility and sacrifices it brings.

It would be pointless to hold anger toward you because you have shown me nothing but love. Yet, living in your home forced me to confront some difficult truths. The elders say the road to hell is paved with good intentions, and the decision to have me there led me to face challenges I hadn't anticipated.

Your mother's dismissive words and the animosity I felt from her and your sister made me feel like an outsider, and it cut deep. I also saw how the circumstances surrounding our traditional introduction were poisoned by her heavy disapproval. I endured disdain rooted in the belief that I'm a leech who took advantage of you—her beloved son—and trapped you with an unplanned pregnancy for financial gain, and your father chose to stay silent. Even in my struggles, like when I was too sick to stand, exhausted from vomiting all day long, I still tended to your family. Yet I was treated more like a slave than family.

I tried my best to measure up, but I was seen as less than deserving of your love—lowly village girl.

As I've come to terms with a few of these realities, I'm still grateful for the opportunities I've had, especially through the scholarship your mother provided. I initially wanted to keep these thoughts to myself and stay, but the weight of resentment became unbearable, especially when I knew that love waits for me at home.

Now, I must focus on what's best for me and our child. I've completed my second year of school and have decided to take a break before starting my third year. My mother will help care for our baby while I pursue my education. I wish it didn't mean being apart from our child, but I'll visit often and cherish our holidays together. Completing my university education is my dream, and I won't let anything hold me back.

I also need you to understand that I can't bring our child to your house. With your frequent travels, I will not in good conscience expose her to the same treatment I received, in hopes that they will accept her.

As for our relationship, I don't want to be the cause of conflict in your family. It's evident they love you but are unable to accept me. If I were to marry you, it might force you to choose between your family and me, or I'd have to constantly fight for my place. I can't endure either option. So, for now, at least until I carve my own place in the world, I need to focus on building a life where I'm valued and respected.

This decision hasn't come lightly, and it breaks my heart, but I hope it leads us to a place of peace and a better future. I am thankful to have you as the father of our child, and I look forward to seeing you soon, with the hope that we can discuss better arrangements when you return.

With Enduring Love,
Angel

nineteen

FACE-OFF

The corridor was loud but dimly lit.

Sola knocked multiple times in quick succession, the sharp sounds competing with the football noise filtering out of Derin's apartment. After a long wait, Derin finally opened the door, shirtless, bleary-eyed, and unsteady on his feet.

"What's up, Sola? I wasn't expecting to see you this late," he said gruffly.

"I tried to call you, but you weren't picking up." Sola looked Derin over. "Are you okay?"

"Yeah." Derin's hands were shaking. "Do we have to talk tonight?" he asked irritably, holding the door halfway open and looking back into his apartment. "I'm busy and planning to come to the office tomorrow. We can catch up then."

"I came all this way, and I'm not leaving till we talk." He gestured at the door. "May I come in?"

Shifting his feet, Derin opened the door wider. The living room looked like a tornado swept through it. Empty bottles littered the floor, some toppled over, the pungent smell of stale alcohol hanging in the air like a fog.

"You've been drinking," Sola said, eyeing the mess.

"Stating the obvious." Derin scoffed. "Only a little bit to take the edge off. So, what do you want to talk about?" he said, plopping on the couch.

"Who is it?" a lady's voice called from inside the room.

"None of your business," he bellowed.

"Whatever!" she yelled back.

"Who is that?" Sola asked.

"A woman, of course! You aren't the only one who can score," Derin shot back.

Sola clenched his fists, fighting to keep his composure. "I can't deal with you like this. Can you at least turn down the TV volume?"

With an exaggerated sigh, Derin reached for the remote and clicked it.

"I ran into our former finance intern last weekend," Sola said, ignoring Teju's warning in his head. Derin froze for a split second.

"Who? We have increased staff intake lately, so can you be more specific?"

"Ada. She came to me a few weeks ago about some overdue vendor payments that she wanted to resolve. I figured you'd take care of it."

"And?"

"Turns out your idea of resolution was firing her. Why would you do that?"

Derin let out a dry laugh. "You're never interested in these issues, so why the sudden curiosity? Is she one of your babes?"

"Derin, watch yourself," Sola sternly warned.

"Okay, okay. My bad," Derin says, raising his arms in mock surrender. "Learn to take a little joke."

"I'm listening."

"I didn't know she spoke to you before. If I did, I would have carried you along. I don't know what she told you, but she manipulated records. Her manager brought it to my attention, so we fired her."

"That makes no sense. She was trying to resolve the payment issues."

"Damn it!" Derin shouted. "I don't have to explain myself to you! I do enough running of the business while you stick your head behind a laptop screen. I made a call based on the evidence I saw. So, what else do you want?"

"There's no point talking to you when you're in this state," Sola hissed, seething with anger.

Derin scoffed again, chugging a bottle of beer.

"You'd think that was obvious when I said we should talk tomorrow. But no, Sola always has to get his way."

"What does that even mean?" Sola's voice rose.

"Nothing," Derin snapped, wiping his hand with the back of his hand. "Look, just tell me the truth. Maybe we can fix it together. We've been working our butts off to make the company a success. We've turned a corner with big accounts and investor inflow. If it were a year ago, I'd blame you for acting out from stress, but now? Things are only going to get better. So, what's the problem?"

Derin's expression turned dark. "Yeah, working out for now. But what if it doesn't get better, crashes, or doesn't grow fast enough? What then?"

"We'll figure it out like we always do."

"No," Derin shouted, "I'll tell you what'll happen. You'll fall back on daddy and mummy's money while I'm left stranded, hustling my way through."

Sola recoiled.

"Where is this coming from? After all these years, you've seen me try to live on my own, away from my father's shadow, and you say this."

"Please miss me with the self-righteous, faux moral, underdog crap. You think I don't know that your brother is brokering some form of reconciliation? Good for you, but don't pretend to be riding with me. Even after that ill-fated night, you had a comfortable life, but what happened to me? I hustled. And I'm still hustling. You don't get to judge me."

"You're a mess, and you, of all people, know that I have no intention of going back to my father. And it's rich of you to bring up that night when I've covered for you repeatedly. You asked me to save you, and I did. We promised each other we'd be straight, and I kept that promise. Did all this for you, returned to Nigeria, built with you, but after all these years, you're still not keeping up your end of the bargain. On one hand, you're one of the smartest and most brilliant dudes I know; on the other hand, you're downright reckless. In the beginning, it was fun, but when it turned wrong, I still hoped that I could be there for you and help you out of whatever chaos you wanted to throw your life into. That's what friends do, right? But again and again, I end up on the wrong side. All I've done is sacrifice my life and happiness on the altar of your selfishness."

Derin cackled so wickedly it raised goosebumps on Sola's skin.

"Yeah, man, whatever helps you sleep at night. Don't you see that this says more about you than it does about me—poster boy for confusion. I thought you came back because you wanted meaning and purpose, which you could only find by being your own man and sticking your success up your old man's butt. Isn't that why you refused to go back to him for any form of assistance? For God's sake, we could have blown by now! You didn't sacrifice shit for me.

You, with your own hands, buried your life in a grave made of guilt and nailed shut with an overinflated ego."

"What?" Sola could not form any other coherent words.

Derin continued his tirade, "You heard me. The truth is, you were lost, and it was easy for you to latch on to me as an anchor. Who knows if you're even the cause of my bad luck? If I'd cut ties instead of waiting around for you to stop punishing yourself and get some sense, I would be in a better place. But look at where being your sidekick has gotten me. Scraping by and begging small rats to buy our services. But you, sir, are no martyr."

Sola's head was spinning as Derin's words landed, like a punch to his gut, bringing bile rising up his throat.

He laughed bitterly.

"You know what? You have a point. It's misguided, but you've said your truth. So, I'll do what I should have done all those years ago, face the music for my actions, but instead of dancing alone, you'll be right on the damn stage with me, in front of the lights and camera, moving in step to your own consequences." Sola spat. "And one more thing, it doesn't matter how you spin it, your miserable life isn't anyone's fault but your own."

Without warning, Derin threw his bottle to the floor, and as the glass shattered, he yelled and lunged at Sola, pinning him forcefully against the wall, elbow digging into his neck.

"How dare you?" he said through gritted teeth.

Choking, Sola started to struggle, pushing against Derin with enough force to shift his arm. But Derin rebounded with a punch to his cheek, pinning him again.

"Don't do this." Sola coughed.

"Dee, stop!" the woman's frightened voice screamed as she ran into the living room.

Derin let go, and Sola fell to his knees, clutching his neck and coughing.

"Get back inside!" Derin yelled, kicking a bottle on the floor. She hastily obeyed.

Sola slumped against the wall, staring at his friend. How did they get to this point? A lump formed in Sola's throat, but he held back the words. The last thing he wanted was to provoke Derin further. As he looked on, Derin's shoulders slumped.

"I'm sorry," Derin croaked, his voice thick with regret. "I don't know what came over me. Just that the past few years ... they've been rough."

"Meaning you weren't meeting up to the ambitious expectations you set in your mind. Who were you trying to impress this time?"

"It's not that simple."

Sola stared wordlessly. He came here hoping to hear that his suspicions were unfounded, but it's painfully clear he miscalculated.

"Guess I was wrong to think you'd clear this up," he replied, standing up. "I'll just leave you to cool off."

As he turned to go, Derin's voice held him back.

"You want to know the truth? Yeah, I took some money from the business. But it's our business, so it's not like I'm hurting anyone. I made some bad choices a while back. I bet everything I had and lost it then I borrowed to buy some promising stocks. But it crashed."

"How much was worth doing all of this for?"

Derin shrugged. "130K."

"Naira? That doesn't make any sense."

"No, one hundred and thirty thousand dollars. And it wasn't only my money. I got in over my head with a loan shark, thinking the payout would save me, but it didn't. So, I turned to the company for a lifeline and duplicated payments. I thought it would be like an advance, to get by, just once."

"Just once?" Sola challenged him, straining to keep his voice from rising.

"Okay, okay, more than once. It was easy, too easy, so I continued."

"Yet it wasn't enough for you. You sabotaged the Tabano account," Sola said, and immediately regretted the slip when Derin's eyes narrowed. Still bitter and unable to hold back anymore, he spilled his final thoughts.

"If you don't fix this, you're dead to me."

Without another word, he turned and walked out the door, leaving Derin and his mess behind.

Outside, unable to drive away, Sola sat in his car, tapping the wheel with each desperate dial tone to Teju. He needed to speak to someone, and Teju, despite the bad blood, was the only one he can trust. Teju always shoots straight, and right now, Sola craved that honesty. One hour passes with no response. At the thought of the situation with Derin, rage rises within him, and he slammed his fist against the steering wheel, the horn blaring unexpectedly.

Startled, he jerked upright. He turned the key in the ignition, and the engine roared to life. As he pulled onto the road home, a memory flashed through his mind, one he wished he could erase, of the unfortunate night that had flipped his life upside down.

JUNE 2010

"I don't think we should drive this way," Sola murmured, feeling dizzy. "I could call my mum and explain everything. She might be upset, but..."

Derin burst out laughing, cutting him off.

"Don't be a coward. It's the last night of school. You're supposed to be independent and have fun."

Sola frowned, feeling his stomach lurch. "Fun? This doesn't seem like much fun. Let's call a taxi then I'll sneak back for the car in the morning."

With an exaggerated sigh, Derin snatched the car key from Sola's hand and jumped into the driver's seat.

"Get in," he yelled in defiance. "I'll drive!"

"No, Derin!" Sola protested weakly, but his friend was already revving his engine.

"Come on! It's just a few minutes' drive to your house."

Reluctantly, a lightheaded Sola climbed into the passenger seat.

"Woo hoo!" Derin shouted as he sped out of the parking lot and down the highway.

"Slow down!" Sola yelled, jamming his hands onto the dashboard. "You're going to get us killed!"

"Chill, Sola. The road's clear, it's almost midnight, and no one is out here."

Derin fiddled with the radio till he tuned to a station blasting their favourite song.

"Yeah. That's our jam," he cheered, and Sola joined him, singing loudly and drowning out his anxiety for a while. Then, seemingly, out of nowhere, a red stoplight came into view, and Sola's heart leaped into his mouth.

"Red light! Stop the car!" he shouted, tapping Derin's arm frantically.

But Derin only laughed, his foot pressing harder on the accelerator. "Whoa!"

Another vehicle flew into the intersection. Time slowed as Derin pressed the brakes, but it was too late. The impact was brutal; metal crunched, glass shattered, and his night became a din of screams, blaring horns, and exploding airbags.

Then darkness hit him like a heavy blanket. He was screaming one second, and everything faded to black the next.

When his eyes opened, he was being wheeled down a corridor, the bright lights blinding him temporarily before everything faded again. The next time he woke up, he was in a hospital bed, surrounded by the rhythmic beeping of machines and the shuffle of feet.

A sudden cough escaped his throat, and he picked up his mother's voice amidst the chaos.

"Oh my baby, you're okay, you're awake. Jesu seun," she cried, leaning over him.

"Mum?" He croaked, attempting to sit up, only to be met with sharp pangs of pain.

"No, rora," she gently urged him back down. "Don't sit up, just rest. The worst is over, you're alive." She wiped his forehead with a cloth and pressed a comforting kiss to his cheek.

"Mum, I'm sorry …" he whispered.

Before she could respond, his father stormed into the room, his eyes red with anger, and Derin hovered shakily behind him.

"Efosa," the police are here, and we need to talk to them," his father announced.

"Honey, what's the problem?" his mother asked.

"Dad?" Sola whispered, but his father wouldn't look at him.

"I don't want to upset the boy further, but he and Derin both know there'll be consequences for today. He should focus on recovery, but we have to face the police now," his father insisted, his tone left no room for argument.

"Police?" Sola echoed shakily.

"It wasn't enough that you snuck out with the car while both of you were drunk; you didn't have the common sense not to drive!" his father yelled. "I thought I raised you better than this."

"Honey, take it easy," his mother pleaded.

"Stop coddling him! He should have known better. Your son was drunk driving, and now a man is dead!"

"Egbami o!" His mother stood abruptly, chair scraping against the floor, and her wail echoing in the cold room. "Please tell me it's a lie. Ah, Oluwa mi o."

His mind spun as he looked from his mother to his father as they rushed out of the room.

After they left, Derin walked into his room, clutching a bandaged hand, desperation in his eyes as he grabbed Sola's hand.

"I panicked! I didn't know what to say when they started asking questions, so I said you were driving," he confessed, his entire body shaking like a leaf.

"What?" Sola whispers in stunned disbelief.

"I know I shouldn't have," Derin continued, his voice spilling out in a frantic rush. "I'm so sorry, I didn't have a choice." His eyes darted around the room like he expected someone to burst in any minute.

"I should have listened to you. I almost killed you, and I killed someone," Derin cried, tears streaming down his cheeks. "I'm over eighteen, I'd go to jail. Please, you have to help me. I don't want to go to jail. My family won't survive this. Please cover for me."

Sola could barely process the distraught pleading but nodded weakly as exhaustion swept over him. His eyes fluttered shut once more, and he drifted back into unconsciousness.

OCTOBER 2024

Rebecca sifted through the stack of letters, trying to find the ones that followed the earlier notes from her mum. Instead of heartfelt messages, these letters were practical updates—her mum explaining how her dad's financial help was being spent, shared moments from her childhood, and requests for school supplies. Her dad's responses mapped out travel plans and listed when he would visit them. Over five years, the letters painted a picture of family life as co-parents living apart. She also found letters celebrating milestones: her dad's promotion, her mum's graduation, and her first job. Then there were discussions of love, with her mum enthusiastic about marriage, now that she felt secure. But strangely, the next letter was dated almost four years after the last one, and despite searching, she didn't find any other letters within the gap.

She opened it and it's from her mother. As she read, a gasp escaped her lips. The truth was startling. Her father provided for them financially for years, writing letters and visiting regularly, until he vanished. Her mum went looking for him, only to discover from his sister that he had started a new life with another woman abroad.

The letter dripped with the bitterness of her mother's anger, emotions she bottled up for years before finally putting pen to paper. It was a mix of blame toward him for abandoning his family while attempting to cloak her own deep pain.

Then followed a letter from her father, and Rebecca braced herself for the words.

To err is human, but to forgive is divine, the letter read. *My Angel, forgive me.*

Gabriel went on to lament his decision to walk away without so much as a goodbye, leaving she and her mother behind. He apologised for putting his family's scornful opinions over their love, for failing to fight for them, and for thinking that his responsibility started and ended with financial support.

Then he admitted to feelings of inadequacy when she proposed they proceed with their marriage plans after years of postponement.

Why did I leave when you were ready to marry me? I was a small man, he wrote. The realisation that she achieved her dreams without him—education, career—made him feel as if he was no longer needed. Being wanted hadn't proved enough, so instead of facing these insecurities, he walked away.

My conscience told me I was wrong, but I ignored it, he confessed, admitting that he searched for love in the wrong places. He painted a picture of three empty years only to end up more lost. *I thought I found happiness elsewhere, but it only led to disappointment.* He missed and longed for her.

My heart only knows you as home, he declared. *I want to come back to you if you'll have me.*

Rebecca knew what came after—his return to their lives the following year. But she still had questions. Why did he come back to them, and why did her mum take him back? She resolved to speak with her mother once more, hoping that this time they'll finally have an honest conversation about everything, peeling back the painful layers to reveal the truth.

"Mummy, can you hear me?"

After an eternity of convincing herself that only getting answers and clarity can ease her heavy heart, Rebecca finally called her mother.

"Ehn, Nkem, how are you?" her mother's happy voice sounded from the phone. "I've been trying to reach you and was worried when you stopped responding. What's going on?"

"I'm sorry. I'm fine, things got very busy, that's all."

"Eh-ehn. Okay. Have you finished your inventory? Chimezie showed me one of your videos on his social media. It was so funny to watch, and the clothes were so fine. Well done, my dear. I have not collected the new bale, but it will come next week."

Rebecca smiled weakly. "No, Mummy, I haven't finished selling the clothes."

There was a heavy pause on the line.

"What's wrong?"

Tears threatened to spill as she choked out, "Nnem ..."

"My sugar, talk to me. Is work stressing you? Please take it a little at a time, but don't cry, my dear."

"No, Mummy, it's not work." She wiped her eyes. "I found Papa's sister. And the man from the night Papa died."

She can feel her mother's shock through the phone. ""Nkem ...Do you remember him? The man and Papa's sister?"

"Please tell me. All these years, I've been desperate for the truth but convinced myself that it was just misplaced childhood imagination, but it was real. I need to know what happened after he died. We had visitors the next day, and then they disappeared. Why?"

Her mother's sigh echoed back, and she started to recount the story of how they fell for each other and the resulting unexpected pregnancy.

"Obim was overjoyed when I found out I was pregnant and urged me to tell my parents. True to his character, my father insisted on an immediate marriage to save face in the community. I refused the wedding but agreed to a betrothal, vowing to finish school first. So, Gabriel brought his father and some of his friends for a small ceremony. His mother and sister were displeased and didn't show up. I took a semester off after you were born, but my mother, bless her heart, cared for you while I returned to finish my studies. I lost the scholarship, but he supported us."

Each word her mother uttered painted a heart-breaking picture.

"His visits became less frequent as his career took off. I worked hard, finished school, and landed a government job. When talk of our marriage came up again, he disappeared. I tried to reach out to his family, but none responded. He returned on your tenth birthday, apologetic and wanting to make things right, to finally marry me. I didn't agree immediately, but he visited me every month for about six months, and we would talk at length about life and all that had happened to us. I kept him away because I wanted to be sure he had a place in our lives. I didn't want to confuse or hurt you. But as we spent all that time together, I realised that I still loved him and wanted you to grow up with your father. So, I agreed to his proposal, and we headed to Ibadan."

"I remember."

"Yes, but tragedy struck. On our first night, he went out with his friend, Subomi, while I stayed behind with you because you were ill. Obim never came back; only his friend did, and the horrific news was that there'd been an accident involving drunk teenagers. I never got to say goodbye."

Angel paused.

"Why is life so unfair?" Rebecca said softly.

"I thought the same thing," Angel continued, her voice shaky. I'd waited ten years, clinging to hope, only to have my joy taken away. The following day, I had unexpected visitors: first, the Adesesans', parents of the boy responsible. They begged and offered me money to walk away from the case. I turned them down, but I could see their agony. It didn't make sense, but I felt pity for them."

Her mother's pain mirrored Rebecca's own, slicing through her heart like a knife. "My late husband's sister and mother came after, raging and shouting the house down, accusing me of bringing bad luck to her brother and family. From the start, I was a curse to her brother, a bad omen, a leech who wanted to feed on their prosperity. I'd supposedly wielded village charm to make him unable to stay with any other woman but me, which was why he came looking for me despite his family's protest. She threatened to destroy everything I had if I didn't pack my bags and leave Ibadan for good. Even though the world was crashing down around me, I chose to believe that grief made her act that way. Anyway, I left and turned to my parents for solace. I chose to let go, and move forward, pouring all my love into you, my gift. The journey was tougher than I imagined, but God helped me."

As she listened, Rebecca wished she could go back in time and change the hand fate dealt her mother. How could the world be so cruel to a young woman with a child? But since she can't change the past, she listened, soaking up her mother's pain like a sponge, yet unable to reconcile with the choice to show compassion rather than seek justice.

"I can't believe they were so heartless," she spewed. "They abandoned us, living their lives while you suffered. I wish them only pain and disappointment. Sandra deserves every bit of suffering she's going through."

On the other end of the line, her mother's voice trembled, "My baby, please don't say that. Hearing you like this is tearing me apart. I wanted to shield you from all this. I don't want you to be bitter."

"No, Mummy. It's not your fault," she replied hotly. "They are villains here, those terrible people who turned their backs on you like you were nothing. I've wasted so many years wanting their love, only to find that they'll rather pretend we don't exist. They carried on like saints, while we bore the hurt."

There was a heavy pause on the other end before her mother spoke again, "Nkem, this isn't what I wanted for you. I've faced my share of pain, but you're my light, my pride. With you and your brother, I have everything I need in life. I know it's hard right now, but you can't let anger consume you."

Rebecca recalled Hauwa's text message from earlier.

I can't ask you for anything, but please think about it, and if you can find it in your heart to forgive Sandra and her family, please see this as a chance to help them and to do something kind. This is bigger than the past. They need you.

That's not fair! Don't tell me that, Rebecca texted back with bile in her throat. *I don't owe Sandra anything. Just because Mummy may have found a way to move on doesn't mean I have to, too. I don't see a gun to my head. Just because she's your friend doesn't erase what she's done!*

Hauwa immediately replied with an apology, *I'm sorry, I didn't mean it that way.*

"Nnem," Rebecca said, returning to the present. "I only want to make you proud, to give back everything you've sacrificed, not running to help someone who turned you away, cursed, and abandoned us."

Nothing her mother said shifted her resolve. Every plea only fuelled her fire, morphing her grief into burning hatred.

GOSPEL

Sola's arms were sore from his morning session at the gym—hitting the punching bag hard till his arms gave out. Afterwards, at his parents' house, he felt welcomed by the familiar scent of home. A joyful chorus of women singing and clapping floated from the living room.

"Mummy's women's house fellowship just started, but I'll tell her you're here," Yewande informed him before disappearing into the house. She shortly popped back out.

"She said you should come and join us."

Sola opened his mouth to protest, but Yewande shot him a knowing glance. Resisting was pointless, he wouldn't hear the last of it. Considering he was here to ask for a favour, it was not worth it to be stubborn. He grudgingly made his way to the living room.

To his surprise, the circle of women present was diverse. Teenagers sat side by side with women in their forties and fifties. His mother, glowing with pride, introduced him to the group, and he caught a few giggles in his direction. He nodded respectfully at them and took the nearest chair.

Prayers were said, and a young lady, probably no older than fifteen, started to exhort them. She sat up with poise, her voice strong with conviction as she began to share a message.

"There was a younger son, who asked for his inheritance while his Father was still alive and squandered it all. Left in penury and hopelessness, he returned home, hoping to be one of his Father's servants. But when his father saw him from afar, he ran to embrace him and welcomed him with a great party."

Sola's heart tightened in his chest. He was familiar with the parable of Jesus from the bible.

"God loves us so much that He gave his only Son, there's no condemnation for those who believe," the young lady continued and a quiet voice whispered in his heart:

When will you stop running, Sola?

It felt like cool water seeping into the crevices of his guilt and loneliness.

"Even when we stray, he doesn't forget us but pulls us to Himself, offering mercy and grace." The lady's words were an invitation to return to his heavenly Father, to lay down his burdens and step away from the weight of secrets and regret. Let us pray," she prompted, and everyone joined in.

When the gathering ended, Sola exchanged pleasantries with the women, masking his urgency to speak with his mother. Finally, the last woman left, and he settled with his mother, who pulled him into a firm hug.

"Oluwalonsolami. I've missed you." She pulled back to study him, worry etching her features. "Your visits have been infrequent lately. You've even lost weight. This boy. You should take better care of yourself."

Yewande emerged with a steaming plate of pounded yam, vegetable soup, and a glass of juice. Sola's mouth watered at the sight, and he dove hungrily into the meal.

"Mum, could you please help me call Teju? I need to talk to him," he asked between mouthfuls.

Her eyes narrowed.

"Is this the Lord answering my prayers already? Are you and Teju speaking now?"

"Something like that but I want you to call him and ask him to come here. He's not picking up my calls, and... I need to talk to him."

"Gladly!" she beamed, brushing aside the details. "I'm going to the market with Yewande before the afternoon sun comes out, but I'll call him on the way," she said, bustling away, leaving Sola alone with his thoughts.

After he finished his food and cleared the dishes, he collapsed on the couch, his full stomach lulling him into a peaceful nap.

Sola jolted awake to Teju's booming voice echoing through the living room.

"Mum? I'm here."

Sola groggily sat up to see Teju striding in. Their eyes locked, and a silence charged with unspoken disdain settled.

"Did Mum call you too?" Teju queried.

"No, actually, I was here before she called you. I asked her to," Sola cautiously replied.

Irritation flashed across Teju's face, but his forehead was creased with worry.

"You could've texted if it was about business. Is she okay? She sounded frantic on the phone."

"She's good, left for the market a little while ago. I wanted to talk to you on a more personal note, and I couldn't capture that with a message. She called you because of me. I didn't ask her to add the drama, but...you know Mum."

Teju shot him a scathing look and turned to leave.

"Wait, please. I know you hate me, but I need to talk to you." Sola rose from the chair, pleading. "I need your help and don't know where else to turn."

The hard lines on Teju's face softened, but it was fleeting.

"Nobody hates you," Teju snapped, crossing his arms defensively. "Your view of the world is so myopic. It's all about you. You wouldn't have reached out in the first place if you didn't need something. How hard is it to see that I detest your selfishness?"

Sola clenched his jaw but stayed silent, letting Teju vent. He wasn't going to be sidetracked by an argument.

"Anyway," Teju grumbled, dropping into a chair across from Sola. "I'm here now. What is it?"

"Derin admitted to duplicating the vendor payments," Sola blurted, "and I don't know how to handle it. We fought yesterday; he said some nasty things, and now I'm unsure about my decisions."

"You confronted him, and it turned ugly?" Teju asked, a hard, knowing look in his eyes. "Why am I not surprised?"

Sola's voice was shaky as he laid out the situation, leaving out their childhood secret. "He has always had my back. I never thought I'd have to look over my shoulder. This feels like a knife in my chest."

"Yeah, that's typically what betrayal feels like," Teju said sharply. "But has he really had your back?"

"Can you just spare me the sarcasm today and be the brother I used to know?" Sola's voice cracked, betraying a vulnerability he was ashamed to admit.

"I'm sorry, but it's hard for me to have any compassion when you created this situation for yourself. I've extended the hand of reconciliation to you multiple times over the years, even on behalf of Dad. Still, you always turned your nose up at me. All of a sudden, you expect me to drop all of that history to advise you or pat you on the back."

"I don't know what to expect," Sola hung his head. "But you're the only one I can talk to. I can't just cut Derin off, but I need to do the right thing, and it's hard. He refuses to acknowledge how his actions affect me. He isn't just hurting himself; he's hurting my relationship, my business. Do you know how hard I've worked?"

Teju let out a scornful snigger.

"Mehn, life is funny!"

Sola glared. "I don't see what's funny."

"I could say the same words to you, Sola, and they'll paint a perfect picture of how oblivious you are to the mess you created in our lives."

"What do you mean?"

"This family lost so much because of you, especially Dad."

"That's not what I came here to talk about," Sola said through gritted teeth.

"Too bad. You're here anyway, so we'll talk about it. You're no longer fifteen. Mum has shielded you for years, but I'm done turning the other cheek."

"Shielded me from what exactly?" Sola shot back.

Teju's eyes clouded like he was tapping into buried memories.

"You never asked why Dad moved the family from Ibadan to Lagos or how he kept you out of detention. He sent you abroad instead of letting you face your consequences here."

"I didn't need to ask. Mum told me the victim's family didn't pursue the case. Also, Dad himself disowned me, saying he never wanted to set his sight on me until I righted my wrong. Whatever that meant."

"That's the point. You were away for years, and mum and I had to pick up the pieces of what was left of Dad's sense of pride, honour, and commitment. He changed as a man and a father. Not only did he lose you, but we all lost him," Teju said, his voice heavy with pain. "But if you ask him, he may never admit that he did it all because he loves you, but mum and I know that he never stopped loving you."

Sola felt a wave of guilt hit him. He was bursting to tell the truth about the accident, but hesitated under the weight of all that had been said. Some truths may be better left unsaid. The thought of dragging his family through that turmoil again made him shudder, so he chose silence as Teju told his father's story.

JUNE 2010

It had been a long, harrowing week for Chief Adesesan. What begun as a joyful birthday night, a romantic getaway with his wife, was marred by a phone call carrying horrid news. An accident his son Sola was involved in. Upon reaching the hospital, after the relief of finding Sola alive, they were hit with the grim reality that he'd killed a man in the crash. Their entire lives were upended, and a deep sense of helplessness had held him since then.

In the dimly lit office, his wife, Efosa, walked in, carrying a bowl of boiled plantains and vegetable soup. But he waved her away, his mind rolling in turmoil.

"Honey, you haven't eaten or slept in days. You can't keep this up," she urged.

"I'll be fine," he replied, trying to mask his despair, but heaving under its weight.

She approached behind the table, cradling his face in her hands, and he looked up, truly looking at her for the first time in days. Her face was drawn, dark shadows circling her eyes, reflecting their shared agony. He'd been so consumed by the madness that he'd neglected to consider her suffering as well.

"I'll eat soon," he said, changing his mind. "But let's eat together in the dining room."

"Okay," she replied, but as she turned to leave, he gently grabbed her hand, guiding her to sit with him. He pushed his chair back to take in her full frame, not wanting to speak but knowing she needed the silence to find her voice. It wasn't long before the pent-up emotions burst forth.

"I can't stop thinking about the woman and her poor child. I can't wrap my head around the devastation. She came to Ibadan to start a life, and now... it's all gone," her voice broke, tears spilling down her cheeks. "And it's my son who is responsible. Ha, my heart can't take this."

He held her hands tightly, feeling her trembling beneath his touch. They had visited the widow the morning after the incident, offering apologies that felt woefully inadequate. They'd offered her a substantial amount of money as consolation, a desperate attempt to ease not just her pain but their own fear of public scandal. The widow had barely spoken, turning down their offer, but a few nods of consent to let it all go. He hoped that her promise would hold up.

They weren't the kind of family that usually settled matters this way. But the inspector general of police, whom he considered a friend, had advised them to settle with the man's family to dampen the fallout. He was torn, and it felt all wrong, but he and his wife had agreed that it was the best path to take.

Tears streaked down Efosa's face. "She's just like me, and she's lost everything. She now has to raise her child alone. I feel like we are all responsible for this. If only we had stayed home that night. If only I hadn't ignored that nagging voice telling me something was wrong."

"No, it's not your fault," he fought to keep his voice firm, trying to soothe her. "We did our best as parents. We couldn't have known what would happen. Sola has been a handful with his friends, but he knows right from wrong. We can't change the past, so please don't beat yourself up over this. We'll get through it together."

She nodded, wiping her tears with trembling hands.

They were interrupted by Yewande.

"Sorry, Ma, there's someone here to see Daddy. Should I bring him in or have him stay in the living room?"

"Who is it?" Chief asked.

"Commissioner Ibidun."

A lead weight dropped in his stomach. Efosa sprang from the chair.

"Why is he here?" she demanded an answer, but he could only shake his head in despair. The vultures were already circling.

"We'll find out soon enough. I want to speak with him alone. You don't need to be caught up in this."

"Okay," she replied. "I'll bring him in."

Moments later, she returned with the commissioner.

"Good evening, commissioner. This is a surprise. I wasn't expecting to see you in my house," Chief said.

"I ran into our dear friend, the police inspector, early this morning, and he shared the devastating news with me. I wanted to come and check on you and your family. How are you all holding up?" the commissioner said, the gleam in his eyes exposing a mockery of sympathy.

"We're doing our best," he replied, forcing a tight smile. "Sola is recovering well."

"I'm pleased to hear that," the commissioner said, taking a sip from the drink offered. He swished it around in his mouth before swallowing. "I feel like this is the perfect time to revisit our discussion about the development project."

Chief kept a straight face, trying not to betray his frustration to the gloating man before him. He remembered all too well the conversations they had about the project. The scheme would displace countless families for the profit of a few. He stood firmly against it, with the community's support, but the commissioner was relentless in trying to twist his arm, including offering him a generous cut of the inflated project budget,

"You are a crucial and influential stakeholder, after all. The people listen to you."

The man sitting across from him, clad in his flowing agbada, wasn't here out of concern. He was here to blackmail him.

"I believe there's more at stake now, especially with this situation and the grief of the victim's family. It's in all our best interests to stick together and protect each other, with your reputation and high moral standing. We wouldn't want any sensitive information leaking to the media and community now, would we?"

Chief felt his blood boil. "Are you threatening me?"

"Threatening? I wouldn't dream of it. Only making sure you know that I'm very much invested in making this project happen, and we should be on the same side." His smile widened into something almost predatory. "So, think about everything. You know how to reach me when you make up your mind. I hope you understand?"

"Clearly."

The commissioner rose, smoothing out his agbada and extending his hand. "I'll be on my way now."

Chief kept his seat, his hand clenched in a fist on his lap.

"I won't be able to walk you out."

The commissioner snorted, then left.

"Dad?" Sola's timid voice called.

"Yes?" he bellowed. "What do you want?"

"Sorry, Dad, may I talk to you about the accident?"

"Boy, I do not want to hear a word from you. Do you know what your irresponsibility is costing me?"

Efosa rushed into the room.

"Honey, what's wrong? Sola, are you hurt? I thought you were sleeping."

"I couldn't anymore. I want to talk to Dad," Sola stammered.

Chief seethed. "Get this boy away from my sight this instant. I never want to lay eyes on him again."

"Go back to bed, Sola." Efosa urged and Sola left, shoulders slumped.

"Oko mi, aren't you being too harsh? He's just a boy, and he feels guilty enough as it is. What did the commissioner have to say?" she asked.

He sank lower into his chair, defeated. "Nothing good."

Efosa retreated, leaving him alone with the fear that had snaked its hands around his neck. In the days and months that followed, that fear ruled him, and he in turn ruled the house with an iron fist. Conversations with Sola dwindled, replaced with silent orders and commands that were followed without question until his departure to the university. His wife convinced him it was best to send Sola abroad—a workable compromise to keep the boy out of his sight.

He also signed off on the commissioner's project despite every bone in his body screaming about the injustice of it all. Of course, the government reneged on the compensation they negotiated, and when the loss hit hard, especially for the elderly, who lost their properties and livelihoods overnight, he joined some community leaders in initiating litigation and fighting the injustice, all in a bid to ease his conscience. But when there was an attempt on his life, he left the fight to protect his family, sold his house, and moved to Lagos.

One day, he looked at himself in the mirror and instead of the person he'd sworn to be, a man with a fiery passion to help people, he saw a mere shadow, fleeting, who'd sacrificed his principles in a time of weakness.

twenty-one

IMPACT

Lights flickered and danced in the night, but Rebecca's mind was miles away from the excitement as she exited the theatre with Muyiwa and other laughing patrons. Muyiwa recounted his favourite moments from the performance, but just like the crowd's applause earlier, it faded into a backdrop of her own thoughts. Accepting his invitation had seemed like a good idea, but the thrill had now long evaporated. The jokes fell flat for her, no blame on the performers, but she had endured the two-hour show, forcing an empty smile with each laugh from the audience.

Sliding into the car, she remained in a daze as Muyiwa turned on the engine, barely noticing when the vehicle remained motionless.

"Rebecca?" he said, breaking through her reverie. "Are you okay?"

She snapped back to reality, shaking her head slightly. "I'm fine. Just... distracted."

"Are you sure that's it?" he probed gently. "You've been off since we left the house. I thought tonight would lift your spirits. Didn't you like the show?"

"I did, it's just ..." she faltered.

"You know," he softly interjected, "some of the best conversations with my dad happened in his beat-up Volvo. We'd drive out at night, just him and me, leaving my mum at home. We'd talk about everything, and some days, it felt like therapy. What I mean is, you can talk to me here."

"You have a father ... I lost mine too early to even know what that feels like." She avoided Muyiwa's eyes. "His family wanted nothing to do with me and my mum, and I spent so long desiring reconciliation and their love, thinking maybe it was a misunderstanding. How foolish of me ... They never loved us. They never wanted us."

"Rebecca ... "

"I know, you're sorry. Everyone's sorry, but it's no one's fault ..." her words trailed off. "Growing up, I endured being picked on because my father abandoned us. I thought I was the reason for my mother's unhappiness because I was an unplanned and unwanted child. So, I begged God to bring my father back. I would have traded my life just to see him again, thinking it would make everything better."

"That's a heavy burden for a child to bear," he whispered.

"When my daddy returned when I was ten, I saw the light return to my mother's eyes. She told me that this was the day God had made. But then I got scared—wondering if having my father back meant God would take me away. So, I made a pact with myself: To be the perfect daughter, never a source of sadness again. We moved to Ibadan, but then he died in a car accident." A tear slipped down her cheek, and she wiped it away quickly. "I don't know what I did wrong for him to die. Since then, I feel like I've just been going through the motions with God, trying to be perfect so nothing fails again. And you can guess how that has turned out—whenever things start to go well, something bad happens. It's the same at work; I'm trying so hard, but nothing's working."

She heard Muyiwa sigh and could sense that he was trying to choose his words carefully.

"It's terrible what happened to you and your family. I'm sorry you had to live through that," he finally said. "But God loves you very much, and the blessings we receive aren't based on how good we perform. His love unconditionally takes us at our worst."

Rebecca turned and locked her eyes with his, listening.

"You're God's child, and He gives good gifts freely to His children. So, you can expect good things to happen to you, not because of what you've done but from knowing that you are loved by Jesus."

"It sounds so simple." She rocked in her seat, wrestling with his words. "But my life proves that anything can be taken away as fast as it's given. How can I live like this without knowing if good things will come to me?"

"You know, we all have things we want badly, and it's frustrating when it feels like they're just out of reach. But God is actually in control, and while trusting God is easy when things are going well, it's tough when we face disappointment, hurt, or loss. But instead of trying to force things or getting discouraged, it helps to take stock of the blessings we do have while trusting that He'll take care of us. So, throw out the net and start believing again. You can dream and have faith that God will make a way and bless us in greater ways than we expect."

She sighed, wanting to be alone even though Muyiwa's words and presence were comforting. "Let's head home, please," she said softly.

They left the now-empty car park and drove home. Ushering her into the apartment, Muyiwa studied her face.

"I'll let you get some rest, but if you need some company, I'm just a call or knock away, okay?"

"Muyiwa," she called softly

"Yes?"

"Thank you."

"You're welcome." He opened his arms, inviting her into a hug. Slowly, she moved to him, resting her face against his chest and losing herself in the soothing rhythm of his heartbeat. Muyiwa cleared his throat, breaking the spell hanging between them. She pulled away slowly, lingering, but he held her hands gently and planting a light kiss on her head before leaving.

Alone in the brightly lit office, the faint hum of the air conditioning was Sola's only company. Papers were scattered across his desk—auditor reports he had reviewed with a team earlier that day, as Teju had advised.

"You can't assume Derin's fraud is limited to vendor payments," Teju said, and the auditors had proved him right.

Sola's fingers were busy on his phone, alternating between calling Tiffany and trying to reach Derin, but each attempt was met with silence. A few days ago, Tiffany's single text message broke him.

"We are over."

He tried everything, sent messages, pleaded, even stalked her social media for any hint of where she might be. It felt like the last fragments of his happiness had slipped through his fingers. He'd blown it, as he feared he would. He wanted to fight for her, but needed to resolve with Derin first.

Then he would make his way to Abuja to beg for his life.

As for Derin, Sola dreaded involving law enforcement like Teju was advocating, but Derin wasn't giving him much choice. Four calls had gone unanswered, so he typed out a text message.

"Let's talk face to face. You already know about the audit. The results are in, and I'm sure you know what we've found. So, step away from the company until the investigations are complete. I'll decide what to do next." He paused, biting his lip before adding, "Teju is now involved, and while I'm trying my best to protect you, we'll have to bring in law enforcement if you don't come to the table. We also need to talk about the other thing; it's killing me, and I think it's time to come clean."

He hit the send button, and a few minutes later, his phone rang. It was Derin.

"Hello?"

"Hey, man, You have every right to be disappointed and angry," Derin's voice was strained. "But we've come so far together, we can't let this tear us apart."

"What do you suggest?"

"Let's meet tonight. I'll text you the location. Nine PM?"

"Okay."

"I know I haven't said how sorry I am, Sola, but I truly am sorry."

"Sure. See you later." The call ended, but an unease gnawed at him as he leaned into the silence. Something felt off in the way Derin spoke.

Still, when it was 8:40 PM, Sola headed out to meet him.

Downing a glass of cold Sprite, the thumping bass of music playing from the bar's speakers drowned out the anxiety Sola had felt earlier. He glanced at his watch; it was 9:20 PM. He pulled out his phone and saw that Derin still hadn't replied to his last message. His ire grew with every passing minute.

His phone buzzed.

"Finally. Where are you?" Sola snapped.

"Sorry, bro. Got caught up in something," Derin slurred "Are you drunk?"

"Lay off me, man. I'm here." Derin's gentle demeanour from earlier had vanished.

Sola scanned the crowded room. "Where? I've been watching the door, and there's no sign of you."

"I found another spot across from the bar. It's quieter, so just come and meet me."

"On my way."

Sola weaved through the dancing crowd, opened the door, and stepped onto the road to cross to the other side.

A chill ran down his spine as a high-pitched squeal reached him. Screeching tires.

His heart thumped violently, but his feet couldn't move. Only his head turned, just in time to see blinding headlights closing in on him fast, like a predator.

"No!"

The word echoed in the night as the car collided with his body—a violent crash that sent him flying into the air. Time stood still. The air left his lungs. Then, silence.

He hit the asphalt with a sickening crack, pain exploding through him. And for the second time in his life, everything faded to black.

twenty-two

EXPOSURE

Rebecca was pulling hours upon hours of virtual presentations and training of teams in West Africa on what she tagged the 'Capable Tribe' tour as they deployed her commercial team engagement program. But it wasn't courage that was pushing Rebecca, it was chaos. She desperately needed an escape from the turmoil in her mind and throwing herself into it work, despite the doubt that it would end well, was the easier option than fighting a losing battle with her mind.

She expected little but had received multiple rounds of applause from the teams, with even Imade openly crediting her for leading the initiative, much to the chagrin of Adonai and Eric. It was as if Imade knew what transpired in her absence, because Rebecca couldn't explain the kindness she'd received from Imade lately.

"A win is a win …" Rebecca mused. At the end of the day, the end justified the means. "I did it." She gave herself a mental pat on the back, letting a small smile flit to her lips. "Anyhow, there's such a thing as too much talking," she muttered as she rubbed her aching jaw, relieved to be done with the first phase of the project.

As she leaned back to catch her breath, her phone beeped, and a message from Muyiwa flashed on the screen.

"I miss you," it said. "I can't wait to see you later."

She responded quickly, explaining that she'll be home late and he shouldn't wait up for her.

Imagery from the scriptures he sent her played in her mind, especially the one about Jesus' disciple calling himself John, "The one whom Jesus loves."

She can't explain it, but there's something in her heart that feels less vindictive and less fearful. She's allowing herself more grace, a concept she hasn't entertained in a long time.

"*The girl whom Jesus loves,*" she muttered, a soft smile crossing her lips.

Suddenly, Tari came running over, her eyes wide with worry. "I have bad news. Your friend, Sola, got into an accident."

"What!"

Tari leaned closer, zooming in on the screen of her phone, revealing the news. Rebecca gasped at the image.

"What do we do? Should I head to the hospital?" she blurted.

"But his family doesn't know you. I doubt the hospital will let you in. He's been there since yesterday, and they say he's critical but alive. I'm sure he's getting the best care," Tari replied, obviously trying to soften the blow.

"I'll just go home and try tomorrow?" Rebecca suggested, her eyes wide with uncertainty.

"Yeah." Tari nodded, but there was a catch in her voice.

"There's something you aren't telling me. What is it?"

"It's nothing ..."

"Tari?"

With a resigned sigh, Tari finally answered. "How well do you know him?"

"Obviously not well enough if you're asking me that. Just tell me, please ..."

"Well, your friend's full name is Sola Adesesan," Tari blurted out.

"And?"

Tari paused.

"Adesesan," Rebecca whispered, a slow realisation settling. She froze.

"It can't be. Was it Sola? But ... but his name nor picture never came up in all of my web searches, so how is this possible?" A cackle escaped her lips, and she clutched her stomach.

"Are you okay? This is the opposite of how I thought you'll react." Tari stared at her, puzzled.

"I honestly don't know how else to react," Rebecca said, shaking her head. "I've exhausted my anger. It's ridiculous, isn't it? I've been wearing blindfolds, not wanting to know, yet all this while ..." she hissed the last words bitterly, "he'd snuck into my life. But to what end?"

"You're scaring me."

"I'm fine. Just amused by the wicked irony of him being in a car accident. Life is already taking out its trash," she spat.

"I think you should head home," Tari advised gently. "You're dissociating. When reality hits, it won't be pretty. You don't want to be here when that happens. I'll come to check up on you at home once I'm done closing over here," Tari promised.

Driving home, Rebecca cranked up the music to drown out Tari's words, blasting the volume as she sped through the roads. It was a miracle she made it home in one piece. Pulling onto her street, she spotted Muyiwa from a distance. Her heart jumped but then dropped as she watched him hug a woman closely. Pressing on the brakes, her heart sank deeper as they shared a laugh. He kissed the woman's cheek and waved her off.

Another one lost to the street.

Rebecca parked the car and prepared to go inside, but Muyiwa appeared from behind the gate, smiling widely, a contrast to his usual tame demeanour.

"Rebecca. I'm so happy to see you," he said.

"Sure, you are," she replied coldly, walking toward her flat.

"Is something wrong?"

"You're so perceptive, aren't you?" she retorted.

"What?" His smile gave way to a perplexed frown.

"I'd like some space, okay? I'm not a project for you to adopt and manage. I can take care of myself."

He recoiled. "Sure, I get it. Sorry for pushing," he said, turning away.

Once inside the house, the walls felt like they were closing in on her, sucking any trace of comfort, so Rebecca climbed back into her car and headed to the hospital.

"What am I doing here?" she wondered, as she idled in front of the building. Her phone rang, and Tari's name flashed on the screen.

"I'm at your house, but you aren't here."

"I'm at the hospital,"

"Rebecca ..." Tari groaned. "They won't let you in. What's the point?"

"I don't know," she admitted, frustrated.

"Just wait there. Don't do anything rash."

But as luck would have it, Rebecca spotted Sola's friend, Derin, rushing through the hospital exit.

"Derin!" she called, stopping him in his tracks.

He turned. Dressed in a black hoodie and joggers, his face was partly hidden by his glasses and the brim of his cap.

"I think I just found a way in!" she excitedly told Tari over the phone. "Got to go." She ended the call, cutting off Tari's protests.

Derin stepped back, clearly anxious to leave, but she wasn't going to let him go without saying her mind.

"Wait, please!"

He paused, his eyes vacant and red.

"Did you know that your friend is a killer?" She asked calmly.

"I need to leave," he mumbled.

"No, you'll listen to me first, then tell your friend I know who he is and what he did."

"What are you talking about?" his words slurred.

Tears started pooling in her eyes as her emotions rose to the surface. "Sola killed my father in a car accident years ago. Did you really not know?"

Derin's face was transformed by an eerie smile. "I can see you're upset," he said, his voice low but urgent, "but his family is in there now. I was heading home to get some supplies for an overnight stay. Come with me? We can talk about it and come back later."

Before she could process his words, he stepped closer, wrapping an arm around her shoulder and guiding her away from the hospital's glaring lights. She was too exhausted to resist, so she allowed herself to lean into his comfort and be led to his car.

Sola's eyelids fluttered open to the persistent beeping of machines surrounding him. He blinked against the fluorescent lights, trying to make sense of his surroundings. As he attempted to shift, a jolt of pain shot through his back, leaving him breathless. He couldn't feel his legs. His gaze shifted to the familiar figure sitting beside him.

His mother, with eyes closed, was feverishly whispering comforting bible verses. He reached out to her and whispered.

"Mum?"

She looked over at him and shouted with uncontainable joy.

"Oluwalonsola mi! You're awake! Ha Oluwa seun!"

A nurse appeared at the sound of her cries, but Sola's focus remained on his mother.

"Mum, you're trembling."

"I can't help it." Tears glistened in her eyes. "This is the second time I've almost lost you. Thank God for the good Samaritans who rushed you here. What would I have done, ehn?"

The reality of what had happened rushed back to him, and a wave of panic hit him.

"Where's Teju?"

"He was here earlier, but he had to leave. He'll be back this evening," She reassured him, but her voice faltered. "Your father was here, too. We were all so worried. They are working with the police to find the driver who did this to you."

Sola's heart raced. "I need Teju here."

"Why? What's going on?"

Suddenly, a bright-haired woman entered the room, capturing his attention. He squinted, trying to place her face while his mother turned to the newcomer.

"Are you a nurse?" his mum asked.

"No," the woman stuttered. "I'm his friend ... I mean, a friend of a friend. Rebecca?"

Recognition washed over Sola. It's Tari. But a knot of confusion tightened in his gut. "Why are you here? Is Rebecca with you?"

The woman's face paled as she stared at him.

"I thought she was here, because she came here to confront you about—about killing her father."

His mother's shocked gasp rippled through the room, echoing his own. "Who are you? You can't be here," she demanded.

"Mum ..." Sola reached for her hand, desperate to calm her and focus on the situation.

"I don't understand ..."

Shadows crept in at the edges of his vision, and he felt his grip on consciousness slipping. Teju burst into the room, and he sighed with relief.

"Derin ..." Sola murmured, the name slipping from his lips like a plea.

"What are you saying?" his mother asked, panic threading her voice.

Sola reached out to Teju, trying to hold on a little longer.

"Derin. He tried to kill me."

The last image in his mind is of Tari's expression morphing into alarm, just as he slipped into unconsciousness.

Derin's house was in disarray. Clothes lay scattered as if tossed in a wild fit. He grabbed a hefty pile from the couch, chucking it aside while offering a half-hearted apology.

"I wasn't prepared for a guest."

As he stumbled over another pile on the floor, Rebecca instinctively reached out to steady him, but he swatted her hand away with a ferocity that made the hairs on her skin stand.

"You said you wanted to talk to Sola about something important?" Derin asked.

"Yeah, well, I found out tonight that your friend is Sola Adesesan." Rebecca swallowed hard. "The news today mentioned that Sola is the son of Chief Adesesan. Is it true, or is there another one?"

Derin froze.

"Okay, from your reaction, I think you know about the accident." She pressed on, her heart pounding as he grabbed a bottle and gulped its contents, the glass flashing dangerously in the light.

"Would you like some water?" he asked, almost too casually.

She nodded. "Yes, please."

Derin handed her a glass of water, and she took a long gulp, relishing its coolness against her throat.

"Was he really the one?" Rebecca asked, her voice barely above a whisper. She felt dizzy, and the room started to spin. "He was the one, right? I just need to hear him say ..." she trailed off.

As her vision blurred, she saw Derin hovering, his silhouette dark against the fading light. Her chest tightened as he spoke.

"I'm sorry," he murmured. "I was afraid you'd tell Sola I was at the hospital, so I brought you here. I didn't plan for it to go this way. But you mentioned the accident ... How much did Sola tell you? Don't worry, it's just some sleeping pills, more than you should have, but it'll keep you quiet till I figure this out."

As his voice slipped farther and farther away, her dry, heavy lips parted to protest, but no words came. Her consciousness faded, and she surrendered to a dark, heavy sleep.

"Rebecca!"

The distraught voice cut through the haze, yanking her back to reality. She blinked against the darkness, the jarring sound of sirens ringing in her ears, and overlapping screams around her.

"She's awake! She's awake!" a familiar woman's voice screeched near her ear. Confused and disoriented, Rebecca tried to sit up, but a wave of dizziness washed over her, knocking her back down.

Then she caught a glimpse of an unfolding situation: Derin had his hands cuffed and was being led away by officers. A shiver ran down her spine.

"What's going on?" she managed to croak out.

"Shhh, you're okay. You're fine," Tari said, tears streaming down her cheek. "Thank God you're okay."

Her words calmed Rebecca, and she soon felt gentle hands guiding her away from the scene. The world blurred once more as she fainted.

When she woke up again, the disinfected smell of the hospital greeted her, and she saw two familiar faces hovering beside her—Tari and Muyiwa. In a matter of minutes, they were filling her in on what had happened.

"Tari heard Sola mention Derin's attempt on his life," Muyiwa explained breathlessly. "You weren't answering your phone, and your car was still at the hospital. One of the security guards remembered seeing you with a young man matching Derin's description. They checked the CCTV and saw you leave with him." Rebecca's heart pounded as she listened.

"Wha—what happened?"

"He was trying to take you away," Tari cut in, her voice shaking. "We arrived just in time, as he was carrying you to his car, trying to escape.

Rebecca shuddered.

"He drugged me," she whispered, horrified at the thought.

"I was so worried. I thought I'd lost you," Muyiwa said.

"Water," she croaked, her throat dry and scratchy. "Bottled, and please open it in front of me."

They laughed as Muyiwa went to fetch her request.

It was still dark and windy as Rebecca sprinted through the empty streets.

The events of the past months played in her mind like a carousel, each memory a reminder of her desperate need for approval and love. It took facing her anger and inadequacy head-on to find refuge in God's embrace and finally discover how to love herself. But the weight of grief was still heavy on her heart. She mourned the loss of her father, the life they could have shared, the little moments of joy, lost to regret, and the pursuit of his family's approval.

In her reflection, she recalled the faces of those who'd stood by her: Hauwa, Tariebi, and Muyiwa. A small smile crept onto her lips at the thought of Muyiwa. He was there for her when the world felt dark. The embarrassment from Felix was a distant memory, obliterated by this man who was genuine, caring, and charming.

"Maybe once all this settles down, we can give it a shot," she whispered, hopeful but unsure after what she saw. He'd given her the space she requested, even after the hospital visit.

Panting, she stopped to catch her breath, hands braced on her knees as her chest heaved. When she straightened, a whisper stirred in her heart:

Nothing can separate me from the love of Christ. God chose me not for my performance but for His grace. I am His.

When she finally arrived home, her mother, flanked by Muyiwa, was seated in front of the house.

"Nnem. Is this a dream?" Rebecca shouted with joy, rushing into her mother's arms. Tears sprang in her eyes. "What of Chimezie?"

"He's on holiday with your grandparents, so I took the night bus to surprise you. But I didn't find you at home," her mother said with a smile. "This kind gentleman heard the knocks and offered me a chair while I waited."

"I'll be on my way now, ma," Muyiwa said. "It was lovely to meet you."

"I'll be right back!" Rebecca opened the door quickly for her mother, then dashed after him.

"Muyiwa!" She shouted after his retreating figure as she closed the gap between them. He turned, his expression unreadable.

"Uh ..." she stammered. The silence stretched uncomfortably, and she shifted her weight awkwardly. "I wanted to thank you for being at the hospital, for keeping my mummy company ... for everything."

"That's alright. It's what anyone would do," he replied curtly, turning away.

"No, wait, please," she said. "I'm sorry for being short with you the other day. It's been overwhelming, and I didn't mean to pour my frustrations on you."

"Thanks for apologizing," he said.

"Listen, I was thinking ... maybe we could go for a game night and dinner later? If you're up for it?" she suggested.

"Hmm. Why the sudden change of heart? Thought you didn't want me around."

"It's not like that at all. I just think you've been incredibly good to me. I'll feel bad not returning the gesture," she quickly explained.

"Do you even like me?" he asked, his voice dropping a notch.

"I guess so? I mean, yes?" she replied, glancing away.

He chuckled, closing the gap between them and gently lifting her chin so she met his gaze.

"I don't have to guess. I know I like you. At first, it was admiration, but getting to know you over these past months has shown me how exceptional you are. You're beautiful, fun, principled, ambitious, I could keep going, because just the thought of you takes me to a place that I've never been with anyone else."

She swallowed but remained silent, eyes locked on him as he continued speaking.

"You don't understand, do you?" He dropped his hands. "I don't want to be your last choice—someone you settle for after trying out all your options. I'm not trying to be a fixer, neither am I interested in waiting for you to realise you want me."

"I'm not a project," Rebecca whispered.

"You made that clear," he replied. "I was only trying to support you, but I think I need to step back. It feels like you enjoy being wanted without wanting the commitment in return, and that's not something I can handle. If you need me, you know where to find me."

He started to turn away.

"Yeah, I know you won't be waiting, especially when you have another woman lined up. You're no different from Felix."

Her words broke his stride as he glanced back, brows furrowed.

"Another woman? And you're seriously comparing me to your deadbeat ex?"

"Yeah, and I'm not sorry about it. I saw you with that woman, and you looked pretty cozy before you acted all surprised and happy to see me," she snapped back.

His confusion was evident, and he shook his head, a slight laughter escaping his lips. "You thought I was trying to play you?"

"I was genuinely starting to trust you," Rebecca ranted on. "To believe each time you said a kind word to me, eager to see you, or hear your voice. Maybe it was wrong to crave your attention or expect your companionship because you said you'll be there for me. But for how deliberate and disciplined you are about everything in your life, it couldn't have been a mistake that you would be all over me one day about going out with you, then the next, you're too busy to return a call or text. Disappeared without explanation, and to rub it in, you were basically falling over yourself to kiss the lady."

"One time, Rebecca, I wasn't available that one time, and you label me the villain. I can't measure which hurts the most: the lack of grace, the comparison to your ex, or that you didn't stop to ask if I was doing okay. You didn't ask, but that was my sister Sope, and if you'd come over, I would have introduced you.

She came over to pick me up because of my persistent complaints about stress and feeling down. I've also been facing difficult decisions in my life, breaking down due to work stress. I finally admitted to myself that I was burning out, and thankfully, Sope was here to encourage me and give me a much-needed boost."

Blood rushed to Rebecca's face.

"You didn't tell me."

He shook his head.

"You had your own share of troubles, and after her visit, I was in a much better headspace, excited to see you, only for you to hurl hurtful words my way. No thanks for letting me know what you think of me," his voice dripped with hurt as he turned and walked off.

"Muyiwa, wait!" she called, but he didn't respond, leaving her reeling with the realisation that her selfishness and haste had cost her another chance at happiness.

twenty-three

HARMONY

Lying in bed alone, surrounded by blankets and pillows, Sola welcomed the solitude. He sank into the pages of his Bible, losing himself in verses that spoke of hope and grace, a reminder of the life he's thankful to have despite his pain.

Although the house was busy, most of the visitors were downstairs. Since he came home from the hospital, a steady stream of visitors had flooded in, from his mother's church community, his father's colleagues, and friends with bowls of food and stories to lift his spirit. And then there was Tiffany, who'd rushed to the hospital as soon as she heard the news.

"You came," Sola had said to Tiffany.

"I did. If I want you dead, I'll kill you myself. That's not the case, so here I am." She took his hand in hers, and he felt a slight tremor. He squeezed.

"I'm glad you're okay," her voice broke.

"Me too."

She had visited the house every day since his discharge.

The door of his room creaked open, and he tried to sit up.

"Dad?" Sola took in his father's intimidating frame. They'd spoken a couple of times in the past days, but this was the first time that they were alone.

His father motioned for him to relax before sitting next to him on the bed.

"I'm happy to see you're feeling better. We have an update on the case. The boy confessed, and the state is prosecuting him for attempted murder and kidnapping. Teju and I are keeping a close eye on it, so you can check in with either of us if you need information or have concerns."

"Yes, sir."

Sola was saddened by the idea of his friend behind bars, but it was out of his hands now.

His father lingered so Sola continued.

"Thank you for all you and Teju have done and the grace that you've shown me. I took a lot for granted, and I'm very sorry that it's taken me this long to come around. I was too focused on how hurt I felt and failed to see how much it cost you and took away from the sort of life you were building for us. I should have been honest instead of covering up, yet you still supported me while I studied abroad. I realize how ungrateful I've been considering the circumstances."

"Well, the worst is behind us, and an honest conversation is due between us, my boy. I never stopped being your father, but I did a terrible job of it. It took you almost dying for me to wake up from what has been a long-overdue delusion. We're too much alike. Everyone pointed it out since you were a child. I didn't think those common threads would tear us apart. I sacrificed some things and blamed you as the cause, but I had a choice. I always had a choice, and I wish I chose to pay more attention to you instead of being engulfed by rage. I lost sight of what actually mattered, which was being your father and modelling the love and heart of our Lord and Saviour. So, forgive me, my boy."

Sola thought he saw his father tear up a bit, but he wasn't too sure.

Looking up to the ceiling, he blinked back his own tears, and his father stood to leave so that Sola could get some rest. But before he left, he looked back and said words that he didn't imagine he'd ever hear again.

"You've done well for yourself, my boy. And I'm proud of you."

Sola had barely processed those words when Tiffany slipped in with a tray in her hands.

"Your mum made pepper soup. Eat up so you can take your next dose of painkillers," she chimed, placing the steaming bowl on the bedside stool. The spicy, savoury aroma wafted up, teasing his senses. He shot her a thankful smile.

"Thanks, Tiff. I don't deserve you.

"That's right, you don't," she shot back, a glimmer of mischief dancing in her eyes. "But here I am anyway."

Sola chuckled but immediately winced as a sharp pain shot through him. Tiffany's laughter faded, and concern took its place as she sat on the edge of the bed.

"How are you feeling?" she asked in a soft whisper.

"Broken," he replied with a wry chuckle. "But, grateful to be alive," he continued.

"Stay strong, okay? The road to recovery may be long and hard but take it a day at a time. You have a session with the physiotherapist today, right?" she asked.

He nodded.

"I'm just grateful you're here. I'm sorry for not being open about my life and family. I should have told you everything before now: the history with Derin and the dynamics in my family. You've always been so open with me. I took so much for granted, hurt those I care about, then carelessly put your business and reputation in harm's way. Beyond being business partners, you're the love of my life, and I don't want to lose you," he continued, his eyes searching hers. "I was scared to commit and felt unworthy of happiness. But you brought back joy into my life, and I won't trade what we have for anything."

Tiffany bit her lip as he spoke.

"I'm cleaning up everything on the business side. I want to operate with transparency, so Teju will be a silent partner. I also have a lot of change ahead, and I want to learn to love you the way you deserve. So, can you forgive me?" he spoke with laboured breath.

Her smile softened.

"I almost lost my mind when I heard about the accident," she confessed. "I was hurt and lashed out, which pushed you to confront Derin. It was my fault that you almost died."

Sola shook his head. "You did nothing wrong. In fact, I owe a lot to you for making it all unravel, even if it came with broken bones." He reached for her hand, fingers intertwining as he looked into her eyes. "I love you, Tiff."

"Slow down, cowboy," she teased. "By the way, you're lucky to have your family supporting you. That's a precious gift."

"I realize that now."

She stood up. "What about that lady? The one that Derin almost hurt? Rebecca, I believe. Have you spoken to her?"

A pained laugh escaped Sola as he rubbed the back of his neck. "Not yet.

I feel like such a coward. I don't know how to face her."

Tiffany leaned closer, her voice unapologetic. "She deserves better than that. The past is behind you, but you can only start afresh with honesty and genuine remorse. Go see her. You owe her that much."

Sola nodded slowly, acknowledging her words.

"I'm going out with your mum. She invited me to join her for a visit to the orphanage."

"Yeah, she loves spending time with those kids." A small smile played on his lips. "But what about the other thing?" he asked, holding his breath.

"I know you want me to say that we're back to normal and that everything is water under the bridge, but I need some time to think. I'm here now, but I can't decide just yet if I should stay. I laid all my cards on the table with you, Sola, but you didn't reveal your full hand, and that hurt. Your secrets caught me off guard, so I can't just move on and pretend that all this—" she gestured around "—didn't happen."

"I didn't mean to. I didn't know it would turn out this way."

"You can't continue to hold on to not knowing as an excuse. It's flimsy at best and unaccountable at the worst. It was the culmination of your choices that brought you here. The company you kept, the secrets you held, the lies you told, and the people you hurt—all those were your doing. Admit that you made mistakes, then take control of your life, not leaving it to the whims of someone else."

"You're right."

"Somehow, I want to believe that you're a good guy because of how you still pull at my heart strings, but I hate being wrong. I leaned too much on my instinct and too little on the Holy Spirit's leading. Even when I felt uncomfortable about you holding back little details, I shrugged it off to a phase, and that once we got together, you'd be more forthcoming. But you weren't, and I almost got burnt. I could have easily lost years of work because you didn't trust me. I want to do this right, but that means I need to step back to see things clearly again. So, I'm going to take some time to think about if there can still be a future for us, okay?"

"I understand." Sola swallowed. "And whatever you decide, you'll always be special to me."

"Good. Now eat, and I'll see you later."

Sola was left alone with her words, and resolved to face Rebecca at last.

You know that feeling you get when you unwrap a present at Christmas to see an item you've wanted desperately but thought it was too hopeless to ask for, the giddy realisation that someone cherishes you so much that they fulfilled your deepest unspoken desire? That's what it felt like spending the past few days with her mother.

Rebecca hadn't even thought to ask for it, but she wouldn't trade it for anything in the world. They shared stories, and worked on her mother's daily crossword puzzles, a familiar routine. Together in the kitchen, they were cooking while Onyeka Onwenu's songs played in the background.

Her phone beeped with another message from Sola. He'd been blowing up her phone for over a week.

I'm sorry for all the pain I've caused you. I'd give anything to take it all back. I know nothing would fix it, but please give me a chance to talk to you. I'm begging, the message read.

Her mother paused, holding a knife over the vegetable on the cutting board. "Is all well?"

"Yes, it's just that Adesesan boy. He wants to talk," Rebecca replied with a hiss.

"Hmm ..."

"Yeah." Rebecca sprinkled salt into the simmering pot on the stove and dropped the shaker, which clattered against the counter. She leaned against the surface, feeling a mix of emotions.

"It's just ... now that I'm finally grieving the loss of Papa, hearing from Sola is like opening a fresh wound. So, I don't know what to say or do. I thought by now, the pain would have faded. Nnem, how did you heal?"

"For me, the grief is not gone. I miss your father every day. You see, grief can hit you in waves, unexpected and overwhelming. We don't only mourn what we had, we ache for memories that no longer have a face, voice, smell, touch, or warmth. And we long for what we could have had, future experiences that disappear when the person ceases to exist. But I cope by remembering the good times we spent together and the joy Obim brought to my life. Then I go to God's word to remind myself that although time may not heal all wounds, God binds the broken-hearted and comforts us. He knows the number of hairs on our heads and cares."

Just as Rebecca was about to say more, a loud knock on the door startled them.

She headed to the living room and opened the door slightly, only to be met with the unexpected sight of Sandra and her family standing on the doorstep. Goosebumps rose on her skin.

"Please, don't shut the door," Sandra pleaded. "We just want to talk. Hauwa told us what happened, and we came to check on you."

"Who is it?" her mother called, walking into the living room.

Rebecca stepped aside and opened the door wider.

Sandra's face paled, as if she's staring at a ghost. "Angel ..." she whispered. "I'm sorry, I didn't know you'll be here."

"It's okay. Let them in," her mother urged."

They entered, and Sandra fell to her knees, tears spilling down her face.

"I committed a grave sin against you," she sobbed. "I was lost in my own grief after losing my brother, my best friend. I allowed bitterness to blind me to your pain and ignored your love for Gabriel instead of honouring what he wanted. Afterward, I was too ashamed to reach out, and now I regret everything. Please, I beg you both."

Rebecca's mother walked over and offered her hand to help Sandra to her feet. She took both hands in hers. "Wipe your tears. I forgave you long ago. Gabriel wouldn't want me to hold onto anger, so I let it all go. And although it was hard sometimes: I spent many nights praying, weeping, and asking why. But even without answers, I found peace. God has been a good Father, guiding us through our trials. We walked through fire, and He was there to keep us safe. So I hope you can forgive yourself too."

Wiping her tears, Sandra turned to Rebecca.

"It was selfish of me to think only of my own health needs instead of genuine reconciliation. I'm sorry."

Rebecca still struggled to let go. Her heart still ached so she could only manage a nod.

Her mother extended her hands, and prayed over them, asking for healing not just for Sandra but also for herself. As they prepared to leave, another knock echoed through the house.

This time, it was Sola sitting in a wheelchair, his brother Teju at his back. Sola looked desperate, his eyes searching for understanding.

"I'm sorry for showing up here like this," he blurted. "You weren't picking up calls or responding to messages. You have every right not to, but please, give me a chance to ask for your forgiveness."

Rebecca stepped aside, letting him in and introducing him to her mother and Sandra's family. Sola's eyes widened with guilt as he grasped who they were, while Sandra buried her face in her hands, loud sobs wracking through her body as her husband tried to console her.

"Sola?" Teju encouraged his brother quietly.

But Rebecca spoke first, "I have only one thing to ask. Why did you sneak into my life without telling me who you were?"

"I didn't know," he stammered. "It wasn't intentional, and after everything that has happened, it's flimsy for me to say that. Although you felt familiar the first time we met at the restaurant, there was no way to explain it. Maybe things would have turned out differently if I had told you who I was."

"Maybe."

"I don't know if Derin said anything to you the other night, but I wasn't behind the wheel when the car crashed. It doesn't take away the guilt I feel for being there that night, and I wish there was a way to go back and change it all. But I swear none of it was meant to hurt you."

"That's hard to believe," Sandra cut in sharply.

Rebecca tilted her head at the irony of this woman who had just been shown mercy and yet was being harsh. Surprised at her own defensiveness of Sola she didn't speak. Sandra continued her attack.

"Your family's actions to cover up the truth make it seem like you could have run a con, so why should we take your word for it?" Sandra folded her arms across her chest.

"Yes, my family covered up to protect me," Sola admitted, shame clouding his eyes. "It started with me wanting to shield Derin; my family, in turn, protected me. It then wove into a tangle of secrets that spiralled out of control."

Rebecca studied him closely, her heart softening in compassion. Carrying such a burdensome secret for so long must have tormented him. Here he was, his friend in jail, and he'd lost the use of his legs. The raw pain in their history wouldn't be erased in a day, but maybe they could try to make a new path toward healing.

"I actually brought something," Sola said, his hands trembling as he removed a bracelet from his wrist, revealing it like a peace offering. The inscription *"my angel"* caught Rebecca's eye.

Angel released a sharp wail.

"Where did you get that?"

"On the night of the accident, the officers gave it to me, thinking it was mine. I couldn't bring myself to tell them it wasn't. I've held onto it all this time, but I'm returning it now to its rightful owner."

A single tear slid down Rebecca's mother's cheek as she reached out, accepting the bracelet. Then, she bent to her knees, squeezing him into a heartfelt, tender hug that spoke louder than their words could, a soothing balm for all their wounds.

twenty-four

CLOSURE

"Every good gift and every perfect gift is from above, and comes down from the Father of lights, with whom there is no variation or shadow of turning."

Morning run - check.
Quiet time - check.
Brand influencer contract signed - check.

Rebecca reflected on the last part. She finally got around to taking advantage of Suleiman's offer to use his studio, and switched up her content. Acting out a dramatic scene as different characters in carefully curated outfits. One of the popular fashion designers reposted the reel and, from there, it went viral. What followed was an avalanche of new followers, DMs for partnerships, and a contract as brand ambassador for a couture brand. She was carrying her shoulders high today.

Tari appeared, bubbly as usual.

"Hey, girl. An impromptu town hall is coming up soon. Are you ready?"

Rebecca glanced at her watch. "Yeah, the invite dropped a few minutes ago."

A glint appeared in Tari's eyes.

"What?"

"Nothing," Tari sing-sang.

"Come on. What are you hiding?"

"Do you seriously not know what the town hall is about?"

"Nope. But since it's so short, it seems like an announcement."

"Okay then ... you won't hear it from me." With that, Tari twirled on her heel and sprinted away.

Rebecca's laptop buzzed with a message from Imade asking to see her. Smoothing her shirt, she straightened up and walked over to Imade's office. The door was open.

Imade was wearing a coy smile and speaking with Director Jimi when Rebecca walked in. Director Jimi turned to leave them, winking as he exited the room.

What are these two up to now? she wondered, shutting the door behind her. When she turned back to Imade, the smile had been replaced by her signature serious expression.

"Boss, you wanted to see me?"

"Yes, have a seat, please."

Rebecca sat down.

"I understand you went through a traumatic incident. Although you're back, I want to confirm that you're okay. So ... how are you?"

"I'm much better, thanks. Although I still shake a bit when I think about what could have happened if my friends and the police didn't show up when they did. I'm thankful it wasn't worse."

Imade's gaze softened. "I'm happy you got through unscathed. The company has a free counselling service if you need someone to talk to."

"That sounds great. I'll check it out, thank you."

"Don't be shy to reach out if you need extra support at work, okay? I mean it. After my own health scare, I had to take a step back to reexamine my priorities and how to better manage work and life going forward. I reached out to them, and the sessions are teaching me to be kinder to myself and others."

Rebecca was blown away by Imade's openness.

"Now that we have that out of the way, on to business." Imade switched gears. "The leadership team has a lot of positive things to say about your performance, and I'm proud of you."

"What?" Rebecca blurted.

"I thought I was doing you a favour by letting you take baby steps in your role at your own pace. I was concerned that if you were thrown into more responsibility too soon, you might struggle. From day one, I saw your great potential, but you weren't confident in yourself and often hid behind excuses. However, my leave turned out to be a blessing in disguise. I had no choice but to let you step up, and they saw you live in action. Haven't you noticed how people now lean over to listen when you speak? That's a result of your bravery to rise to the occasion. There's a premium on your expertise, and the global capability team is adopting your templates and rolling them out as an essential commercial toolkit worldwide. You've also been invited to participate in the next ideation session in Detroit for the upcoming fiscal year."

Rebecca could see Imade's lips moving, but she was struck with disbelief at the words forming.

"I don't understand ... I mean, I understand, so thanks, I guess?" she stammered.

"I'll give you a minute," Imade said, growing silent.

"Wow!" Rebecca finally exclaimed, jumping up from her seat as the words finally sunk in. "I can't believe it! Thank you so much, Imade. For everything. I don't even know where to start ..." she gushed.

"That's not all. We reviewed our team's development plan while you were out of the office. The company is redesigning the commercial department, changing some roles for better productivity and introducing new ones. Effective two months from now, we'll have a new manager role focused on commercial intelligence capability for West Africa. This position will involve training teams on adopting new tools for data analysis and enhancing decision-making through better interpretation of data. There's a 25 percent travel requirement. I recommended you for the role, and the sign-off is unanimous."

Rebecca felt her mouth drop open in disbelief. "What?"

"The role reports to me, so there's no need for an interview since I already manage your KPIs. Anyway, congratulations on your new role if you're accepting it."

"Of course! Thank you so much for the opportunity and trust. This is amazing, and I honestly didn't see it coming." She clapped her hands over her mouth, giggling.

"Alright then." Imade waved her away. "It'll be announced at the town hall."

"Thank you again, boss. I promise I'll make you proud.

"Yeah, yeah, I know, you can go now."

As Rebecca walked out, joining her colleagues heading toward the conference room, Tari grabbed her by the elbow and whispered, "Hottest chick on the block. Congratulations, sweetie."

"I appreciate you, girl."

"You owe me dinner for being your biggest cheerleader," Tari added, and they shared a high-five.

Rebecca walked into the room feeling different, confident, and eager to receive what good things will come next. But a small part of her heart felt hollow, empty as if it's holding space for something or someone else.

Later that evening, Rebecca found herself at Muyiwa's apartment, a bowl of peppered snail stew in her hands. She knocked tentatively at first but hit harder when there was no answer.

"One minute!" Muyiwa called from inside, and shuffling footsteps soon approached the door.

When it swung open, Rebecca felt a rush of pleasure, but it quickly wavered as Muyiwa's smile turned into a firm line upon seeing her.

"Rebecca?" he asked questioningly, almost guarded as he glanced back into his apartment, then back at her and the bowl in her hands. "What are you doing here? Is there a problem?"

"Oh, no." She forced a smile. "I got some good news earlier today and wanted to celebrate with you, so I brought food."

"Okay ..." he said but didn't move to take it. Neither did he step aside to let her in.

"Yeah ... I got promoted at work," she added.

"That's nice, congratulations." His eyes shifted back inside the apartment again.

"Sorry." She tried to peek into the house. "Am I interrupting something?"

"Yes, actually. I was on a call with my siblings. I should get back to that ..."

"I see," she replied, swallowing her disappointment. "Well, can I drop this somewhere inside for you?"

"No, that's okay; I'll take it." He reached out to lift the food from her grasp, and the quick, soft touch sent flutters in her stomach. "Thank you. If that's all ..." his voice trailed off as he began to close the door.

Instinct kicked in, and she reached out to stop it from shutting completely. "Also, I'm sorry," she blurted out.

He paused. "What did you say?"

"I was wrong. I shouldn't have said those things to you before. I was upset and, for no reason, channelled that to you when you've been nothing but kind and supportive."

He leaned casually against the door frame, a small smile betraying the stoic façade. "Hm ... I'm listening."

"So, I ... um, brought a peace offering ..." She pulled out two tickets from her pocket and waved them. "I snagged tickets to the show you wanted to see. They have slots for the weekend, and I'd love for you to go with me."

He studied her briefly, then opened the door wider. "You know what? Just come in. Give me a few minutes to wrap up the call."

He dropped the food on the dining table and gestured to the sofa. Rebecca's eyes drifted to the gamepad on the centre table, a paused game flickering on the screen.

"May I?" she whispered, picking up the gamepad.

"You play?" he asked.

"A little."

"Okay, there's a guest profile you can use."

"Thanks."

"Muyiwa, do you have a guest?" a man's voice queried from the phone.

"Do you have to ask?" a woman chimed in. "I heard a lady's voice, and Muyiwa invited her in."

"You guys were eavesdropping? No wonder you went quiet." Muyiwa said.

"Can you blame us? You never tell us anything, so we snoop for bits whenever we can," another male voice added.

"You're shamelessly intruding on my privacy, and proudly so."

"Whatever, who is it? Tell us if you have a woman o," the woman insisted.

"Guys, you're on speaker and starting to embarrass me, so I'll go now," Muyiwa said.

"Wait, first, can we say hi?" the woman pleaded, voice full of mischief. "Let's meet your friend, now—don't be shy."

Muyiwa groaned. "Sope, this counts as bullying." He muted the call and turned to Rebecca with an apologetic and helpless look. "They want to say hi. Do you mind?"

Rebecca chuckled. "Not at all."

He squeezed beside her on the couch, bringing her into view of the camera. Suddenly, three smiling faces—two men and one woman—burst onto the screen.

"Hello," Rebecca greeted with a slight wave.

"Hi ..." the first man said.

"Hello ..." the other echoed.

"Nice to meet you," the woman said genially. "I'm Sope, Muyiwa's sister."

The name brought heat to Rebecca's face as she remembered her rant to Muyiwa. "I'm Rebecca. It's nice to meet you, too."

"Ooh ..." Sope said, her eyes sparkling. "The Rebecca? You're the one who curated the housewarming gift box on behalf of my brother, right?" she asked.

"Yes ..."

"Oh my God, I absolutely love it. The diffuser is my favourite. The smell is heavenly, totally to die for. You nailed my preference. My brother could never have."

Muyiwa quickly jumped in as Rebecca giggled, "Yeah, Sope, thanks for mentioning." He pointed at the screen. "And that's Bare and Seyi, my brothers."

They waved enthusiastically.

"That'll be goodbye from us," Muyiwa said.

"Later then!"

The chorus of voices immediately ceased as Muyiwa cut off the call.

"What was that about? The Rebecca?"

"Nothing."

"Hm, if you say so."

"Yeah, I do," he said, leaning closer. "So, it sounded like you were apologizing earlier but didn't get to finish."

"Well ... I was done ... I think," she stumbled over her words. Her breathing was shallow, and her heartbeat sounded louder in her ears.

"That was all you wanted to say?"

"Yeah, I'm really sorry and would like the chance to make it up to you."

"I see. So, the food and tickets are a bribe to accept the apology?"

"Something like that."

"Just a few words, food, and an outing I initially invited you for, and it'll all be over? Hmm, that sounds like a brilliant plan. You thought it'd be that easy, huh?" Although his words sounded like a challenge, his eyes were smiling, and she recalled doing the same thing to him at the health walk.

"I didn't think it'd be easy, but it's a start, right?" she pushed back softly.

"Hmm ... what's the continuation?"

"You're enjoying this, aren't you?"

"Very much so. It's not every day a beautiful woman comes to me with food and an apology. So, forgive me if I try to milk it for what it's worth."

"That's not fair!" she squealed, playfully pouting as the heat rose to her cheeks.

He sighed softly. "You are adorable, you know." He took her hand, his touch feather-light, sending a spark racing up her arm. "If it's worth anything, the past few days have been tough because I couldn't look forward to catching you unawares, chatting with you, or seeing you, especially when you're only a few steps away."

Rebecca coughed, trying to rid herself of the lump in her throat, searching for composure.

"I have a bottle of wine in the fridge that would have found its way to your house later tonight, with me as a desperate delivery person. So, thank you for coming first," Muyiwa said.

She nodded, but he suddenly pulled away, breaking the proximity, and she bit her lip to suppress her disappointment. *What do I say now?* she wondered.

Muyiwa swiftly grabbed a second gamepad from the console, returning to sit beside her.

"I hope you can stay and play a few rounds with me. Please say yes," he said.

"Sure!"

"Great." He beamed and selected a car race game. "Ready to lose?" he taunted.

She shot him a feisty look, scooting forward in her seat. "No way!"

He relaxed back on the couch. The game began, the countdown ringing out, 3 ... 2 ... 1 ...

The cars zoomed forward, engines roaring, and she was completely absorbed in the game. Colours flashed on the screen, and their excited shouts filled the room. Minutes flew by, her car lagged, and Muyiwa chortled beside her. Their banter mixed with the game's chaotic crashing sounds and jaw-breaking manoeuvres.

"If this were a crash tournament, you'd be winning!"

"I give up!" she declared, dropping the controller on the table, breathless from laughing. But in a move to catch her breath, she leaned back and found herself against him, his arms wrapping around her tenderly.

"Rebecca," he whispered, his breath soft against her ear.

"Yes?" Her heart danced.

"I've missed you in so many little ways that made me ache. Like the way your eyes light up when you smile, and that cute gap of yours that shows every time you do. Being with you feels like home. And not just because we happen to be in the same place, but because of how content and happy I am whenever we are together. I want to always remember this but I don't want it to stop here. I want to spend my life with you, to be part of your moments—the big ones, minute ones all of it. There's nothing I'm more certain of."

Lost in his voice, Rebecca felt her fears start to fade.

He continued. "You have my heart. Seeing you happy makes me happy." He turned her to face him fully, their faces so close, she could see the longing in his eyes. "Let me in, Rebecca. Give us a chance. We'll be good together. There'll be good and bad days, but we can be there for each other through them. I promise to treat your heart gently and love you with everything I have."

I want another chance at love, she thought. *And somehow, in all of the chaos, I've fallen in love with him.*

"Rebecca? Please say something."

Taking a deep breath, she cradled his face and leaned in. Their lips meet in a soft, gentle kiss. She pulled away slowly, resting her head against his chest.

"Is that a yes?" Muyiwa asked, his voice raspy and emotional.

She nodded. "It's a yes."

He jumped up, pulling her with him, then wrapped her in another long, tight hug. When he stepped back suddenly, his face was scrunched like he just remembered something. "By the way, I got an offer from the EdTech company whose application link you sent me."

"What! That's incredible and much more than by-the-way news. It's amazing. Congratulations, my love."

She tested the word on her tongue and decided she liked it, especially when Muyiwa's lips curled into a wider smile.

"Yeah, thanks, love," he said, pulling at his ear. "I'll go grab that wine!"

Rebecca watched him stride to the fridge, her heart dancing with happiness.

Mrs Adesesan was positively beaming as she glided through the house, all while giving instructions to Sola, Teju, and Yewande. The delicious aroma of food infused the air and mixed with the family's joyful disposition.

"Yewande, have you finished setting the table?" she called out from her place at the sink.

"Yes, Ma!" Yewande replied cheerfully.

"Sola, are there enough drinks in the fridge?"

"Yes, Mum," he answered, grinning and rolling his eyes at her exuberance. "Don't worry, we have our tasks covered."

"Teju, make sure Tiffany and Irawo are resting," she said, referring to Sola's fiancée and Teju's pregnant wife. "Go check on them to see if they need anything. I don't want them lifting a finger. They must be comfortable!"

"Sure, I'll go check," Teju replied gruffly before heading to the living room.

"Sola, I'm so happy today. God has answered my prayers. Our family is all together. Isn't He faithful?"

He hobbled slowly toward her his mother, leaning on crutches for support. He hugged her, feeling her joy wrap around him like a warm blanket.

"You never gave up on us. We are all here today because of you." Sola kissed her forehead.

The doorbell rang.

"I'll check," his mum said, heading out. He whispered quickly for Yewande to get Tiffany for him.

Tiffany soon walked in, talking as she approached him. "Your mum's sister just arrived."

He shrugged, extending a hand to her.

"Come here, baby ..." He leaned his back against the counter and pulled her to him. "That ring sure looks good on your finger."

"You mean this beautiful rock?" She raised her hand and the diamond ring on it to the light. "My husband-to-be has good taste."

"If that isn't the truth. You're proof of that."

He cradled her head in his hands and planted a light kiss on her lips.

"I can't believe I have to steal you away from my mum and sneak around to get alone time with you. I'm the one who's marrying you, yet she's got more facetime."

"She's a delight and knows how to plan a party. And you know I love it. Teju tells me it'll be a carnival soon, that the private lunch is just the beginning."

"He's right, that's why I pulled you away before it goes into full swing, and I lose sight of you. I wanted to take a minute to tell you that I love you."

He planted a kiss on her lips.

Tiffany cooed.

"I cherish you." Sola kissed her neck. "And you mean the world to me."

Finally, he took her palms in his, lifted them to his lips and brushed another kiss against them. Tiffany giggled, wrapping her arms around his neck, staring lovingly into his eyes... his soul.

It was in this house he first declared his love, but she walked away, justifiably so. But after working through counselling and earning her trust back in deliberate bits of honesty, she's in his arms, a personification of the second chance he received in his life.

"You know, there are some people who change the trajectory of your life and don't even know it. But I want you to know that you changed mine. I was confused and wondered what meaning life could possibly have. But then, I met you, and without a doubt, I knew I wanted to live life to the fullest. You brought me back to life and took another chance on me. I'm lucky ... I mean, I'm blessed you chose me. I can't wait to declare my love, loud and bold in the presence of our families."

"I could listen to this all day," Tiff said, gently rocking in his arms to the melody that filled the house. "You're special to me and I love you too."

He pulled her closer, but Yewande entered, and he groaned.

"Your guests have arrived," Yewande said.

"I'm sorry to cut this short." Sola said to Tiff.

Tiff nodded, carefully handing him his crutch before following the housekeeper. He followed suit slowly. His face lit up when he saw Rebecca, her mother, and a boy he knew was her brother.

"Rebecca! So happy you're here!" he exclaimed, greeting her mother with a respectful bow and giving Rebecca a light hug. She introduced her brother, Chimezie.

"Welcome!" Mrs Adesesan appeared. Her joy was unmistakable as she rushed to greet Rebecca's mother. "Thank you for accepting our invitation. It's so lovely to see you again after so many years!" She led them toward the living room.

Inside, Sola's father was watching a home video with the other ladies and Teju, who had ditched his share of work in the kitchen. As introductions were made, Sola's father moved quickly to Rebecca's mother, taking her hands in his. They shared a soft exchange that no one else could hear.

Rebecca's mum wiped away a tear, and it felt like time stood still.

Mrs Adesesan broke the silence. "The table is set. Let's head to the dining room."

As the family moved, Sola and Rebecca hung back.

"You and Luna Pay have been in the news lately. Another huge raise," Rebecca said. "Congratulations."

"Thanks. It's been a lot of work because we scaled pretty fast with new customers while expanding our services concurrently. But our revenue blew up. Most of the praise goes to Teju and my fiancé. I may have lost my mind if they didn't hold me up."

"Lucky you. By the way, Tiff is gorgeous," Rebecca teased with a playful smile.

"I know, right. I won in life." Sola winked, slipping back into the friendly teasing they shared at the beach club. "I'm glad you came. Easter lunch is a family tradition for my mum, and she definitely poured her heart into planning this one."

"I'm also happy to see you out of the wheelchair and moving around."

"Yeah. I can now move around with support, and hopefully, I'll be back to my full self in a couple of months."

"I hope so, too."

"While on the subject of recovery, how's Sandra doing?"

"Oh, she's well. The donor that came through in January—after I wasn't a confirmed match—was like a new year miracle. Her surgery went well, and she's healing nicely. Tiwa and I spoke this morning and shared some lovely family photos. Sandra looks so much better, glowing even."

"Amazing news," he said.

Laughter rang out from the dining room, and Tiffany called for Sola.

"Be right there!" he shouted back, and looked around with a dizzying sense of completeness. When he crashed through that red light so many years ago, his soul was mangled as totally as the car he was in. He'd then stayed stuck at that unyielding reminder of loss and pain, his heart twisted out of shape with regret. But love found and fought for him.

Sola glanced at Rebecca, who looked just as happy as he felt.

For them.

Now, surrounded by laughter and family, they shared a knowing smile. With hearts full of hope and belonging, they stepped into the room and toward beautiful new beginnings.

THE END

ACKNOWLEDGEMENT

It's a beautiful thing when a dream drifts from the unseen into your hands, like a seed in your heart breaking through the soil and blooming into something real. As this book did.

When I started writing When the Light Turned Red, my time and energy felt limited, so progress came in tiny bursts; single sentences here and there, half-formed ideas, unfinished scenes. There were seasons when I couldn't quite sit still, and others when everything slowed to a crawl. Through it all, this story was as persistent as I was, and somehow, we made it here.

Thanks be to God, the faithful Gardener, who planted this seed and walked me through every season until it flowered.

My heartfelt thanks to everyone who watered both me and this story with encouragement, patience, love, and thoughtful acts of kindness. For those who showed up in words, in deeds, in presence. Every gesture meant more than you'll ever know.

To my cherished readers. Thank you for picking up this book, for reading, sharing, and believing in me. You make it all worth it.

My priceless tribe—Semilore, Oluwadamilola, Iyinoluwa, Oluwatobi, Oreoluwa—your handprints are all over these pages. You lent me your eyes and gave this story real estate in your hearts. The feedback, rants, insistence, concessions, laughter and space for the grief when I had to let something go. You extended grace to me and it mattered.

To my editors and reviewers, thank you for helping prune and shape this manuscript into its best version.

To Bamise, Susan, Boluwatife, Kayode, Blessing, Sheun, Ayanfeoluwa, Oluwadamiloju, and my ARC team: thanks for championing this story and helping bring this book to more readers.

And to my Demola: Thanks for being my anchor— for the cheers, the assured reminders that I could do this when doubt tried to take root; for listening to my rambles when the story was raw; for helping before I asked; for loving me. To many more dreams coming to life.

ABOUT THE AUTHOR

Simi Joel writes Christian fiction, suspense, and emotionally resonant love stories that explore faith, second chances and healing.

With a professional background in business development and customer marketing, Simi believes strategy and creativity do not exist in separate worlds, instead they fuel each other.

Born in Nigeria and now based in Canada, Simi weaves stories that are easy to get lost in, taking complex, real-life issues and explores them in ways that feel real and relatable. Her characters are layered but familiar—people readers can see themselves in. At the heart of her work are hope, redemption, and grace.

When she isn't writing, she's endlessly curious; burying her nose in mystery novels, tackling puzzles, crafting, or enjoying time with her family.

OTHER BOOKS BY SIMI JOEL

Scarred - A Novel: Teni is only a woman working hard at her craft, and looking forward to her upcoming marriage. Until she encounters a young girl's story that forces her to confront the painful scars of her past. Burdened with the responsibility of helping the girl and her family, Teni must find the strength she isn't sure she has.

On other hand, Ranti appears to have it all—a thriving career, a loving family, and a promotion. Then tragedy strikes and an old flame reappears, offering her a second chance at happiness.

Scarred is a story that poignantly depicts the struggles of two women as they try to navigate life in the face of the changing landscapes of their emotional lives.

Missing - A Novella: Away from home, in the service of her country, Eunice is relishing her independence. Everything changes when in one fleeting moment of curiosity, she is abducted. In the days that follow, Eunice's friends have to work through their personal issues and search for her. The clues they find lead them to uncover a mind-boggling conspiracy.

The Deal: *What's the Price of a Life?*

In a stroke of ill-fate, Kolade, a struggling job seeker finds himself in debt to man who saved his life. To pay his debt, he has to do one job. So, he makes a deal, but the stakes are higher than he imagined.